I0737222

ELITE OF ELMWOOD ACADEMY

TURMOIL

USA TODAY BESTSELLING AUTHOR

J.L. WEIL

THE DIVISA SERIES

(Full series completed – Teen Paranormal Romance)

Losing Emma: A Divisa novella

Saving Angel

Hunting Angel

Breaking Emma: A Divisa novella

Chasing Angel

Loving Angel

Redeeming Angel

LUMINESCENCE TRILOGY

(Full series completed – Teen Paranormal Romance)

Luminescence

Amethyst Tears

Moondust

Darkmist – A Luminescence novella

RAVEN SERIES

(Full series completed – Teen Paranormal Romance)

White Raven

Black Crow

Soul Symmetry

BEAUTY NEVER DIES CHRONICLES

(Teen Dystopian Romance)

Slumber

Entangled

Forsaken

NINE TAILS SERIES

(Teen Paranormal Romance)

First Shift

Storm Shift

Flame Shift

Time Shift

Void Shift

Spirit Shift

Tide Shift

Wind Shift

HAVENWOOD FALLS HIGH

(Teen Paranormal Romance)

Falling Deep

Ascending Darkness

SINGLE NOVELS

Starbound

(Teen Paranormal Romance)

Casting Dreams

(New Adult Paranormal Romance)

Ancient Tides

(New Adult Paranormal Romance)

For an updated list of my books, please visit my website:

www.jlweil.com

Join my VIP email list and I'll personally send you an email reminder as soon as my next book is out! Click here to sign up: www.jlweil.com

This book is for my readers! Your kind words and friendship inspires me every day. Thank you for following me through genres and worlds.

PROLOGUE

What a fucking shit show!

This was by far the worst night of my existence. And it felt as if it would never end, an infinite tunnel of darkness with no light in sight. That was the definition of my life.

Most people cried tears of joy at weddings. My tears were of utter despair. The moment my mother said "I do" to Steven Patterson, Elmwood's most eligible bachelor, my world ended. Nothing would ever be the same.

I slammed my fourth glass of champagne back, letting the bubbles pop and tickle down my throat. Hell, maybe it was my fifth. Who was counting? I sure wasn't. Keep the liquor coming. It was the only way I would get through this awful event.

What a damn joke.

My fingers slipped over the glass as I clumsily went to set it down on one of the fancy white-clothed tables.

2

Crash.

Glass shattered at my feet, and I giggled, a watery little laugh of hysteria that was covered up by the clichéd wedding music blaring through the reception hall.

Oops.

No one noticed.

Story of my life.

"Fuck them all."

Shit. Did I say that out loud?

Across the table from where I stood, a dark brow lifted. I guess I had spoken out loud. A small lopsided smirk tugged at the corners of a sensual mouth that would be so easy to get hung up on. I dragged my eyes from those luscious lips to take in the rest of the face. And what a fucking face. This guy had the kind of looks poets wrote about and girls drooled over in romance books. His dark hair had a slight curl to it, purposely styled messily like he'd just gotten off a motorcycle. He was striking.

Sculpted cheekbones.

Full, kissable lips.

A sharp jawline I wanted to trail the tip of a fingernail over.

But it was the eyes that hit me straight in the gut with a punch of unexpected desire.

Nothing prepared me for the piercing color of his eyes. It was like looking into an infinite tropical ocean, such sparkling aqua. I felt myself drowning in them, all the noise in my head fading.

Holy hell.

My breath caught with the full effect of him. God, was he hot, in an intimidating way that made me bite my lip. His white shirt stretched across his firm chest, unbuttoned at the top where his tie hung loosened around his neck. The urge to grab him by the tie and pull him to me inundated me. That was the champagne talking. The bubbly liquor went straight to my head... and apparently other parts of my body too.

What was it about this guy that drew me? Perhaps it was the wicked smirk on his lips as he lifted his glass of champagne to his mouth, but I wanted him.

Right now. On the table.

A quick vision of sweeping the cloth off the table, glasses and half-eaten cake scattering over the floor, flashed through my head.

Aggressiveness wasn't one of my usual personality traits, but again, it was the champagne. And this horrible night that had me all twisted up and out of sorts. I didn't feel like myself.

So why the hell should I act like me?

For a single night, I wanted to pretend I was the type of girl who was reckless, sexy, demanding, and who didn't give a damn about anything. Morals? I didn't have them. Not at this moment.

Besides, anything I could do to ruin my mother's night the way she ruined my life, I was up for. Assuming my toast earlier in the night hadn't already made wedding history. *Cheers, Mom. Hope you and sugar daddy rot in hell.*

Without thinking, I grabbed Dreamy Eyes's hand and mumbled, "Let's dance." I didn't wait for a response, and I didn't care who he was, only that he was willing. My lips curled as he went with me, a soft chuckle caressing my ears behind me. I turned around, finding him taller than I had initially thought, and I craned my neck back to meet those startling eyes. Again, a bolt of desire struck me. This guy was too damn attractive for his own good, and the way he carried himself with such arrogant confidence, he damn well knew it. A characteristic I normally found irritating, but on him it was alluring.

What is wrong with me?

The question didn't stop me from putting my arms around his neck and swaying against him, letting my body brush and press into the hardness of his. He hadn't spoken a single word and in truth, I didn't want to talk. I just wanted to dance, to lose myself in the music with a gorgeous guy and forget who and where I was.

His lips danced over my ear as he murmured, "And to think I thought this party would be boring." His fingers tightened reflexively at the small of my back.

I grinned along his jaw, close to his ear so he would hear me, and said, "The party is just starting." My fingers slipped into his as I pulled back, staring him in the eye. The look I saw sparkling there sent a shooting star of lust through me.

This guy was wicked... wickedly bad, not someone I should probably toy with, but I couldn't stop myself. I wanted danger and recklessness.

But that wasn't all I wanted.

The dance floor grew crowded, so I led Dreamy Eyes out of the reception room, snatching a pair of champagne flutes on the way. In the common room, the double doors drowning out the music behind us, I clinked my glass to his. *To random hookups with hot guys,* I toasted in my head right before I drained my glass.

He followed, tossing his back like he majored in drinking. Grinning, I gave into my earlier temptation, grabbing the end of his tie and tugging him into one of the other rooms. I stumbled once or twice along the way. The room was a lounge with a big picture window of the gardens where fireflies danced through the flowers. A quick scan revealed that it was empty.

Perfect.

The door clicked shut behind him, and I lifted up on my toes, twining my fingers around his neck. "You have incredible lips. And eyes," I added, rambling thanks to the boost of liquid courage. "In fact, everything about you is pretty incredible."

"Is that so?" he replied, bemused. "Let me take that," he offered in a husky voice that had me trembling. He took my glass, setting his and mine on a little round table just to the right of the door. His hands came to rest at the side of my hips, and heat seeped through my dress. Something in his touch was possessive.

"Thanks," I replied, my teeth grazing along his jaw. I had to keep touching him. I was desperate to feel those glorious lips on mine.

He seemed to read my mind, leaning down to brush his lips across mine in a teasing kiss. I let out a soft moan and tilted my head to give him better access. He chuckled at the invitation, a deep, raspy sound laced with an arrogance that turned me on even more.

But I wasn't in the mood to play. I wanted the pleasure of his lips, so I closed the very minuscule distance between us and fused our mouths. Parting my lips, I glided my tongue across his teeth, waiting for him to give me what I desired.

At the first contact of his tongue darting between my lips to touch mine, I shuddered.

My eyes closed, and I let my body take over.

With his lips on mine, he started to guide me across the room, but kissing and walking were proving to be difficult. My feet got tangled together, and I stumbled into him. A giggle escaped my lips, breaking the kiss momentarily. I kicked aside my shoes, hands clasping his shoulders for stability. Once the heels were gone, he lifted me, and I wrapped my legs around him. Good thing, because my weak knees were about to give out on me. It was so much easier being carried to the leather couch and allowing my lips to explore every angle of his face.

He sank us into the plush couch, and I straddled him. A low-lit electric fireplace nestled into the wall in front of the couch, the flames flickering and dancing in the dim room. Neither of us had bothered with the lights.

The truth was, I had no intention of ever seeing Dreamy Eyes again. Tonight I only wanted one thing from him. To forget where I was—who I now was. I just wanted to lose myself in the pleasure his body offered.

Pressing tightly against him, my arms wound around his neck so I could tangle my fingers into his mess of silky, dark hair.

"What's your name, Firefly?" he murmured as those glorious lips cruised down the column of my neck.

My stomach fluttered at the nickname. How very appropriate, since the room seemed to be surrounded with fireflies prancing in the gardens. "Names aren't important," I replied, sinking my hands into his hair and pulling his mouth back to mine, successfully silencing any more questions. But soon kissing wasn't enough. "I need you."

His eyes darkened, like a turbulent storm. His fingers slid the thin straps of my black dress over my shoulders, all the while watching me with those intense eyes. His brow lifted in a silent question. *Are you sure?*

I bit my lip and nodded. *Hell, yes.*

He sealed our mouths together in a kiss born of desperate hunger. I heard the zipper undo along my spine, felt the silky material of my dress fell to my waist. The warmth from the fireplace, from his body, and my desire kept my skin blazing hot, despite the exposure.

Holy shit.

I am doing this.

My first one-night stand.

I don't know what this guy saw in me, didn't care in the heat of the moment, but it was a question that would haunt me days after when I remembered the feel of his lips on mine—tasted him on my tongue.

He handed me a condom, which I quickly unwrapped and slipped over him, my fingers lingering. His kiss grew more demanding, his hands more urgent on my body, and yet I met him touch for touch, often the one pushing harder, faster. I couldn't seem to get enough from him. His fingers cupped my breast, squeezing before brushing gently over my nipple.

God, yes. This is what I need.

My head fell back, body buzzing and basking under the glow of firelight as he slammed into me. It wasn't gentle, but it was exactly what I craved. Hot pleasure like molten honey seeped into my veins, making me dizzy with the scent and feel of him. My nails raked down his damp back, the muscles there tight and firm. He held me against him as he moved in and out of me at a mind-blowing pace.

My orgasm tore through me just as his tongue swept in between my parted lips, swallowing my cry of pleasure. *Sweet Jesus.*

The door creaked open, letting a stream of light into the room. Laughter and voices trickled in, and I turned my gaze to see my mother's shocked face, which quickly morphed into unbridled rage. She stood in the doorway in her obviously expensive wedding dress, clutching the door handle with white knuckles.

I grinned, running my hands through Dreamy Eyes's disheveled hair. I didn't bother to untangle myself from him or cover up, and I was pleased he made no move to let me go either, regardless that he damn well knew someone was at the door. His eyes remained focused on my face. Without a word, my mother closed the door, and I rolled my hips, letting my eyes flutter closed.

I never claimed I wasn't a rainbow of fucked-up. I had my mother to thank for that.

CHAPTER ONE

My plans for the future seemed so simple until they became a dangerous game of life and death. Something I never thought possible until I attended the Academy.

The rules of life weren't the same.

And I found that out the hard way.

"Do you know how hot school uniforms are? Guys go nuts for that short skirt preppy shit. Instant boner," my best friend, Ainsley, assured as she flipped through a row of designer jeans. We were shopping at another overpriced boutique where you couldn't buy a G-string for under a hundred bucks.

This was her attempt at cheering me up. The problem was, I wanted to sulk in my misery. It was bad enough I was forced to transfer schools my senior year, but I was also being told how I could dress. Fuck Elmwood Academy. "I should show up my first day in a bikini and high heels." That would make a statement. I wasn't sure if it was the statement I wanted to get across, but I wasn't thinking clearly, anger clouding my common sense. "Besides, you don't need a school uniform to look good."

And it was true. My bestie was a hottie. She was petite in a way that made guys feel strong, once they got past the gothic makeup. Ainsley Fisher was too damn cute, but she could lighten up on the eyeliner.

She threw a dark look my way with her pretty, mossy-green eyes. As usual, they were heavily lined with black mascara and smudged in smoky eye shadow that emphasized the beautiful slant of her eyes. "I think you are confusing me with you. I'd kill for your long, golden legs."

"But at least you have a perky ass," I retorted and slapped her on the backside. A pair of women shopping a few racks down shot me a dirty look. I glared back, lifting my middle finger in the air. They huffed and spun around, shaking their heads. Bunch of stuck-up hags. They were the kind of women my mom would love to be friends with: rich socialites with all the right connections.

Ainsley giggled. "I can't believe you did that," she muttered with a playful smirk, turning to check out her ass in the full-length mirror. "It is a pretty stellar ass, isn't it?"

I gave her a grin in the mirror, my pink hair flashing in the corner. "You'd give Kim Kardashian a run for her money."

"Right!" A tie-dyed shirt caught Ainsley's eye, an identical match to her rainbow hair, and she paused to check it out. "You can't get away with that shit anymore. You're not anonymous. You're *Steven Patterson's* stepdaughter. And in this town, he's a big freaking deal."

I let out a low breath. "He owns two football teams. Whoopie." Except in a town where football was as important as breathing air, it was a big deal.

Ainsley looked at the price tag and put the shirt back, moving on to the next rack. "You need to accept this shit. The sooner you do, the easier it is to play their games."

"I don't want to play any games," I grumbled, gazing out the display window into the street.

She shrugged, tossing strands of hair over her shoulder. "That's not how their world works."

"God, you sound like Angie."

Ainsley gasped, a hand flying to her heart as if I'd wounded her. "Never compare me to your mother again. That woman is batshit crazy. Nothing she says makes any sense, and I know what the hell I'm talking about." She held up a cute T-shirt, and I nodded, so she slung it over her arm. "There are worse things than school uniforms."

She had a point. In the scope of things, being forced to wear a uniform was really a first world problem. If I was going to get into Hamilton University, I needed to put my focus on my grades, not what I was wearing. It was one less thing to worry about. I wouldn't have to wonder how everyone else would be dressed and how far out of place I'd look.

All those designer jeans my mother had slapped on Steven's credit card would continue to collect dust in my closet. I refused to wear them.

Stubborn? Maybe.

Probably.

Ainsley and I left the store with a single pair of jeans she'd decided to splurge on. It was close to one in the afternoon as we stepped out onto Walnut Street, the sun warming my skin. Downtown Elmwood was bustling with people rushing to get their last-minute back-to-school shopping done. My stomach growled at the smell of food from the local vendors, reminding me that I had skipped breakfast—unless coffee counted as one of the food groups.

"Do you have time to grab something eat?" I asked as we came upon a casual restaurant with sidewalk seating. "I'm craving a burger."

Ainsley blinked at me, swinging her shopping bag on her finger. "I just bought the skinniest pair of jeans on the planet and you want me to eat a burger."

My lips curved. "I'm buying. Or I should say, Steven is." I pulled out a platinum credit card from my back pocket and dangled it from my fingers. Giving me a credit card was such a horrible idea. Did he have any idea the kind of damage I could do with a card like this? It was like giving candy to a baby.

"Gimme," she said, grabbing the card.

I laughed, letting her snatch the glittery little piece of plastic.

"It's so shiny and new." She stroked it like the thing was something precious. "My ass is going to hate you," she relented with fake venom.

Her metabolism wasn't half as bad as she complained. Some people carried weight in all the best places: hips, ass, and boobs. Ainsley was one of them. But she had a tiny little waist and curves every girl dreamed of.

I, on the other hand, had a decent rack. *Thank you, Angie.*

My legs were probably my best feature, combined with my natural golden skin. I'd been spending most of my time at the pool swimming at the Pattersons' mansion. I still couldn't bring myself to call that house home.

We sat at one of the sidewalk tables under a big black-and-white plaid umbrella. I took a chair that faced the street and watched the cars roll past. It was a typical Sunday. Everyone was out enjoying one of the last few days of summer. I grinned at the cutest little corgi as he pranced by on the sidewalk, looking all proud of himself.

"I wonder if I could get a dog," I mused, watching the puppy's tiny little butt bounce away. Just looking at him made my smile grow, but really, a dog wasn't in my plan.

"Isn't your mom allergic?" Ainsley reminded me.

"That was always her excuse. Maybe I could find one of those hypoallergenic breeds, like a Maltese. I think they're okay."

"I'm not trying to rain on your parade, but could you trust Carter with a dog?"

Her question was valid, and the mention of my stepbrother was enough to make my stomach churn. Carter couldn't be trusted with shit. My heart sank, and I wasn't so hungry anymore. "Good point." I picked up the menu and scanned down the list of items, needing to occupy my mind with other thoughts than Carter. No way would I subject a dog to the evil torment of my stepbrother.

Talk about the biggest douchebag in existence. The Pattersons' mansion, no matter how huge, was not quite large enough to keep Carter far away. Obviously, the universe decided I needed to be punished every single day of my life.

Carter made it clear from the second Mom and I moved in that he was onto our game. Meaning, he pegged my mom for the gold digger everyone knew she was, but somehow I was lumped into the equation. He had it all wrong. But it was a waste of breath to argue with a stubborn asshole like him.

Why the hatred he felt for her had to come out as bitterness and assholery against me was another story. It's not like I put his dad and my mom together. I didn't ask my mother to cheat on my father and divorce him, just to turn around and have the splashiest wedding Elmwood had seen in a decade. I wasn't the cause of either of our problems. And I wasn't the one who'd made my mother a complete narcissist who only cared about how she looked to the rest of the world.

Her daughter be damned.

Fuck Carter Patterson.

That was my motto until graduation.

He could shove his expensive cars and flashy clothes right up his saggy ass. Okay, Carter's ass wasn't saggy, but it sure as hell should have been. Not that I checked out his ass. Ever.

Cringe.

If I'd had my way, things would've stayed the way they were. Life with my parents hadn't been full of roses and beams of sunshine. They hadn't been happy for a long time. I picked up on the hostility that lingered in the air between them fairly young. Sure, some of the digs and insults went over my head, but from the overall vibe, I understood things were wrong. Broken, even. Kind of like me.

What was the old saying about ignorance being bliss?

But I'd give up a thousand mansions to be back in the little ranch I grew up in.

That was home.

"Oh, shit. Here comes *trouble*." Ainsley said "trouble," but the infliction in her tone implied otherwise.

I lowered the menu and followed the direction she was staring in. It didn't take long for me to make out the black Range Rover cruising down the road in front of us, bass-heavy music thumping from the open windows.

Ainsley straightened up in her chair as she brushed aside any flyaway hairs from her face. "Why do the assholes always have to be so damn gorgeous? It seriously isn't fair."

The Elite.

Those were the assholes Ainsley referred to—four guys who were deemed the Elite of Elmwood Academy. They had quite a reputation for getting into trouble, drinking, fighting, getting laid, and partying. You name it; the four of them had done it.

And yet, every girl I knew was far too eager to drop her panties at the prospect of banging one of them. Except me. I only knew them by reputation; never cared enough to look them up.

"When is life fair?" I mumbled, toying with the corner of the menu. My gaze wandered past the bleached-blonde in the passenger seat to the driver.

The world spun. My stomach dropped, followed by my heart.

"Holy fuck," I whispered.

This can't be real. This isn't happening.

Hoisting the menu in front of my face, I sank deeper into my chair.

Ainsley gave me a funny look. "What are you doing? Are you hiding from someone? Is your mom here?"

"It's him," I hissed, peeking out from the side of the menu at her.

"Who? The Elite?"

The Elite. The fucking Elite. Those words echoed in my head.

I wanted to crawl into the nearest manhole. I had slept with one of the Elite.

Someone kill me now.

"Ainsley," I groaned. "The driver."

"Brock Taylor," she supplied. "Unbelievably gorgeous. Killer smile. Quarterback at the Academy," she stated like she was reading his bio. "What about him? You interested?"

I swallowed. "I had sex with him. He is the guy from the wedding."

Her eyes bulged. "Are you shitting me?" Then she started to giggle. "Oh, Josie. That is goddamn classic. You had sex with Brock Taylor. He isn't just one of the Elite. He is *the* Elite."

"You are so not helping," I complained, daring to inch the menu down so my eyes peered over the top. Shock hummed through my bones. I was going to faint.

This was worst-case scenario. The guy I never thought to see again went to the Academy—to the school I would attend in a week. Was it too late to convince Angie to let me homeschool?

How was I going to face him every day at school?

Ainsley's eyes bounced from the sleek SUV to me. "I can't believe you didn't know who Brock was."

"I know of him. I just didn't know what he looked like," I said in my defense, dropping the menu onto the table. My gaze landed back on the car's driver. If he saw me sitting here, would he recognize me? Probably not. He laughed at something someone in the back seat said. The Range Rover was loaded with people. Presumably the other three guys, Brock's best friends, and whatever girls they considered worthy of them this week.

I hated the ever-so-slight flutter in my chest at the thought of having been one of those girls for just a single night.

"No wonder you've been torturing yourself with memories of the hottest sex of your life." A knowing grin spread over Ainsley's glossy lips. "He looks good," she purred, eyes devouring the car.

I averted my gaze back to the menu. "Which one?"

"Don't play dumb with me."

"Fine. Brock Taylor looks good," I begrudgingly admitted.

She tapped a black-painted nail against her lip and raised a brow at me, a menacing smile on her lips. She had her diamond stud in today, and it winked above her lip, twinkling at me. "I bet even their dicks are gorgeous." Ainsley was known to be crass. It was part of her charm.

I shook my head, biting on my lip so she wouldn't see the stupid smile trying to break over my mouth. "You're making me lose my appetite." I didn't want to think about the Elite's junk, and still, I couldn't stop my mind from going back to that night.

She eyed the black car stopped at the red light directly in

front of the restaurant as if it were a piece of candy she wanted to lick. "I'd fuck them all. Probably at the same time."

"Ainsley!" I hissed before it turned into a laugh. "You are unbelievable." The light turned green, and the Range Rover took off. I watched the rear license plate as it drove down a few blocks and disappeared, Brock Taylor with it.

She snorted. "Don't tell me you wouldn't jump straight into Brock's bed again given the chance."

Dammit. She had me there. I shouldn't want to go anywhere near Brock-fucking-Taylor, and yet, the mere mention of his name did unmentionable things to my lady parts. He was off-limits now that I knew who he was. "I wouldn't give him a second of my time."

Liar!

"Liar," she echoed my thoughts.

Not a single person in town hadn't heard of the Elite. Their infamous pranks and parties were legendary—headline-worthy. They were also on the football team with Carter—teammates. Just another reason to hate my stepbrother.

Of course, the four of them came from old money—the kind that established fucking cities and ruled the world. I'd heard one of them had a father who was a big-time movie producer, but that was as in-depth as my understanding went.

"I can't believe you had sex with him," she shrieked, still hung up on the idea of Brock and me together.

Hell, I was still having a hard time believing it. "Jesus, Ains, why don't you stand on the table and shout for the whole town to hear. Josie James had sex with Brock Taylor."

A deep voice cleared his throat beside me.

Shit. I closed my eyes for a brief moment and dropped my head. FML.

Ainsley sat back in her seat grinning. "I think you just did," she replied.

My cheeks flamed as I glanced up to see a guy not much older than me with sandy-blond hair smiling at me. He set down two glasses of ice water and a little bowl of lemon wedges. "Can I get you something to drink?" he asked.

I wanted to crawl under the table and die. This guy not only probably went to the Academy but also definitely knew the Elite. *Why me?*

"We're good with water," Ainsley said, shooting him a cheeky grin. "But I think we're ready to order." A minute later, our server left to put in our orders, dazzled by my best friend.

Ainsley picked up her water and took a slow sip, condensation already pooling on the glass. "Relax. You act like it's something to be ashamed of. Do you know how many girls would kill to have a night with one of the Elite? Besides, you could do a lot worse than Brock Taylor. You could have slept with your stepbrother."

"For fuck's sake, please. Stop talking about it. I just want to forget it ever happened." I wanted to forget everything. The feel of his lips. The touch of his hands. The way he moved inside me. His fucking unforgettable face.

I was seriously banking on Brock Taylor not remembering me. At all.

"I don't want to be one of the millions of girls he screwed," I explained in a whisper, reclining back in my chair.

"Wow. Millions?" she proclaimed with mock astonishment. "Guy is talented. Besides, I think it is too late for that."

He was talented all right—fucking gifted—but I didn't want to get into that. The Range Rover was long gone when our sandwiches arrived. "Don't make me throw a perfectly good sandwich at your head. You know what I'm saying. How the hell did I get myself into this mess?"

She took a bite of her BLT, chewing on the side of her mouth as she replied, "It seems that Brock isn't the only one gifted." She swallowed. "Your specialty happens to be creating drama. It follows you around like a dark cloud."

"It sure does," I said as I glanced across the street to the smoothie bar. *This has got to be a joke.* Brock, along with the other three guys who I assumed were the Elite and two girls I'd never seen before, headed inside.

I couldn't tear my eyes off him. Brock slid his sunglasses up onto his head, where they nestled in black waves. Were his aqua eyes just as I dreamed, sparkling in the sun like the ocean on a hot-ass day?

"Oh, shit," Ainsley gasped, noticing what snagged my attention.

And from across the street, those damn dreamy eyes clashed with mine, as if he knew I was staring at him.

My breath halted, waiting to see if he would recognize me. I did nothing, just met his gaze head-on, unable to look away.

The jackass lifted his chin.

I shot him my best fuck-off smile.

That was all the confirmation I needed. Brock hadn't forgotten.

Damn it. Why did that even matter? Why were my insides fluttering with excitement?

My gaze darted back up as one of the girls threw her arms around Brock's neck, whispering something in his ear. The desire to rake my nails down her pretty face tore through me. He slid an arm around her waist, yanking her closer to him. As they walked through the door, he pressed his lips to hers in a kiss, giving her ass a squeeze.

That clarified it. I was just another notch under the Elite's belt.

CHAPTER TWO

Before my hookup with Brock at my mother's wedding, I had no reason to be interested in the Elite. Our paths never crossed. Academy kids rarely mixed with those from the Public, and I never went to any Academy parties.

Perhaps if I had paid more attention to the gossip swirling around school, I wouldn't have made the colossal mistake of sleeping with one of them.

The damage was done, and all I could do was face the music next Monday morning. That night meant nothing... so I kept telling myself. It sure as shit didn't mean anything to someone like Brock.

But I couldn't help recall that night of the most shattering orgasm of my life. It was also my only orgasm, which might have been why it was so mind-blowing. Brock Taylor was no stranger to the pleasures of the female body, unlike Harvey, my ex-boyfriend, who had been my first and only sex partner up until that night. Poor Harvey had been fumbling and unsure the few times we hooked up.

I had heard so many cruel stories about the Elite the last two years, yet that night, Brock had been... nice, dare I say. Another reason why I wouldn't have pegged him as one of the asshole Elite. It never crossed my mind. I assumed he was from out of town, the son of one of Steven's acquaintances. The wedding had been large, and hardly any of the attendees were friends or family of my mother. They had mostly been Steven's guests, exactly how my mom wanted. Her old life was the past, and she planned to keep it there, buried forever.

Brock had made me forget for a short time where I was and the future that waited for me. I had been grateful in the moment, but now... I wasn't sure who the hell Brock was or what his agenda was with me. Why would he hook up with a nobody? Or was that just his game?

Having sex on my mother's wedding day was one of the worst things I could think of doing to her. Although part of my decision to be so reckless had been about me and my feelings, a larger part had been a big F-you to Angie. Her newfound image didn't include a slut for a daughter. I was expected to act the part of someone with class, dignity, and self-respect.

The idea made my eyes roll. As if my mother ever had any of those qualities. It was all an act, the best performance of her life.

Well, I sucked at acting, so she was just going to get me, whether she liked it or not. I refused to be someone I wasn't, to lose myself, my values at the sight of dollar signs. She constantly preached that she didn't want me to end up like her, pregnant and forced into marriage. It was so nice to know that I was wanted.

I snorted.

The look on her face when she saw me with Brock that night had been priceless. My hair a wild mess, my dress wrinkled and slightly out of place, and the purple-red hickey on my neck had been the clincher. Thinking about it brought a smile to my lips.

Now I wanted to forget that night ever happened.

"There you are!" I knew from the sound of my mother's voice that she had been drinking.

Joy.

She had the whole *everything's splendid* tone going on. Her bright, wide smile was as fake as her tits. I stepped out onto the screened-in back patio where she and Steven were having a cocktail by the pool. Arms outstretched, she lifted her glass in the air.

I rolled my eyes. *I wonder how many of those she's already had?*

Mom loved a good drink. And far too frequently. It was something Ainsley and I had in common: parents who didn't know their limit. When Angie drank, she had two personalities. I never knew which one was going to come out. The overly loving mother, with her high-pitched voice that almost sounded as if she had a British accent. Phony, in other words.

Or the queen bitch.

Tonight it was clingy mom who just wanted to smother me with love.

"Hey." I nodded to Steven. He smiled warmly at me before

I faced my mother. "I wanted to let you know I'm home from shopping."

"And how is Ainsley, *sweetheart*?" she asked, crossing her long tan legs. She was wearing a two-piece bathing suit with a white sarong tied around her waist. Mom didn't actually swim. She just liked to dress the part.

Her voice grated on my nerves, and I made a face. Jesus Christ, would she don a tiara and start calling me *darling* next, like she was royalty? "She's okay. Same Ains. You know."

Angie's lips turned into a pout, pieces of her dark hair falling out of her low ponytail to frame her oval face. "I haven't seen much of her since we moved. You should invite her over for a swim. We could grill, couldn't we, honey?" she said, turning to Steven with a bat of her false lashes.

I swallowed back a mouthful of bile at the sickening endearments.

Eighteen couldn't come soon enough. I was dying to get the hell out of here.

"Sure," Steven agreed. "Whatever you want." He couldn't have cared less who I had over at the house. Couldn't care less what I did. Steven was an average-looking dad. Beefier than most because he hit the home gym daily to keep up his fit physique, but it wasn't his looks my mother was interested in. He had the same sandy hair as Carter, but his nose was just slightly crooked, unlike his son's perfectly symmetrical facial structure.

"I'm surprised she hasn't been over sooner. You guys are normally inseparable. Is there something going on between you? She isn't jealous, is she?" Just like my mom to somehow make my relationship with my best friend about money. It was all that was ever on her mind. I found it exhausting.

"No, Ainsley and I are just fine," I said between clenched teeth. "She's been busy working all summer."

"Working the entire summer before senior year." She took a sip from her drink and scrunched her nose. "Where is the fun in that? You're fortunate you don't have to work."

Fortunate indeed. That was one way of putting it. I shrugged, switching the majority of my weight to my other foot. "I wouldn't have minded a summer job." It was the truth and would have made the summer bearable.

"Well, Steven has been so generous. There is no need for you to work." She reached over and rubbed his bare knee, and I straight-up vomited a little.

"Now, Angelica, there is nothing wrong with learning the value of a job and earning a few bucks," he countered, surprising me. Never thought Steven would take my side in a discussion. "If Carter didn't have to put all his focus into football, I'd have him interning at the office."

Right... because playing football was all that mattered. It should come as no surprise that Steven pushed his son into football, seeing as he owned professional teams and had been a huge college football hero himself. Like father, like son.

If it had not been for a torn ACL, Steven would have signed with a pro team. But then he would not have met my mom, and I would not be living in the lap of luxury. *Oh, what a fucking shame that would have been*, I thought with heavy sarcasm.

Mom dropped the sunglasses down the bridge of her nose to

peer up at me. "I think it's time, don't you?" she asked Steven, the corner of her lips tipping up.

My eyes narrowed as I stared at my reflection in her shades. "What are you talking about?" I looked from Angie to Steven. "You know I hate surprises," I groaned, my mouth twisting into a scowl.

"I swear, Josephine, you take the fun out of everything." Her voice pitched as her eyes glared at me. They were the same chocolate shade as my own, but hers lacked warmth and were a little glossy. I took after my mother in the looks department. Same dark hair, when mine wasn't dyed pink, and same curvy, slim figure. But that was where our similarities ended.

She stood up from her lounge chair and put an arm around my waist like we were friends. I wouldn't have cared so much if it were genuine. Did she have any idea how ridiculous she made us both look? "Come on. I think you'll like this surprise."

Steven stretched to his full height as he accompanied Angie and me to the side of the house where the four-car garage was. This was only one of their garages. I stared at the driveway, looking for this supposed surprise, but all I saw was my powder blue Corolla along with Mom and Steven's cars. Carter was out, thank God for small wonders.

Steven punched a code into the far right garage, and as the door unfolded, he said. "Now, use of this is contingent on your grades and behavior. If you can show you're dedicated to having a good year and starting school on the right foot, then it's yours. If not, we'll... have to talk about rules." I could see the idea of laying down rules for me made him uncomfortable. He rubbed at the back of his neck, waiting for the door to fully lift open.

"What is...?" I trailed off as my eyes landed on a shiny cherry-red Lexus. My mouth hung open. "Holy shit," I whispered. It was the most beautiful piece of machinery I'd ever laid eyes on. Did they just give me a fucking—

"Surprise!" My mother's hug engulfed me, but I could barely feel her. "We wanted to do something special for your senior year at a new school. I know it is difficult having to switch schools."

"So what do you think?" Steven asked, his hazel eyes sparkling.

I blinked hard. What did I think? I thought this was the biggest crock-of-shit bribe in history. "You didn't have to buy me a car," I started in a whisper. "Really. It's too much."

"It's not too much for you, baby." She even stroked my damn hair. The hair she said she hated at least once a day since I'd dyed it pink. "We know there have been a lot of changes these last few months, and I wanted to give you the best start to your new life. You deserve to drive the sort of car—"

I wiggled out of her grasp. This car ensured I looked the part of a rich kid when I arrived at the Academy. Unbelievable. "My car runs just fine." Dad had given it to me on my sixteenth birthday. Didn't she see that I wanted to hold on to something from my old life?

My dad was a mechanic who managed to make ends meet. We hardly starved. But it wasn't enough for Angie, who left my father for the first millionaire who sniffed up her skirt. I didn't want to think about the number of affairs. Dad deserved better. We both did. Angie... or Angelica, as my mom now referred to herself as, wasn't winning any mother or wife of the year awards.

I almost felt sorry for Steven.

"Yes, sweetheart, it's a very reliable car. But it doesn't fit your new lifestyle." Her voice had an edge I recognized too well. She wanted me to squeal and thank her for the generous gift.

"Why don't I get to decide what I want my lifestyle to be? Dad gave me that car!"

All the excitement from before was gone from her face. "And your stepfather is giving you this one."

I stared my mother down, not budging.

"Josephine," she said sternly, prompting me to show my appreciation, which I refused to do.

The pain of everything I'd lost came crashing down on me, and instead of risking I'd say something terrible, I turned around and stormed into the house.

Angie was hot on my heels, cursing the entire way. I tried to get through my bedroom door and close it before she reached me, but it was too late. She was fast when she wanted to be. Drunk or not. Maybe faster because she was two sheets to the wind.

"You ungrateful brat." She shoved her way into the room and slammed the door behind her, then marched up to me, her face as red as a lobster, fists clenched at her sides. "How dare you be so rude when all he's been is giving and accepting."

"I don't want it!" I snapped back. "I won't drive it."

She crossed her arms over her chest, and I couldn't help think how ridiculous she looked in her bikini top. "Nobody asked whether you wanted it. People don't get asked when somebody wants to give them a gift. And when they get the gift, they have the grace and the decency to accept without whining and complaining about their piece-of-shit Corolla!"

"Maybe you care about the sort of car I drive, but I don't. You know damn well—"

"Watch your language!" Her chest heaved, rising and falling with ragged breaths.

"—Dad gave me that car," I continued right over her. Like she ever cared about my language. "You can't take everything away from me. It isn't fair. He made sure it would run for me. That was the last thing he was able to do before we left."

The hardness etched in her face softened some. "It's a vehicle, Josie."

It had been so long since she called me by my nickname. "Reality check. So is that Lexus, *Mom*."

Her mouth pinched, and she lifted her chin. "Yes, but don't you at least want to try to fit in here?"

"Here we go." This was a battle neither of us would win. "Was it even Steven's idea to buy the car, or was that you? I don't accept it. Your relationship is your problem."

"How dare you?" she clipped out, making a noise of disgust in the back of her throat. "You are an ungrateful, disrespectful, spoiled little bitch, and I won't have this from you anymore. Do you hear me? I won't. I am your mother whether you like it or not and whether you like me or not. You will not disrespect my husband or me in our house. You will learn to obey. You'll be the nice, sweet, respectful little girl I deserve, or else..."

My voice cooled at the unspoken threat she dangled in the air between us. "Or else what?"

She took a step toward me, a gleam of rage glimmering in the depths of her brown eyes. Her hand pulled back like she wanted to hit me, but stopped herself before the impulse went past her control. I don't know what I would have done if she had slapped me. She'd never put her hands on me before, but the verbal lashings were just as damaging. "Or else I'll make your life a living hell. And you can forget Steven paying a cent for anything this year, and sure as hell forget college. Better hope you get a full ride."

I knew she meant it. She was just evil enough to carry through with the threat.

My eyes went flat at the look of triumph on her face. It made me want to scream, but that would have only made her happier.

"That's what I thought. We sold your car. The new owner is coming to pick it up tonight."

My shoulders sagged in defeat, my hands falling to my sides. Silence stretched between us, and when I didn't object, she spun on her heels and left, thinking she had won.

"I'll walk to school then!" I shouted after her, and I half expected her to fly back into my room. I was so looking forward to slamming the door in her face.

My hand rested on the knob and tightened when I saw a shadow traveling up the stairway. I figured it had to be her...

But as the shadow grew closer, a lump formed in my chest. *Fuck.* It was obvious from the size and the way the shadow moved, it wasn't my mother. Then I saw the sandy hair and moved to quickly close the door.

A hand pressed on it before I could get it shut, and Carter's smirking face appeared. To some girls, he was the perfect golden boy, the all-American football hero, a guy made for fantasies. Trim waist, toned muscles thanks to the hours he spent bulking up at our home gym, a chiseled jawline. To me, he was the devil in disguise. I shuddered to think what he would do if he found out I had slept with Brock.

My chin lifted at him. "Do you need something?" I snapped.

He leaned a broad shoulder against my doorframe, taking up the entire exit with his body. "Nice car."

I plastered on a condescending smile of my own. "Oh, you like it?"

His eyes ran over me in a way that made me wish I was wearing sweats and a bulky hoodie. "What did you do to get a Lexus? Suck the old man off."

I scowled, reaching for the door again. "You're disgusting."

He didn't budge regardless that it was obvious I wanted him to leave. "Like mother, like daughter."

"I'm nothing like my mother." My voice dripped with venom toxic enough to kill.

"Bullshit." What might have been a handsome face twisted up in a snarl. "If you ever want to put that pretty mouth of yours to good use, I'm just down the hall."

My hand itched to slap him across the face. Instead, I forced my lips into a sneer. "That's the best you can do?" I held the smile in place.

"Oh, I'm just getting started. At least your mother doesn't pretend to be anything more than a gold digger. You're just a bitch." It was a cold hiss, like ice water running down my back in a thin stream. He took a step closer, using his size to intimidate me. "But I'd still fuck you."

It took every ounce of my self-control not to step back away from him. I refused to shrink in front of him. "Problem is, I'd never fuck you."

He leveled me a look. "We'll see."

I tilted my head to the side. "I get it. You're pissed off I moved in. Well, newsflash, asshole. I don't want to be here. How about you just stay out of my way and I'll pretend like you don't exist. Deal?"

His snarl morphed into something of a self-righteous grin. "Where is the fun in that? I have big plans for you, sis." He pushed off the doorframe and shoved his hands into his front pockets, strutting down the hall.

I slammed the door shut, the sound echoing down the hall. "Asshole," I muttered as I flipped the lock.

CHAPTER THREE

Turning, I pressed my back against the door, my chest heaving. I stayed like that for a minute, focused on the bed until my breathing evened out. I stared at the large room with its white furnishings. It wasn't my bedroom. Not really. And the sight of the soft gray walls and blush pink decor caused a pang of sadness in my chest for my old room. It was too damn whimsical for my taste but was probably my teen mom's bedroom of her dreams. I preferred splashes of color to soft pastels.

How had I been here for three months already? And yet, the feeling of being a guest wouldn't go away. Nothing about this place felt like *home* to me. I slept in a stranger's bed.

The house as a whole lacked charm and character. No warmth. Just modern coldness encased in soulless white bricks.

Who cared about making a life inside these walls when what really mattered was how the grounds looked on the outside? The only opinion important to these people was everyone else's.

I decided to change and forgo the shower I intended before bed. After the altercation with my mother and then Carter, I just wanted to sleep, forget where I was and all the drama in my life.

Slipping the too-damn-tight jeans past my hips and wiggling out of them, I tossed my clothes on the floor and rummaged through the dresser drawers. I changed into a tank and shorts before staring down at the four-poster bed framed in a gauzy white canopy. About thirty-seven pillows were piled on top. Just looking at it, I couldn't even tell there was a bed under all those decorative pillows in various shapes. Who the hell needed that many on one bed? What was the fucking point? To annoy me each night before I went to bed?

Mission achieved.

Sweeping my arm across the bed, I knocked off half of them before shoving the rest over the edge with my feet. Tomorrow, they'd be right back, neatly made on my bed. Nothing like a discreet household staff, though I wished they would spare themselves the trouble. I didn't care whether my room looked picture-perfect. Nobody ever cleaned my room for me before. The best part: everything had been right where I'd left it.

I turned out the lights and slipped under the cool satin sheets—they were nice. It pained me to admit it. Rolling over to my side, I closed my eyes, willing myself to sleep, but the crickets were happily singing outside. They were happy.

And I was miserable.

I had never been so alone in my life.

Ironic, considering I was surrounded by so many people. The staff. I still didn't know all their names. Carter constantly had his jagoff friends over. Steven often conducted business meetings at the house. Mom organized and hosted her committees and charity events. It seemed as if something was always happening.

It was times like this I missed Dad. I wished he had fought harder for me during the custody battle. Time and time again, I expressed my desire to stay with him, but the judge seemed to think a life with my mother in the Pattersons' household was a better *fit*. My ass. It probably helped that Steven's lawyers had thrown his money around like it was raining cash in the courtroom. I wouldn't doubt if the judge was somehow on my stepfather's payroll. Money talked in this part of town.

There was a time when Dad cared about what I had to say, listened to my opinions as if they mattered. I couldn't help feel as if he abandoned me to the wolves.

I stopped thinking of Angie as my mom after the divorce and her rushed wedding a month later to Steven. It pissed her off when I used her actual name, which more or less made me want to continue calling her Angie. I shouldn't provoke her, but I had so much pent-up anger. She had changed so much these last few months. I hardly recognized the woman who ran this household. She wasn't my mother.

On the surface, she presented herself to be a cultured lady. Classy. Respected. Dignified. The picture made me laugh. She was actually just a small-town girl from a poor family who had big dreams. Those visions of flashing lights and red carpets all ended when she became pregnant with me and that translated into me ruining her life.

No one forced her to marry my father. Or have me, for that matter. Those were choices she made. Choices she had to live with.

Perhaps she had a hard life growing up with a single parent and having to watch her mom die from emphysema and cirrhosis. She had been left alone at the age of seventeen to face the world on her own.

In other words, I had some pretty amazing genes. I was really batting a thousand in the DNA department. I don't know what that said about me... probably that I needed to find a good shrink.

Fuck me.

I was nothing like her. And I vowed never to be. I would graduate from the damn Academy with honors and get into Hamilton University. I would make something of myself without her help or the Pattersons' money. I didn't need a damn thing from anyone.

* * *

My best friend was bouncing off the walls on the other end of the phone. I flipped over on my back, staring at the trimmed-out tray ceiling above the bed. "Ains, I'm not going," I said into the phone for the third time.

"Pleeeease," she begged. "It is the party of the summer."

I fumbled with my bracelet, propping the phone between my shoulder and ear. "You said that about the last one."

When it came to parties, Ainsley wasn't easily deterred. "This is our senior year. We have to start it out with a bang. And... it's one of the Elite's parties. Aren't you the least bit interested in seeing you-know-who?"

I frowned and replied, "Nope."

"Josie." She let out a dramatic sigh.

I made a face at the phone, not wanting to admit there was a teeny part of me that wanted to see Brock. I shouldn't, but a little sliver of intrigue lived inside me, whispering in my ear. "I honestly don't give a shit about the Elite."

She made a snorting sound in a way that called me a liar. The thing about only having one best friend was that they relied on you to be their sidekick for everything. "A ton of people from the Academy will be there. It would be a great way to scope out your class." Leave it to Ainsley to find a convincing argument.

I had to admit, it would be nice to know one person when school started next week. I closed my eyes and knew I was going to regret this, like I almost regretted picking up the phone.

"Everyone from Public is crashing. It will be epic," she insisted. Through the phone, I heard her fumbling around in a drawer, probably her tower of makeup. It was such a mess, but Ainsley loved beauty like I loved mint chocolate ice cream.

This wouldn't be the first or probably the last party I'd crashed. It was a common occurrence in Elmwood.

I put her on speaker so I could check my social media. She was right. In the half hour since the last time I scrolled through, my feed had exploded with updates about the party at Grayson Edwards's house tonight. "One last party," I murmured while scrolling past one update after another.

"Don't make me go alone, Jos," she whined. "Who else is going to carry my drunk ass home?"

I sat up on the bed and ran my hands over my face. "Fine. I'll go, but you so owe me big-time for this."

She squealed in my ear. "Pick me up in an hour."

* * *

It took me thirty minutes to shower, dry my hair, apply some simple makeup, and get dressed. I checked myself in the mirror as I smoothed a loose pink curl back into place. The white tank top I wore opened in the back, showing off my tan shoulders. I turned to check out my ass in the dark denim shorts, satisfied that I was revealing just the right amount of skin.

Snatching my keys and phone off the dresser, I shoved my phone into my back pocket and headed down the stairs. Quiet echoed through the halls as I walked toward the garage. I waved at Edmund, the head of security and Steven's driver, and headed through the door.

I halted in the driveway. "Shit," I mumbled, staring at the spot where my car had been parked. It was gone. "Motherfucker." I couldn't believe it. She actually sold my car.

"Looking for this?" Edmund asked from behind me.

I turned around to see him holding a gold ring with a key fob attached to it, a warm smile on his lips. Edmond looked like he was in his late thirties and was built like a linebacker. The black suit he wore fit snugly against his wide shoulders.

Giving him a less-than-thrilled expression, I walked up to him and took the key. "Thanks," I muttered.

He chuckled, shaking his head. "She drives like a dream," he said, "I promise. But if you don't want to take out the Lexus, I could always drive you to where you need to go, miss."

I coughed. "Uh, no. Thanks for the offer, big guy. I can drive myself." Reluctantly, I dragged my ass to the Lexus and slid inside. The rich, black leather glided underneath me. I hated to admit, but it was the comfiest seat I'd ever sat in. My fingers wrapped around the steering wheel, testing out the feel. As sick as this ride was, it wasn't my Corolla.

Emotion swelled up, and I took a deep breath, willing the hurt away. Later, when I had a minute to myself and I wouldn't risk ruining my makeup, I would bawl my eyes out.

I pushed the start button, and the car purred to life like a panther kitten. I exhaled and backed the car down the driveway, then shifted it into drive. As the gate swung open, I pictured my mother's face and slammed my foot on the gas. The Lexus shot down the road, trembling with power.

Fifteen minutes later, I pulled up to Ainsley's house, a record time. She was waiting at the curb, her hair pulled into a high ponytail, a waterfall of colors. She leaned down into the open window, peering inside at me. "Holy. Shit. Please tell me this is yours?"

I grimaced. "Yeah. Now get in before I change my mind and go home."

She was grinning like an idiot as I pulled away from her house.

The party was insane by the time we arrived, cars jam-packed on the street and more than a few on the lawn. Only an Elite party would have valet parking. I cruised past the large iron gate onto the paved semi-circle driveway and stopped the car, handing the key fob over to some guy who promised to treat her right.

I rolled my eyes, not caring if he drove the Lexus into a brick wall.

Ainsley swung her arm on my shoulders and did a little dance of excitement as we walked up the pathway. Music greeted us, blasting different genres from various stereo systems. I couldn't tell one song from another, but no one cared.

Grayson's house—correction, mansion—was jaw-dropping. I craned my neck back, taking in the impressive sight of the cream-colored exterior with four massive columns that climbed up two stories.

"Hey! No empty hands tonight." A guy with shaggy brown hair that reached his shoulders handed two cups to Ainsley and me. "No one enters without a drink. House rules."

I offered him a smile of thanks. "If you insist." I needed a drink to dull all the emotions swirling inside me.

Ainsley bumped her hip to mine. "Loosen up, girl. This is a party. Try to have fun. You need a bit of fun in your life." She took a drink of whatever concoction filled our plastic cups.

We wedged our way through the crowd gathering inside the house. "Damn," Ainsley said in awe, her eyes wide as she took in the rest of the house. "This place is ridiculous."

I thought my house was over the top, but this place... It was another level of rich.

Through the floor-to-ceiling windows, I saw that a crowd congregated outside around the pool and down to the beach where a string of bonfires burned.

"This is the kind of place that has a bowling alley in the basement," she shouted in my ear.

No doubt.

We'd only been at the party for a few minutes when trouble found us. Typical.

"Who let the trash in?" a girl beside me sneered.

I turned to glare, knowing damn well she was talking about Ainsley. The hoity bitch looked down at my best friend like she was a pile of shit her Jimmy Choos stepped in. I cocked my head to the side and eyed her. "You must be part of the bitch welcoming squad." I seriously hated mean girls, and seeing as this was my last year of school, I wasn't taking any shit. "I heard you guys suck, if you know what I mean." I made a lewd gesture with my hand and mouth.

The girl gasped in outrage, blinking her magnetic long-as-shit lashes at me.

Ainsley snickered beside me.

No rich bitch was going to mess with *my* best friend. I didn't give a crap who she was or how high up the cheerleader pyramid she ranked.

"Oh, you definitely go to Public," she said, lips puckered like she just drank a glass of dirty water.

It was the first time I was actually glad to be going to the Academy, just so I could see the look on her face when I said, "Sorry, but unfortunately, you're going to have to put up with seeing my evil face every day."

She let out a short laugh, flipping her unnaturally red hair. "I can't believe they would let someone like you in. The standards must be dropping."

"Obviously, if you go there," I snapped back.

I was only on my first drink, and already I was about to throw down in a catfight. This had to be a new record for me. I was contemplating tossing the contents of my cup into her face when a deep voice to my right interrupted.

"God, Ava, are you starting shit already? Give it a rest." The voice belonged to a platinum-haired guy. He rolled his light blue eyes, a grin of amusement on his full lips. He had an aura about him, like everything in the world was a joke. Up close, he was dazzling.

He was also one of the Elite.

Ava's eyes scanned up the guy, her mouth twisting into something sultry. She angled her body toward him, an invitation twinkling in her eyes. "I thought this was an Academy-exclusive party, Micah."

"It is," he replied, those mischievous eyes turning to me with keen interest, and the way he leisurely glanced me over left me feeling naked before him, as if he could see straight into my broken soul.

I fought the urge to cross my arms over my chest. So this was Micah Bradford. I couldn't stop staring at him, and I wouldn't have been surprised if my mouth hit the ground.

Beside me, Ainsley's fingers dug into my arm. I hadn't even felt her grab me.

Ava twirled the end of her hair, causing her pink crop top to shift up to show more skin, a smug smile on her lips. "Then what are they doing here?"

Brows lifted, Micah asked, "Who are you?"

I'd had enough of this shit. I was done. This was not how I

wanted to spend my night, getting the third degree by a bunch of entitled assholes. "Does it matter? We're leaving."

"You can't leave without telling me your name. I swear you look familiar. Plus, I make it a point to know all the hot girls at school."

"I just bet you do," I mumbled under my breath, ignoring the thrill that ribboned through me at being called hot.

"It's Josie," Ainsley piped up. "She's Steven Patterson's step-daughter," she announced proudly.

I groaned, wanting to crawl under the nearest table. Why did she have to mention who I was?

"Patterson. Right." He snapped his fingers. "I heard he got remarried. Didn't Brock say he hooked up with some chick at that wedding?" A knowing glint came into his eyes.

I stared at him blankly while my mind whirled. He told them? Did that mean he knew who I was? That I was the girl? FML. Did everyone know? "Brock who?"

Ava looked put out at the mention of Brock hooking up with someone that wasn't her. She quickly hid her annoyance with a snide smile that made me want to tear her red hair out at the roots. "Carter told me his stepsister is a real skank," she said tartly.

That bitch.

"Why don't you go contract another STD, skank," Ainsley snarled, coming to my defense. I could always count on my best friend to keep it real.

If Micah hadn't positioned himself between Ava and me, a deliberate move on his part, I would have slapped her. He noticed the fire jump into my eyes. "Carter's a dick," Micah said with a wink. "Enjoy the party. I'll be seeing you around, *new girl*." He grabbed Ava around the waist and threw her over his shoulder.

What did he mean by that? I couldn't help thinking there was a double meaning to his statement. Did he think because I had recklessly and flippantly hooked up with Brock that I would be willing to sleep with him?

Fuck, what had I done? I wished to God I'd never slept with Brock Taylor.

Public enemy number one squealed with a bubbly laugh as Micah carried her through the crowd. "Put me down," Ava said halfheartedly.

Micah slapped his hand over her ass, which was out for the entire world to see.

I shook my head, hands clenched at my sides.

"Come on." Ainsley took my arm and yanked me in the opposite direction. "We need another drink before I toss that bitch into the pool."

"I'd pay money to see that," said a voice behind me.

I cringed, wondering if I could ignore Carter and hope he just went away. Of course my stepbrother would be at the party.

"Here." Carter offered me a drink. "Peace offering. Just for the night." His smile might have looked genuine, but I knew better.

"Whatever. Just stay away from me," I said, already on edge from my encounter with Ava.

His eyes scanned over Ainsley. "Suit yourself," he said with a shrug, setting the drink down on the table and disappearing into the crowd.

It didn't take long to see how different the parties Public threw were from the Elite ones. "Are those girls strippers?" Ainsley asked, her gaze on two girls standing on the kitchen counters. When we walked by, they were only in their bras and panties, but those were about to come off next as one of the girls slipped her finger under the straps.

Things got crazy at the Public parties we went to, but this was... intense.

I saw a table with what had to be cocaine or maybe crushed Adderall spread out, and a pair of blonde girls used flashy credit cards to cut the white powder into lines.

"Found the Oxy!" somebody shouted, and suddenly the room was raining pills. Cheers went up as people nearby scrambled around, grabbing for the ones that hit the floor.

Not long after, we spotted a group of people from Public. There was safety in familiar faces. I drank. I danced. I laughed. I drank some more. "I have to pee," I announced, handing my cup to Ainsley, my feet still moving to the beat.

"Hurry. I need my dance partner," Ainsley hollered back, her arms swaying over her head.

I went in search of a bathroom, not exactly an easy task in a place this big. The first one I stumbled upon on the main level had a line that wrapped down the hall. "You've got to be kidding me," I grumbled. My bladder would not wait.

I hooked around the corner and took the left side of the double staircase, heading to the second level. One of the bedrooms had to have a bathroom.

I sighed in relief when I spotted a girl leaving one of the rooms and hustled down the hall, relieved to find a bathroom. It was clear from the décor and styling products this was a guy's domain. It even had a scent that just screamed male. No soaking tub, just one massive walk-in shower. There were two doors, one leading to the hallway and the other to a bedroom, I assumed.

I made quick use of the toilet and was washing my hands when the door from the hallway opened. What the hell? I swore I'd flipped the lock, but since I was more or less done, I didn't care all that much... until I heard her voice.

"I'll be right out." The lock clicked, and I lifted my eyes in the mirror, connecting with Ava's.

Shit.

It looked like I was about to go round two.

Wiping my hands on a little white towel folded neatly on the sink, I kept my gaze locked on hers as she moved to stand behind me. "He doesn't do girlfriends," she said.

I knew precisely *who* she was referring to, but I wanted to hear it from her lips. Turning around, I leaned against the bathroom counter. "Who are we talking about?"

She wasn't buying my dumb, innocent act. "Brock Taylor. You might have slept with him, but you'll only ever be an easy lay."

"Convenient, since that was all I was looking for," I replied dryly. I didn't want her to think she had gotten to me. "If this is you staking your claim, he is all yours. I want nothing to do with him or the Elite."

Her lip curled up in a sneer. "You say that now. But just wait. They all want a piece of them. All of them."

"And let me guess, you're the only girl that matters?" I

snorted, shaking my head. She was a fool if she thought she could leash someone like Brock. Not that I knew him well.

Something flashed in her eyes as they narrowed, but then she shrugged it off. "I'm just letting you know how things are done here."

"How very thoughtful of you." Because she was blocking the door I came in through, I took the other one and found myself inside an endless closet of clothes, mostly jeans and T-shirts. An entire section of one wall was devoted to sneakers, color-coordinated in rows from shelf to shelf.

It was dark, but the light from under the bathroom door illuminated just enough for me to see. I meandered through the closet into the attached bedroom, halting at the doorway as my ears picked up something.

Shit! I wasn't alone. Of course the bedrooms would be occupied. It was a party full of teenagers who had nothing but sex on their brains.

The rustling of sheets was followed by faint whisperings. I stood frozen, deciding what the fuck I was going to do. Try to tiptoe out undetected, or go back the way I came and face Ava in the bathroom?

A soft moan filtered over the dark room. *Screw this. I'm out.*

I took a step backward, and the fucking floor creaked. My heart thundered in my ears as I stopped moving, afraid to breathe.

Sssshit!

A head lifted from the bed, a gaze colliding with mine in the dark, and I could do nothing but stare back, caught in the heat that brimmed from those aqua eyes. I didn't have to see the rest of his face to know who it was. A sinking feeling spread in my gut.

"Why did you stop?" the girl underneath Brock complained, sinking her fingers into his hair.

He ignored her, his lips twitching into a wicked smirk as his head angled to the side to regard me. "Do you want to join?"

Uh. I wanted to run from the room and pretend I'd never seen Brock's hands on another girl, knowing damn well just how seductive those fingers would feel over my skin. "I'm a selfish lover. I prefer not to share." I didn't know how I managed to keep my voice level, but I was damn proud of myself at that moment.

His chuckle was husky, and I hated that my body responded to the sound.

The girl with him suddenly caught on that they weren't alone. "Who is that?" she asked, sounding miffed.

Brock pushed himself off the girl as he climbed out of bed, strutting straight for me. I lifted my chin as he approached, halting when he was just inches away. The scent of his cologne teased my nose, and I really wanted to take a deep inhale.

"Are you sure I can't change your mind, Firefly? Or should I call you Josie?" Damn him and his sexy voice.

So he knew my name. Big deal. I knew who he was too. And yet, I wasn't prepared to hear it from his lips. But it was the nickname that made my knees tremble, a definite reminder of that night—a night I only wanted to forget.

His shirt was off, the front button of his jeans open, and I couldn't figure out why I was still there. "You wish," I replied dryly, putting my hands on his chest to shove him aside, but the plan backfired.

Brock caught my fingers, keeping my hand secured against his bare chest. I swear, I must have done something to piss someone off in another life to put me through such torment. Heat sweltered between us, and I glared at him, hardly believing this was the same guy I had slept with at the wedding. "I think you misunderstood. What happened between us, that was retaliation. It had nothing to do with you." My fingers curled against his chest.

A dark brow lifted. "I know. I also don't care."

At that point, all I *cared* about was finding Ainsley and getting the hell out of there before I did something utterly stupid. And rash.

Like have sex with Brock Taylor. Again!

"Brock, are we going to fuck or what?" the girl, still lying in nothing but a bra on the bed, whined.

I matched his raised brow with one of my own. "It seems like you have your hands full tonight, *Brock*." I yanked my hand free and rushed out of the room, slamming the door shut behind me. Two steps into the hall, I stopped and pressed my back into the wall, releasing the breath I'd been holding. I gave myself only a few seconds before dashing down the stairs, half afraid Brock might come after me.

It took ten minutes to find Ainsley by the pool. In the short amount of time I'd been upstairs, it seemed as if the number of people at the party had doubled. I recognized more faces from Elmwood Public.

"There you are," I said with a slight edge of irritation.

Relieved to have found her, I didn't notice Trevor until he said my name. I'd been so focused on grabbing Ainsley and getting the hell out of Dodge. My nerves were rattled from my encounter with Brock.

"Hey, Josie." Trevor Jones was a guy I'd known most of my life. He was like a brother to me, but I wasn't sure he felt the same about me. One too many times, I'd gotten the vibe he was interested in something more than friendship.

After my run-in with Brock, I wasn't in the mood to deal with anyone sporting a dick. "Trevor," I greeted before turning back to my best friend. "I've got to get out of here. Will you be okay to get a ride home?" I could tell she wasn't ready to leave. Ains lived for parties, loved to be where the action was. She suffered from a serious case of FOMO.

Her wide, shining eyes dimmed a little. "Are you okay? Did something happen?"

No. Yes. But I said nothing about what happened with Brock or Ava cornering me in the bathroom. "I have a headache and just need to lie down," I admitted, not entirely a lie either.

"Okay. I'll grab a ride with Trevor." She looked at Trevor, who nodded.

"Have fun, okay? And call me tomorrow." I gave her a quick hug. "Make sure to use a condom."

She playfully hit my arm.

I made my way through the sea of people and out the front door, where I waited for someone to bring the Lexus around front. The sky was scattered with stars tonight, a sliver of moonlight breaking through a cluster of trees that lined the property.

It was amazing how quickly a person could sober up. I felt stone clearheaded.

The sense of someone watching me tickled at the back of my neck, and I shifted my gaze over the front of the house. On one of the second-story balconies stood a figure in the shadows.

I knew instinctively who it was.

Brock leaned against the railing, a ribbon of moonlight hitting the side of his face. A midnight curl fell forward, partially shielding his eyes, but even from this distance, I could make out the startling hue.

He was alone.

We continued to stare at each other, neither one of us flinching, and I wondered what was on his mind to cause him to scowl in such a manner. Was it me?

Did I give a flying fuck if it was?

No. I decided right then and there, I didn't care one bit why Brock was unhappy.

He wasn't my concern.

I turned away and hopped into the little red Lexus, but not before I gave Brock the middle finger.

CHAPTER FOUR

The rest of the weekend went by in a rush of nerves and boredom. I texted Ainsley a dozen times, relieved to know she had gotten home from the party safe and sound.

If there was one lesson I'd learned in my seventeen years, it was to go into every new situation with the lowest possible expectations. That way, I wasn't disappointed when things fell apart, which they usually did.

Some might call me a pessimist.

I said realist.

I'd been dreading my first day at Elmwood Academy all summer. Despite this being my senior year, I was feeling like a freshman instead of someone who ruled the school.

Divorce sucked.

Macy, the day maid, had laid out my Academy uniform on the bed while I'd been in the shower. Not even the steaming hot water eased the knots of tension that worked themselves into places I didn't even know tension could exist.

I dried my hair and stepped back into my bedroom clad in nothing but my undergarments and stopped short at the sight of the uniform.

"This actually can't be my life," I muttered, picking up the blue-and-black-plaid skirt. I knew I had to wear a uniform, but this... It was damn clichéd.

And shorter than I expected. As I inspected the skirt, I wondered if it had been altered. I wouldn't put it past Angie to take it upon herself to have my uniform tailored. She would see it as helping me fit in. I ignored the heels at the foot of the bed Macy had placed beside the uniform and went in search of my boots. No one could pay me to wear heels all day. Screw that shit.

I skipped breakfast, my stomach unable to handle food, and grabbed my bag. Carter was in the kitchen as I passed by on the way to the garage. He scowled in my direction. Unable to help myself, I offered him my usual morning one-finger salute.

"Sit and spin," he yelled after me.

Ugh. Did we have to be linked, even if only by marriage?

Ten minutes later, I cruised the Lexus into the Academy student parking lot, guiding the car into one of the empty spots near the exit. It meant a longer walk to the building, but easier access on the way out. And I had a feeling I would want a quick getaway after ninth period.

I might hate the car, but it did blend in beside all the Land Rovers, Audis, Mercedes, and every other brand of luxury car. Not that I gave two shits about blending in.

Flipping down the overhead mirror, I took one last glimpse at my appearance, making sure there was nothing wedged in between my teeth or dried toothpaste on the side of my lips. I'd taken the extra time this morning to curl my hair, mostly because I didn't get much sleep. My makeup was natural and light, just the way I liked it.

I grabbed my bag and braced myself for what was to come. As I got out of the car, I did a quick skirt adjustment and started across the parking lot. A handful of kids hung around their cars, talking and catching up. I focused my attention on the three-story brick building looming up ahead in a U-shape. The Academy was actually older than the public high school, and it showed in the school's preserved charm. The grounds were gated and edged with tall, manicured hedges. All the windows were arched, and three gothic gables framed the front of the building, giving it the feel of a castle. The sidewalks were paved with bricks, leading up to the main entrance flanked by the school's mascot—two stone gargoyles.

I had to admit the school itself was magnificent—a piece of history. Hell, I already felt smarter just gawking at it.

This wasn't the first time I'd been to the Academy, but as someone who appreciated architecture, the beauty of the structure struck me every time. Public was in the same conference as the Academy and they often played against each other during homecoming games. It was a longstanding rivalry between the two schools. Seeing as I wasn't into school spirit, I never cared much to get involved with the rivalry.

Inside, the marble floors shone spotlessly, reflecting the light from iron chandeliers that hung from the high ceilings. My combat boots thudded down the hall as I headed to my locker. During registration this summer, I'd scoped out the school's layout, getting a general idea where my classes were.

Seeing everyone dressed nearly identically would take some getting used to. They all looked the same, properly made-up dolls. Like little fashion designers in the making, most of the girls put their own spin on the uniforms of plaid skirts and white blouses, the school crest embroidered on the right side just below the shoulder. The majority of the girls hiked up their skirts, showing off their legs before the knee socks. Others wore loose, thin ties around the neck, the top buttons of their blouses undone a little too low.

My locker was on the first floor near the school cafeteria, which was actually more like a mall food court. With only a few minutes to spare before first period started, I shoved my bag into the metal container and pulled out my laptop. All our textbooks were online. My arms were happy about that. No more lugging around fifteen-pound books to each class. Public couldn't afford to mandate students purchase laptops. It wasn't in their budget, but Academy students didn't have such struggles.

I glanced at the time on my phone and groaned. According to the actual, honest-to-God map I received with my schedule, I had to go across campus for my English class. It would be like running the length of a football field to get there. Here was hoping I could pull off the it's-my-first-day-of-school excuse if I was late.

It was impossible not to notice the glances I received or the whispers as I walked. I was the new girl. I only hoped the novelty wore off sooner rather than later. Word traveled fast.

I didn't need to eavesdrop to know what they were murmuring about. *She doesn't belong here. She isn't one of us—born into money. She's nothing but trash.*

They weren't wrong.

I didn't belong in this world, and I sure as hell didn't want to be here.

One year, I told myself. *One fucking year.*

And then Elmwood Academy could kiss my poor ass.

The bell rang as I turned the corner into my first class, a little winded, a little sweaty, and the center of attention. Most everyone was already seated, and I took one of the only available spots, aware of everyone's eyes on me.

The day continued in a similar fashion of scrambling to classes, avoiding everyone, and praying it would all just end. It was becoming clear that not a single nice person attended the Academy. Nothing but a bunch of stuck-up assholes who weren't worth a second of my time.

The girls openly glared at me with hostility, and more than one guy had not-so-slyly asked for my digits. I lost track of the number of times I told someone to fuck off.

It was my nightmare made real.

And only the first day.

If this was any indication of how my year would go, I had so much to look forward to.

"Nice hair, freak," a girl passing me in the hall snickered.

I contemplated grabbing a fistful of her bleached blonde locks and slamming her head into the wall. Perhaps it would knock some decency into her. "Shit, sorry. You scared the shit out of me. Did you trip and fall on your face?" I said over my shoulder and watched her cheeks turn red with anger.

If the color of my hair was the only thing they could think to use against me, then they definitely needed some lessons in bullying. The thought was enough to keep my fingers wrapped around my laptop as I headed to the cafeteria.

No fighting.

Fighting led to detention and eventually suspension. Neither would look good on my school résumé for colleges.

And I'd be damned if I get stuck in this town.

Sweat broke out along the back of my neck and my nerves mounted when I looked out over a sea of unfamiliar faces. They all knew each other, grew up together, shared lollipops in kindergarten. They were all cut from the same cloth.

I'm not designed for this shit.

Picking a line, I grabbed a water and a veggie wrap from one of the vendors and swiped my student ID. I decided to eat outside because I needed the fresh air—or that was what I told myself. Truth, I didn't want to deal with finding a table to sit at.

As I made my way around the cluster of tables to head outside, someone more or less shoulder-checked me. I didn't know if it was on purpose or if the girl just wasn't looking where she was going when she ran into me, but the result was the same.

I faltered a step or two, my ass bumping into a table, which then had me falling into someone's lap. Before I got the chance to apologize, collect my food, and rush out of the cafeteria, a pair of hands clasped my waist, steadying me. I glanced up, blowing a strand of hair out of my mouth. Four sets of eyes were on me, pinning me with equal glares of amusement.

The Elite.

What were the chances that I would end up looking a fool in front of them?

"God, I love it when hot girls fall into my lap," Micah said, grinning. I recognized him from the party. He had a dazzling smile that just edged on evil.

Brock's captivating glance caught mine, and I told myself not to squirm under those icy eyes, but his unwelcoming frown was unnerving, along with the rest of them.

They were all stunning in their own way. The school uniforms fit perfectly to their frames, each varying in degrees of muscle mass and probably correlated to what position they held on the football team. I tried not to gawk in appreciation. It was nearly impossible. Particularly since I was sitting on top of one of them.

The full effect of the Elite in such close proximity sent goose bumps over my skin. And yet, I couldn't gauge if it was fear or something else I was feeling. Desire?

Talk about being messed up in the head. A shrink would have a field day with me. Perhaps it was time I scheduled that appointment.

The other two were Grayson and Fynn, but I wasn't sure which was which. Not that it mattered. I wasn't sticking around to find out.

"Sorry," I mumbled, trying to shove off Micah's lap, but his firm hands were holding me in place. I ground my teeth and angled my head to glare at the asshole holding me captive.

His light blue eyes sparkled with devilment.

"Let her go," Brock said disinterestedly, as if I was annoying him.

Prick.

"We need to work on your sharing skills," Micah said to Brock, grinning, but his fingers released my waist.

Brock shook his head.

I stood up and got caught off guard by the hostility I noticed in Grayson's or Fynn's cognac eyes. It cut through me like a knife. I don't know what I had ever done to him, but he looked as if he wanted to slice my head off with a machete. Arms crossed defensively over his chest, he said not a word to me, just watched with narrowed eyes as I gathered my shit and left.

No sooner had I rounded the corner toward the exit than I heard a voice pipe up from the flight of stairs above me. "That was quite impressive back there. Day one and you already managed to do what every girl in this school has tried to accomplish since first grade. They all hate you now."

My eyes lifted, and I studied the girl walking down the steps toward me. She had beautiful olive skin, and her brown hair was streaked with honey highlights that framed a heart-shaped face. Her full lips twisted into a smile, but despite the amusement, something like respect shone in her gray eyes.

"And does that include you?" I asked, raising a brow. As far as I knew, this girl could be just like the rest of them. Out for blood, territorial, crazy bitches.

She snorted, her hand trailing along the wooden banister. "Douchebags aren't my type," she said as her feet reached the base of the stairs.

They must be my type, because holy shit, my body was still reeling from my little interlude with the Elite. I felt as if I'd had a brush with death, like jumping out of a plane and my parachute not opening until I almost hit the ground. That was how being scrutinized by them made me feel. Breathless. Dangerous. Impulsive. Foolish.

"Yeah, well, I seem to attract them like flies on shit," I said.

Up close, I could see the cute little freckles that dotted over her nose. "I like you, new girl. I'm Maddy Clarke, but everyone calls me Mads." She had the ends of her button-up shirt tied in a knot that showed a bit of midriff.

Sighing, I leaned against the wall, cradling my water and sandwich. "Josie James. And you might be the only person who does."

She snickered. "Not true. Brock Taylor liked you enough to sleep with you. No judgment," she added quickly. "I don't care who you sleep with; just pointing out that it's a big deal to catch the eye of one of them." Her gaze went to the Elite's table.

I followed her gaze, noticing how a few girls hung around the table. I snorted in disgust. "Does everyone in this school treat them like gods?" Why did they deserve such attention? I was beginning to wonder if Brock was setting out to ruin me. Or if bragging about every girl he managed to bang was his thing. He didn't strike me as someone who needed to brag.

"When you look like them, yes."

I shook my head. "I don't get it. I didn't even know who he was when we slept together," I said, unsure why I was admitting that to a virtual stranger I only just met, but something about Maddy seemed... safe.

"You must have lived under a rock. Let me introduce you to the Academy's Elite." Her voice was mocking, as if she found the whole idea ludicrous. "You know Brock." A smile pulled at her lips. "He is what I would deem the leader of the group. The other three pretty much do whatever he says. That includes what girls they can fuck."

"Wow, that is messed up."

"Tell me about it. He comes from old money and will inherit his family's hotel monopoly. The pretty boy on Brock's left is Grayson Edwards. He is the son of a very wealthy film producer and a bit damaged inside. His older brother, Sawyer, died in a car accident a few years ago. It was a street race. Big news. Made all the headlines."

I felt a pull on my heartstrings. Was that sympathy for the asshole who had shot me daggers of hate?

What was wrong with me?

"On the other side of Brock is Fynn Dupree. Now, if I was into douchebags, he would be my type." She took a second to appreciate the over-six-foot gorgeous football player. His coloring made me believe he came from a mixed heritage. "Fynn's mom is some big shot corporate lawyer. And his dad is in real estate. And lastly, the playboy, Micah Bradford. He's slept with more girls than Hugh Hefner has put in magazines. Including me."

My gaze swung to Mads. "Really?" I was shocked.

She turned away from the Elite to look at me. "A momentarily lapse in judgment that I promised myself I would never repeat." She shuddered. "Don't let those baby blues and cocky smirk fool you. Micah isn't boyfriend material. He will never give up his player life, not as long as the girls keep throwing themselves at him."

My cheeks warmed as I remembered the comment he made when I had fallen into his lap.

Mads grinned as if she knew precisely where my thoughts had gone. "Both his parents work in finance, like stockbrokers or some shit. Or banking. I can't remember the particulars. But they all are swimming in dough. That's all that matters, and it gets them anything and everything they want."

"Thanks for the rundown. I plan on staying far away from them. I don't need the drama."

She scrunched her nose, her attention focused straight ahead. "I'm not sure you'll have a choice in the matter."

I followed her gaze and stared right back at Brock, who was watching me from across the room. His jaw was rigid, but it didn't take away from his flawless beauty.

Mads leaned over my shoulder. "What I want to know is how you ended up in bed with Brock?"

Breaking the gaze, I rolled my eyes. "It was a couch."

She arched a brow, intrigue lighting up her eyes. Looping an arm through my mine, she pulled me toward the school doors. "Let's swap sex stories and bond over poor decisions."

I laughed and strolled with her down the pathway to a courtyard situated at the center of the grounds behind the building. "Your stepbrother is a real asshole, you know. It isn't Brock going around telling everyone about what happened with you and him at the wedding. It's Carter."

My shocked expression only lasted a split second before it

morphed into rage. "That little fucker. God, I hate him. I swear he lives to make my life miserable."

She took a seat on one of the empty wrought iron benches, and I sat beside her. "And before you ask, no, I haven't slept with your stepbrother."

I laughed. "I guess there is hope for you yet."

She rummaged around inside her bag. "I take it everything isn't peaceful blended bliss at the Patterson household?"

I bit the inside of my cheek, rolling my water bottle in my hands. "Hardly. The one thing Carter and I agree on is that we didn't want our parents to marry. Not that it mattered, because we're stuck with each other. At least for a year."

"What happens then?" she asked, unscrewing the top on her Pepsi bottle.

"I get the hell out of here, go to college."

"Solid plan. Do you mind?" she asked, slipping out a slim cigarette from her bag.

I shook my head. "Go ahead. Do they allow smoking?"

She flicked the lighter, producing a small flame before putting the cigarette between her lips and sucking in as she lit the other end. "No," she said, grinning and releasing a puff of smoke. "Bad habit, I know. But we all have our little vices. This helps me deal with the bullshit at this school."

"Is there a lot of bullshit I should know about?"

"You have no idea. It's going to take more than a lunch period to fill you in." She took a long drag on the cigarette. "But you can bet your ass all the garbage that goes on in this school, one way or the other stems back to the Elite."

I couldn't help but remember the shower of pills during the party at Grayson's house.

"Word of advice, new girl." Flicking the end of her cigarette onto the lush green grass, Mads frowned at me. "Watch your back. Thanks to your loose-lipped stepbrother, everyone knows you hooked up with one of the Elite, and some of the girls want to put you in your place for it."

Oh, good. Future bitch fights. I could already see my rule of no fighting going right down the drain. I wasn't about to let a group of jealous psychos put me in my place. "Thanks. I appreciate the warning."

If anyone needed to be put into their place, it was Carter. My stepbrother and I were going to have ourselves a family sit down. Better to nip this shit in the bud than let it go on all year.

I had every intention of confronting Carter the instant I walked through the front door, but it was my mother who was there waiting for me. Then I remembered the asshole jock had football practice after school. He wouldn't be home for hours yet, which only burned my ass more. I wanted to tear into him now. Not later, when I'd had time to cool off.

Instead, I had to face my mother when all I wanted was to escape to my room and shut out the rest of the world, including the people I lived with. *Especially* the people I lived with.

Shit.

"Josie! I'm in the kitchen. I want to hear all about your first day!" Her voice rang out, all high-pitched and cheerful, the moment I closed the door.

She was about to be disappointed. Then again, I always disappointed her in some shape or another, so what made this any different?

I dropped my bag on the floor and meandered down the hallway into the kitchen, heading straight to the fridge. My ass plopped onto the counter stool after grabbing a bottled tea. "Maybe you should ask Carter. I'm sure he could tell you all about it," I grumbled, my voice sharp with accusation.

Angie didn't actually cook. If she was in the kitchen, it was because she was eating or directing the cook about dinner tonight. She tapped on her laptop, a sheet of paper laid out in front of her. "What does that mean? Did Carter do something?" There was only mild concern in her tone.

I didn't bother to tell Mom for a number of reasons, including having to bring up the incident at her wedding where I'd had sex with Brock and she walked in. "No. I just didn't have the best day." That was me glossing over things. Trying to make them sound better than they actually were. All I needed was for her to meet me halfway, maybe ask what had gone wrong and listen sympathetically the way a mother should.

It looked like both of us were in for disappointment.

She muttered a curse under her breath, shaking her head. Her dark hair was carefully arranged into a smooth bun. "Of course you would say that. You're always so negative."

I opened the bottle of sweetened tea and took a sip. "Being the new kid always sucks. That is just a fact. Everybody is talking about you."

"I would think that would be a good thing," she said, lifting her eyes from the computer screen. I had to wonder just what the hell she did all day. It was a mystery. She had no job, other than looking pretty. God only knew what she was doing on her laptop. Online shopping?

"Not so much." I would regret this, but the words were popping out of my mouth before I could stop them. "Carter has made it his mission in life to destroy me. He's spreading rumors about me at school." Maybe if I leveled with her, she would meet me halfway. I wasn't holding my breath, seeing as she disregarded every claim I made against Carter.

"What kind of rumors?"

"The kind that damage your reputation," I replied, picking at the label on the bottle.

She rolled her eyes. "Do you have to be so dramatic all the time? It is part of the high school experience. I'm sure the rumors will blow over, and it will only make you stronger."

Yup. Should have known better. I wished my heart wouldn't sink as it did. "And that's why I can't tell you anything."

Giving me a sidelong glance, she stopped typing on her keyboard. "What do you expect from me? To coddle you?"

I scoffed. "Hardly. I'm not five."

Angie's mouth twisted into a grimace. "I wish you would try to get along with Carter for me, please."

Did she have any idea what she was asking from me? It was like befriending the devil. "Sure, Mom," I said.

The sarcasm wasn't lost on her, but her eyes brightened slightly regardless. "Thank you. This family means a lot to me."

I just bet it did. At least the image of a family. "I had a family," I mumbled.

Her mouth screwed up in a tight line, losing any semblance of a smile. "Josephine, you still have a family. Did you at least try to make any new friends today?"

I let my head fall back with a heavy sigh. "Actually, I did."

"See, that wasn't hard. I want you to be happy here."

Sometimes living with my mom was like having Dr. Jekyll and Mr. Hyde as a mother. Her mood swings gave me whiplash. "I was happy before you remarried."

She shut the laptop and turned to me, crossing her legs as she released a long exhale. "I know this has been an adjustment for you, but attending the Academy is a once-in-a-lifetime opportunity. It can open so many doors for you. You would be a fool to not take advantage of what the school can do for your future."

As if she seriously cared about my education. Attending the Academy was more about the connections and how much their net worth was. If I didn't tread carefully, this conversation could end up nasty, and after the day I had, I didn't know if I had it in me to go a round with my mother right now.

"Do you know how many girls would kill to be in your shoes?" Her eyes glanced down to my boots. "Well, not those shoes."

I snorted, a stupid smile tugging at my lips before I could stop it.

"See, you can smile," she said, tucking a piece of hair behind my ear. "It's been so long since I've seen you smile, Josephine. All we do is fight."

There was truth to that. All summer we'd been at each other's throat, butting heads over everything. It started before that, but things really took a turn for the worse after the wedding—not that we'd ever been super close. Ainsley's mom was more of a mother to me than mine ever was, but sometimes Angie surprised me. More often than not, if she was nice, she wanted something, so I didn't trust this nice version of Mom. "I've got homework to do. Believe it or not, they give out homework on the first day."

She patted my shoulder. "You always were such a good student."

I plucked my tea off the counter and headed out of the room, pausing at the doorway to glance back at Mom. She was on her laptop again, scrolling through a list. At one time, I would have told her about the rumors at school, about Brock, the Elite, and about Mads. I was so angry with her, not just for marrying Steven, but taking away my car, forcing me to live with her, and not giving a shit about my feelings in any of this.

Turning away, I headed upstairs, grabbing my bag from the entryway floor on the way. As I climbed the stairs, my phone buzzed. I paused in the middle of the steps and checked my messages. It was my dad.

Dad: **Hope your first day at the Academy was a success. See you soon. I'm proud of you.**

Pressure clamped down on my chest. Maybe I should go see my dad. I'd only seen him twice over the summer, and I missed him. Today more than other days. Not having him in my life caused a hole in my heart. I felt incomplete, torn between two lives.

Inside my room, I docked my phone next to the bed and cranked the music up loud, needing to drown out the thoughts in my head and the discontent. I was on the verge of crying, my emotions getting the best of me.

But I refused to shed a tear, firming my lip and steeling myself against the sadness as I climbed onto the bed. At some point, I fell asleep, for when I woke up, my playlist had ended and silence filtered through the room.

It was dark, ribbons of moonlight cast over the floor. A glance at my phone told me it was past eight o'clock. *Shit*. I hadn't meant to fall asleep for that long.

I opened the bedroom door a crack and peeked into the hall. It was quiet, only a glimmer of light coming from downstairs. Most of the staff would have gone home, except for Edmund.

Instead of going to the kitchen for something to eat, I put on a simple black bathing suit and went down to the pool. If I didn't do something to rid myself of all the craziness inside my head, I'd lose it.

I liked to swim, especially at night. The water was cool and refreshing as I swam a slow lap, then another. After a few minutes, I started feeling better. Some of the hurt and anger I still held in my chest over the rumors eased.

But it didn't last long.

As I finished a lap and emerged from under the water, running my fingers over my wet hair, Carter showed up.

And the asshole wasn't alone.

"I'll grab drinks." His voice carried out to the patio. God, I hated that smug voice, worse because his friends were with him, and when they were around, his cockiness went up.

A handful of jocks wandered onto the patio. I recognized most, since he'd brought them around before. They were part of the football team, and it had become pretty clear the five of them might have been able to put all their brain cells together and make an entire brain. Maybe.

But that was basic Bad Guy 101. When you were as

scummy as Carter, you surrounded yourself with people lower than you to make yourself feel superior to them. Carter wanted to be king of this crew—like Brock.

A tall, dark-haired moose of a guy—I thought his name was Shawn but I honestly didn't care—snickered when he found me treading water at the center of the pool. He crouched down at the edge. "Damn, I was really looking forward to swimming." He laughed, glancing at his friends. "But it looks like someone took a shit in the pool."

So original. I stayed in place even as a tight ball formed in my stomach. There were six of them, including Carter, and only one of me. Looking at this bunch of brawny football players stirred a ribbon of fear inside of me. I had no idea if Mom or Steven were home, but since Carter was bringing out the booze, I was guessing no. "Go fuck yourself," I bit back.

A round of chuckles echoed over the screened-in pool. "Such a dirty mouth. Perhaps I should clean it for you?" Shawn suggested.

Carter reappeared carrying two six-packs of beer and made a sound of disgust in the back of his throat when he noticed me. "Oh, you're home?" From the glassy look in his hazel eyes, I could tell he had already been drinking.

"I do live here," I snapped, slowly moving myself to the opposite end of the pool. The temperature-controlled water was growing cold against my skin.

Carter pulled a beer free from the plastic ring, handing the rest to his teammates to pass around. "How can I forget? Your shit is everywhere. But just remember, you might live in this house, but you're still nothing but trailer trash."

Shawn chuckled while the others guys winced and exchanged looks. Not all of them were utter assholes. "I don't know, bro," Shawn said, leering at me. "She's looking kind of hot from here. What little I can see? Why don't you come out and have a drink?" His head angled to the side as he regarded me with a leisurely smirk that made my stomach churn. He held up a can in offering.

Glaring back, I replied, "I'd rather drink my own spit."

"Be careful what you wish for, sis." To my growing horror, Carter strutted to the other side of the pool, walking slowly along the edge.

I swallowed, my neck craned up as I glared at my step-brother. What a righteous ass. I refused to let him intimidate me. Lifting my chin, my fingers reached the edge of the pool not far from his feet. "Just get out of my way," I said. My teeth clamped together as I fought against the cold snaking into my veins, my teeth threatening to chatter.

Carter looked downright murderous at me. "Get the fuck out of the pool."

His friend put a hand on Carter's chest as it heaved. "Okay, hey. She gets the point. You don't have to be a dick. Besides, I came here to drink."

Shawn came to stand on the other side of Carter, popping the top on his beer. "Come on, Carter, let her go."

"I didn't ask you, Shawn." Carter only had eyes for me.

Shaking his head, Shawn turned to me and reached down, offering a hand. "Come on. He's in a shit mood because we had a shit practice today. He'll get over it after he's had a few more drinks."

I stared at the extended hand, every bone in my body telling me not to take the olive branch. These guys, they weren't allies against my stepbrother. They were his partners in crime. But I wanted out of the damn pool. Ignoring his hand, I lifted myself over the side, wary of Carter and his friends.

One of them gave a low whistle at the full sight of me in my bathing suit. I was never so glad for my choice to wear a one-piece tonight. Flipping them all off, I grabbed the towel I'd left hanging over one of the chairs, but I was too slow.

An arm shot out like a striking serpent, wrapping around my waist and pulling me tight against a broad chest. "Where are you running off to?" Shawn whispered in my ear. "I'm not done with you yet."

"Let me go, you asshole!" I tried to elbow him in the gut. Bad mistake. The guy had abs of steel, and when that didn't work, I fought and struggled against his arm, but his grip only tightened. I'd never been accosted before, never found myself in a situation where I felt as unsafe as I did now. I'd be damned before I let any of them touch me.

"Too bad you aren't my stepsister." Shawn's breath reeked of alcohol, choking me. "I'd be a whole a lot nicer to you." His implication of *nice* was very clear.

"Why don't you show me, dickhead?" I baited, for good reason, and the arrogant SOB didn't disappoint, spinning me around to face him.

I forced my lips to curve, encouraging Shawn. The booze made his movements sloppy, which worked in my favor. He grabbed onto my chin and I brought my knee up in between his legs. Bullseye.

"You bitch!" Shawn cursed, shoving me away to clutch and cradle his junk. "What the hell is wrong with you?"

I was beyond livid and shaking with more rage than fright. "What's wrong with me? What the hell is wrong with you? Don't fucking touch me again!"

"What are you going to do about it?" Carter sneered.

Maybe it was feeling helpless. Maybe it was genuine fear. Or the anger still streaming in my veins. Maybe it was that these assholes thought this kind of treatment was okay. Maybe it was the laughter. Or the rumors swirling around school. Carter deserved to be punished.

And I was just the girl ballsy enough to do something about it.

Before I had any idea what I was doing, I spun, throwing my hands out in front of me, and shoved Carter as hard as I could. It sent him stumbling backward, over the edge of the pool, straight into the water.

The surprise only lasted a second as I blinked at where he'd disappeared under the surface. And then I was grinning.

Carter surfaced immediately, water dripping over his dark blue eyes. His sandy hair was plastered to his face. "My phone was in my pocket, you psycho bitch," he seethed, spitting mad.

Time for me to go.

Forgoing the towel, I made a beeline straight for the kitchen, dripping water along the way. Voices thundered behind me, followed by the stomping of feet like a herd of elephants. I didn't stop. I ran through the house and up the stairs until I was behind my bedroom door. I flipped the lock quickly in place. If they broke down my door, there would be questions. I held on to that thought as fists pounded on the other side of the door.

"You better open this door, Josie. I swear to God. What am I supposed to do without my phone!" Carter ranted.

I backed away from the door, afraid he might actually bust the thing down. Swallowing the scream bubbling up my throat, I bit my lip, forcing myself to stay silent. I didn't even dare breathe. Not until the bastard gave up. He hit my door one last time and then lumbered back down the hall.

Exhaling, I sank to the floor, wrapping my arms around my bare, not quite dry legs, and buried my face into my knees. The tears I'd been holding back all day finally came. Silently, I cried, letting them roll over my cheeks, shoulders shaking.

Cater was the worst kind of asshole.

CHAPTER SIX

How long had it been since I woke up in the morning and felt hopeful about the day ahead of me? I couldn't remember.

Not that I had ever exactly been a positive person. I was nobody's ray of sunshine. Still, there used to be things I looked forward to. Girl's nights with Ainsley. *The Bachelor*. Art class.

I was supposed to be on top of the world. I had everything a girl could wish for. Yet, I had never been more miserable in my life.

I slept fitfully after the incident with Carter and his jackass football friends. Every tiny noise had set me on edge, which explained the ring of circles around my eyes this morning and the puffiness. No amount of makeup would fix this. I longed to drag my ass back to bed, instead of downstairs to the kitchen.

I had no idea when Carter's friends left for the night, and I wasn't stupid enough to think my war with Carter was over. If anything, this shit was just getting started. He would find a way to pay me back. It was what he did best. And I needed to be on guard. Who knew when he would strike next, but I could bet it would be soon.

The sun shone bright and sunny as I walked into the kitchen, so very opposite to my current mood. My plan was to get out of the house early and avoid any unwanted run-ins with Angie or Carter.

I popped a slice of bread in the toaster and pulled out the peanut butter. While the bread toasted, I poured myself a cup of iced coffee to take with me in the car. Steven strolled in, his shoes rapping over the tile floor.

"Josie," he greeted warmly.

I closed my eyes for a second, gripping the countertop tight. Steven was the last person I'd expected to see. The man was almost always off on a trip somewhere scouting new players, meeting with other owners, and whatever other important details that required his attention.

"Morning," I replied, turning my head to the side. I made it a point to sound pleasant. My toast popped up, and I plucked it out of the toaster onto my plate.

Steven reached for the coffeepot, pouring himself a mug. One of the staff made sure the coffee was brewed and hot. Rich people perks. "I heard what happened last night."

The knife slipped out of my hand, clattering onto the counter, my appetite suddenly gone. I turned around, fighting to keep my expression neutral. "I was only defending myself. One of his friends had his hands all over me. I just reacted." I refused to admit how scared I'd been, even to my stepfather.

His eyes narrowed just a little—they were so much like Carter's, it was enough to make my heart drop. I knew before he even opened his mouth, Steven would somehow defend his son's disgusting behavior. "Carter said they'd been drinking. I'm sure things got out of hand."

Denial much?

I snorted. "Sure. It's totally normal to assault a girl." This time I couldn't stop the sarcasm from leaking into my voice. What world was I living in that this behavior was acceptable? The fucking Twilight Zone?

Steven stirred cream and sugar into his cup. "Accusations like that are detrimental to a player's career. I'm not saying he is absolved of any guilt, but it isn't wise to go around making allegations. Carter is an asset to the Academy's team and has a promising future ahead of him. We take care of our own."

Outrage fell over my expression. "Thanks for the warning. I'd hate to do anything that might upset the team," I said sourly. It was crystal clear whose future was important. And it sure as hell wasn't mine.

It was too early for this bullshit.

Would anyone ever be on my team? Cheering me on?

Yeah. Me.

I gathered my bag and iced coffee, leaving the toast untouched on the counter, and headed out the door.

My crappy morning extended itself throughout the day. Rumors traveled sickeningly fast. It didn't take long to realize Carter had already been hard at work, talking shit about me. Apparently, I had thrown myself at his friends last night like the desperate slut that I was.

As if.

I was between classes, dashing to my locker to grab my cardigan. The halls were chilly today thanks to the storm that had descended upon the school an hour ago. Violent winds railed against the brick building, rattling the windows.

Grabbing the white knit button-down from my locker, I hiked my bag up on my shoulder and whirled around, dropping the sweater in the process. "Are you freaking kidding me?" I muttered, bending down to pick it up.

A pair of squeaky white sneakers stepped onto the corner of my cardigan's sleeve. I groaned, shoving my hair out of my face as I lifted my eyes. Brock, flanked by the other three Elite, hovered above me. Brock's lips twisted as his gaze met mine with an expression that pierced my soul. "Don't get up on my account. I rather like you on your knees." His voice was husky, edged with danger.

I hated how attractive I found him—hated how flawlessly good-looking he was.

Micah let a low husky chuckle. "Are the rumors true? You looking for your next victim, new girl?"

My cheeks warmed, betraying my desire to stay unmoved by Micah's words. Screw them all. Figuratively, of course. I tilted my head to the side. "Are you offering?"

Fynn and Grayson let out low laughs.

"I wouldn't say no," Micah replied with a wink.

Brock removed his shoe from my sweater, and I snatched it up before he could do something else. It was bad enough there was now a dusty shoe print on the white knit. *Asshole*. I straightened up and stared Brock straight in the eyes. Damn. They were so intense. And scary. I could admit that. He had this intimidation factor that would make even grown men uncomfortable, yet, I was intrigued. Along with other emotions I didn't want to admit.

For once, could I be attracted to a guy who was nice and not a prick?

My nails dug into my palms to stamp down my sudden desire to grab Brock by the hair and kiss him senseless. I dragged my gaze from Brock to the grinning Micah. "Are you sure you don't need his permission first? That's how it works between you guys, right?" I asked, my eyes volleying between the four of them before landing again on Brock.

"Watch it," he warned in a low voice, eyes darkening in a way that I couldn't tell if it was anger or desire that caused them to change.

A shiver raced through me. "Or what?" I countered just as the bell rang. I was so late for class.

He tugged on the end of a pink curl. "You don't want to find out, Firefly. But I can promise it will be the worst thing that's ever happened to you."

I made my lips curl. "Funny. The worst thing that ever happened to me *is* you." I poked him hard in the chest, but he didn't budge. My statement was not entirely true, but Brock didn't need to know all the horrible things in my life. That would just be feeding him ammunition, and I refused to allow the Elite to torment me.

His jaw flexed as he took a step closer to me. "You got that right."

"Do us both a favor. Stay the hell out of my way," I scoffed, giving him a long, hard glare.

"That's the problem. You seem to be everywhere I turn." His eyes moved down the length of me. "The uniform might look good on you, but it doesn't make you one of us, Firefly."

"She does have nice legs," Micah added, his eyes sparkling with humor.

"Who said I ever wanted to be one of you? I'd rather be staked in the heart than become one of you," I said, holding his gaze, turmoil rolling within me.

Brock shook his head. "Word of advice. Watch your back." The four of them just stared me down. Then, after a long, awkward moment, they parted down the middle, allowing me to pass by.

On a huff, I shoved my way through and rushed down the hall. It wasn't until I turned the corner that I realized I was headed the wrong way. Cursing under my breath, I pushed through the girls' bathroom door, needing a moment to calm my nerves.

I went to the sink, clutching the sides of the cabinet as my arms shook with equal parts fury and fear. *Deep breath in. Deep breath out. Deep breath in. Deep breath out.* My eyes lifted, and I gawked at my reflection in the mirror. What the hell did Brock Taylor want from me? I wasn't a threat. I didn't have some sort of master plan to tarnish his reputation. It wasn't my fault I had an asshat for a stepbrother. Was that it? Brock was pissed that Carter was going around airing his dirty laundry?

Turning on the water, I stuck my hands under the stream and patted cold water over my face. I turned off the tap and noticed the sweater draped over my arm. "Shit," I mumbled, remembering the stain. Dropping my bag on the ground, I laid the cardigan over the sink. I flipped the water back on, grabbed a paper towel, and set to work trying to get out the stain of Brock's footprint.

As I was scrubbing at the sleeve, one of the stall doors squeaked open. I'd thought I was alone. Guess not. My gaze lifted, meeting a pair of familiar eyes in the mirror. Mads.

"Hey," she said, strolling over to the sink next to mine. She glanced at the sweater and then hopped up onto the counter.

"Hey," I mumbled back, giving up on removing the stain. I was sure one of the day maids would do a much better job at lifting it out of the material than I would in a high school bathroom.

Mads crossed her legs and pulled out a cigarette. The lighter flicked to life as she lit the end and took a long drag before holding it out to me. "You look like you could use one of these."

I'd never been a smoker. The taste turned me off. I shook my head. "Thanks, but I'll pass."

Shrugging, she flicked the end of the slim stick into the sink, little particles of ash falling into the white porcelain bowl. "Suit yourself, but if you change your mind, you just have to ask."

I shoved the damp cardigan into my bag and leaned my butt against the counter. I wasn't going to ask if she should be smoking in the girls' bathroom. From the little I knew of Maddy Clarke, she didn't give a shit about rules. "God, could this day get any crappier?"

She grimaced, taking another drag. "Want to talk about it?"

"Which part? That my stepbrother and his friends assaulted me last night and my stepfather gave me a stern lecture about the football team's future? Or that the Elite just gave me their official welcome to the Academy?"

A puff of white smoke exhaled from her glossy lips. "Yeah. I heard about the incident with Carter. Everyone is talking about how you attacked him."

I rubbed at the side of my temples, the stirrings of a headache forming. "I'm sure he failed to mention that he had it coming or that one of his football friends got a little handsy with me."

"Welcome to Elmwood Academy, where the jocks think they are untouchable and the Elite are kings," Mads said, unfazed.

My nose wrinkled. "Do they really? Think they're kings?"

She pulled a leg up onto the edge of the sink, the other still dangling over the side. "Well, it is more like Brock is the king. The other three are his knights."

I shook my head disbelievingly, but the truth was, I could see Brock on a throne wearing a crown. "That is so messed up. This whole school is messed up."

"You're finally catching on."

"I don't know how I am going to survive an entire year of this shit," I admitted, my shoulders slouching. Like I didn't have enough to deal with at home. I had to add school drama to the list.

Mads waved her cigarette in the air, sending smoke fluttering about. "You need to be careful. This isn't like your other school. The kids here, they not only have money, they have power attached to it. You wouldn't believe the shit they get away with or the problems they can create. With parents that work in law enforcement, the courts, school boards, one phone call is all it takes to make your life hell."

I turned, propping my hip against the sink, giving up any pretense of going to class. I needed a time-out. At least for a period, and hiding out in the bathroom with Mads sounded perfect. "So what am I supposed to do? I can't do nothing. My stepbrother needs the crap kicked out of him."

Something glinted in Mads's gray eyes. Something mischievous. "Well, I have an idea, but you won't like it."

"I don't like being groped by drunk football players. Your idea has got to be better than that."

She grinned, hopping off the counter and putting out her cigarette in the sink. "Just wait until you hear it first."

Her grin was infectious, and I found myself smiling back. "I'm listening."

"There is only one way to get immunity and protection in this school." I was already getting a sense of where this was going. And I didn't like it. Not one bit. "You need to become untouchable."

"Like the Elite," I offered as an example. Did she want me to form my own crew? I didn't have time for that.

Her eyes grew brighter. "Exactly. You need to find a way to get your stepbrother to lay off you, to fear you. The only way to get that kind of status that the Elite has is to get them to bring you into their circle."

I choked. "You want me to become part of the Elite? Are you stark raving mad? No. Hell no," I shrieked.

But Mads was not the least bit deterred. "Think about it. No one in this school would mess with you. No one. And that includes your stepbrother and the entire football team. The Elite owns them."

She had a point, and I could see the logic in her plan, but... Me? An Elite? I didn't even know how to begin weaseling my way in with those four guys. I bit my lower lip, contemplating the craziest idea I'd ever considered. "So many things could go wrong," I pointed out. I could get hurt, for starters. That was my big concern here—that the whole idea could backfire and blow up in my face.

"True. But like you said, do you really want to spend your entire senior year dealing with Carter and his bullshit?"

A chill ran down my spine. "Fuck, no."

Pulling a pack of gum out of her pocket, she handed me a piece and began unwrapping one for herself. "Whether it was intentional or not, you've already captured their attention. You're on their radar. And the fact that you've slept with the king works to your advantage."

I popped the gum into my mouth. "And how is that?" I asked, chewing. I had no plans of sleeping my way into the Elite, if that was what she was suggesting.

"The guys like to maintain a certain reputation, which includes never being tied down. But Brock Taylor, despite his reputation, doesn't sleep around lightly. He isn't a casual sex kind of guy. He has what the Elite call standby girls. An Elite-approved list of girls available to scratch an itch. Brock never has random hookups. Until you."

"Wonderful," I mumbled. No wonder the girls in this school

have been less than welcoming. Brock labeled me without even my knowledge. Why? What made him break his rule of sleeping with strangers? Why me?

Questions that I would have to get answers to another day.

"The other guys are different. They actually live up to the reputation of male sluts and basically fuck anything with two legs and a skirt. So the fact that Brock slept with you gives us an edge."

"How do you know all of this?" I asked curiously. Had she been one of those standby girls? I couldn't believe it. Mads was too damn proud and sure of herself, but she had slept with Micah, so maybe she wasn't as immune to the Elite as she appeared.

"Let's just say, I've been around the Elite my entire life. I hear and see things."

"Even if it works, I still have no idea how to weasel my way into the Elite. Brock was pretty clear when he warned me to stay away from him."

Mads rolled her eyes. "Please. That's just asshole for 'I want you in my bed.' And as far as the details, we have time to brainstorm."

"We?" I echoed.

Mads smile grew wide. "Yes, girl. I so want in on this. If you succeed in infiltrating the Elite, you will make history, and I am so a part of that. We are going to change this school. And as your new best friend, I want all the perks that go with being an Elite friend."

A laugh bubbled out of me, and it sounded a little insane. "This is utterly crazy, you know that, right?"

Mads turned to face the mirror, checking out her reflection. "Probably. But it is so much fun. You in?" Her eyes found mine.

I should absolutely say no. No way I could pull this off. They would never let me into their little circle. I was a stranger. And the Elite had been friends since forever. They trusted no one but each other. And yet I heard myself say, "Yeah, I'm in."

Mads let out a squeal of delight and hugged me.

Only the best ideas were formed in the girls' bathroom.

Said no one ever.

CHAPTER SEVEN

I planned to meet up with Mads tonight and didn't have the heart to bail on Ainsley, so I invited her along. It might not be the best idea to involve her in this stupid plan, but Ainsley would be hurt and pissed if I left her in the dark. Revenge and secret missions. These were right up her alley. She would eat up this idea of me infiltrating the Elite.

I glanced over at Ains sitting in the passenger seat. "Are you sure you wouldn't rather go to Trevor's party?" I asked.

"Definitely not. I want to meet this Mads. I told you that you would have no problem making friends." She flipped up the vanity, assured that there was more than enough eyeliner encircling her eyes, and sat back in the seat.

Right. I knew she meant it in the nicest way possible—she did want me to make friends, but she also didn't want to be forgotten. I could never forget her. "Thanks to my stepbrother, the entire school basically hates me." I turned her way when we reached a stoplight. "I'm almost afraid Mads being nice to me is some kind of joke I'm not in on."

"I could get some of the guys on our football team to beat the living shit out of Carter and his friends for you," she offered sympathetically. I'd told her about the incident by the pool. Ainsley did not take the news well. She flipped the F out. But what are best friends for if not to feel outraged on your behalf? "And that is why I'm here." She grinned. "If she isn't genuine, I will call her ass out on it. But to be honest, this idea of hers makes me like her already. I want to know more."

I seriously hoped the two of them got along. It would make my life a bit easier for once. The light turned green, and I stepped on the gas, the Lexus cruising smoothly along the road. "She isn't like all the other rich girls," I informed her, trying to find a way to describe Maddy Clarke. "She doesn't seem to care about money or status." Or following rules.

"Is she an alien?" she joked, flipping the radio station to one without commercials.

"Maybe," I replied, smiling, my fingers loosening their grip on the wheel. Being with Ainsley allowed me to relax, truly let my guard down for the first time in days.

It felt so good to be out of the house. My mother was prepping for a party she was holding next Saturday—another desperate attempt at fitting in with the snobbish country club ladies. I didn't doubt they all snickered and talked behind her back when she wasn't looking. Or maybe they were as ruthless as their daughters and gossiped about Angie to her face.

My compassionate soul couldn't help but feel a little bit sorry for my mother. In a way, we were both in the same boat, in a new place, looking to fit in and make friends. The only difference: this hadn't been my choice, but it had been hers.

Ainsley settled into her seat and crossed her legs. "Alien or not, she better be nice to you. I missed you all week. It's not the same at school without you."

I gritted my teeth, keeping my eyes focused on the road ahead of us. "I know what you mean."

A few minutes later, I swung the Lexus into the Pizza Shack parking lot. It was a local hangout in the old downtown part of Elmwood. The side streets were paved in bricks, and rustic black lantern lamplights framed the square. The town always went all out decorating for holidays downtown. I adored the specialty shops and family-owned restaurants. Coming here with Ainsley felt like coming home.

This was what I needed. Familiarity. Gooey cheese. And my best friend.

Mads was leaning against one of the charming light poles, smoking a cigarette. Her lips curved wickedly when she spotted me. She had partially pulled up her hair, accenting defined cheekbones and those cute freckles dusting her nose. Dressed from head-to-toe in black, she looked as if she was ready to go on an undercover stakeout.

My lips curled as Ainsley and I got out of the car.

Ainsley grabbed the side of my shirt and tugged me closer as she whispered, "You didn't tell me she smokes."

"Is that a problem?"

"No, I'm just shocked," she replied.

"Hey," Mads greeted when we were close enough, flicking her cigarette to the ground and crushing it with the heel of her expensive-ass designer shoes. Mads looked the part of a rich girl, but without the snobbish attitude. She had a bad girl edge instead. I think that was partly why we were drawn to each other. There was a little bit of rebel in both of us.

"You made it," I said.

She pushed off the light pole, standing a few inches shorter than me, putting her somewhere in between Ainsley and me in height. Her lips turned up into a friendly smile. "Believe it or not, I've crossed the tracks a time or two."

I rolled my eyes. Downtown was what the Academy kids would consider slumming it. They tended to hang out in the newer parts of town, meaning this was the perfect place to hatch the details of operation Elite. "This is my best friend, Ainsley."

Ains tugged on her skirt, offering Mads a smile. "Hey, Josie has told me all about you. I'm glad she has a friend. It's been tough since she moved."

"The Academy doesn't exactly roll out the welcome carpet for newcomers," Mads said.

"I'll say," I muttered under my breath. "Doesn't help that my stepbrother is a dickwad."

Mads and Ainsley nodded in agreement, just as I hoped. I wanted the three of us to get along. It was important to me, a way to merge my old life with my new life. We had a common ground in our hatred of Carter. There were worse things people could bond over. It wasn't like we were plotting his death.

Mads's eyes twinkled. "Come on, let's grab a table in the back. We've got a lot to discuss. And I'm starving."

"Who can say no to pizza and revenge?" Ainsley craved both.

Together, the three of us headed inside the pizza joint, snagging a booth in the back corner that was made for evening rendezvous and inconspicuous plotting. We were all a little giddy as we sat, and I couldn't believe I had agreed to do this.

Even if this plan sucked and I never got the Elite to give me the time of day, it would be worth it just to hang out with these two.

We waited until after the waitress served our drinks and took our pizza order. Then we got down to business.

Ainsley and I sat across from Mads. I rested my elbows on the table and asked, "So, how does one worm their way into the Elite?"

Mads stirred the ice in her soft drink. "Normally, I would say it is impossible, but... I think there is something about you, something that has grabbed not just Brock's attention, but the other guys' as well."

My brows drew together, and I frowned, wondering how she came to that conclusion. It couldn't just be because I slept with Brock. That didn't make sense. Why would the other guys care?

"What makes you think that?" Ainsley asked the question that was on the tip of my tongue.

"Apparently, your name has come up a few times during Elite business," Mads responded.

Did I even want to know what Elite business was? What kind of business would involve me? Unless they were planning on ruining me or something equally as horrifying. I didn't want to be one of those naïve girls who couldn't see a guy for who he really was or fell for his bullshit, but Brock didn't strike me as someone who wasted his time running a girl out of school. Surely he had more important shit to do with his time. "How would you know that?" I took a sip of my drink, my throat suddenly dry.

Mads's expression sobered. "Grayson Edwards is my cousin."

I choked on a piece of ice. "Say what?"

"Are you serious?" Ainsley shrilled, her knees bumping into the table as she jumped forward in the booth, an expression of utter shock on her face.

I recovered much quicker and shot off my next question before Mads could explain. "Why didn't you tell me?" My heart hammered in my chest.

A rueful look passed over Mads's features. "For several reasons, but mostly because I didn't want you to get the wrong impression of me. I'm not just some rich girl who is related to one of the Elite. I wanted you to judge me not for who my family was, but for just me. And I was afraid you would think I was on their side."

Her explanation tugged on my heartstrings, for it was the very same thing I wanted. Not to be judged by where I lived or who my mother married. "Not cool, Mads. How can I trust you?" I could see our plan unraveling before it even began.

Ainsley was scowling across the table at her, and I was half afraid she might throw her fork at Mads.

Mads, sensing the sudden ice freezing in the air between our table, held up her hands like she was waving a little white flag. "Just hear me out. Then you can decide what you want to do. Fair?"

Ainsley and I shared a look. My longtime friend raised a brow, silently telling me that this was my choice. She would back me no matter what I decided. With a heavy sigh, I nodded. "Don't make me regret this."

"Oh, you won't. I'm serious about what I said. About the plan." Her voice lowered and she waited until one of the servers passed our table before she continued. "I can help you. And when we're done, Carter won't know what hit him. The Elite either."

"Why would you do this? Help me? What do you get out of it?" I asked, still unsure this was a good idea. Today, I'd been open, but now...

"I have my reasons for wanting to pierce the Elite's solid circle. You could say I'm still butt sore about Micah. But more importantly, I want to destroy Carter. You aren't the first girl who has been victim to Carter's brutality. He and a few of the other football players have a reputation of harassing girls and taking things too far. Help me bring him down."

Was she one of Carter's victims? Or did she know someone who had been hurt by my stepbrother and his thugs?

"Kill two birds with one stone," Ainsley muttered.

Mads grinned. "Exactly. Getting Josie the protection of the Elite means they will take care of her and anyone who touches her. Especially Carter. Brock has history with him, and I know he is just looking for a chance to take him down."

I couldn't believe I was sitting in a pizza parlor discussing how to destroy my stepbrother and essentially use the Elite to do it. Two days ago the thought would have made me laugh. "I can't believe Grayson is your cousin."

Mads rolled her eyes. "Our mothers are sisters. But you see how this works in our favor. I have inside information."

Ains jumped on that. "Okay, tell us all the dirt you have on the Elite."

"First, we have to agree that whatever we discuss stays between us." Mads started to lay out the rules.

Ainsley and I both nodded.

Taking a sip from her drink, Mads looked us each in the eyes. "This only works if we keep quiet about what we're doing. If word gets out, the Elite will make our lives a living hell." Her voice made it perfectly clear. "We're not just dealing with four high school boys. You guys have heard only the surface stuff of what the Elite does, but it goes so much deeper."

"My lips are sealed," Ains said, drawing an invisible zipper across her mouth.

"Same," I agreed, tucking my hands into my lap.

"Josie, you are taking the most risk here, but you also have the most to gain. You can't let Carter keep treating you like this and getting away with it. Things will only get worse. Trust me," Mads said, an expression of regret and sadness creeping over her features.

I didn't know why, but I did trust Mads. "I can't spend the entire year afraid. I'm not safe anywhere."

"Agreed," Mads and Ainsley said at the same time.

Our pizza arrived a moment later, and the table fell silent as we waited for our waitress to leave. I grabbed a slice of cheese and set it on my plate. "And if the lesser of the two evils is Brock and the Elites, then I'm all in," I said, giving the pizza a few seconds to cool off before I devoured it.

Mads beamed as she picked up a slice for herself. "I was hoping you would say that," she said, right before taking a bite.

It seemed an unspoken agreement had been formed between us. Mads would take point. She was the mastermind behind the plan, so it only made sense that Ainsley and I took direction from her. Something told me Mads had been involved in schemes like this before. It wasn't her first takedown.

And so the plotting began. We scarfed two pizzas between us as we laughed, brainstormed, laughed some more, and stuffed our faces. It was one of the best nights I'd had in a long time.

There was no backing down now. I was in. Full throttle.

CHAPTER EIGHT

The following weekend, the house was in an uproar all day Saturday in preparation for the dinner party. Only an hour left to add any last-minute details. The only other time I'd seen my mother this frantic was when she was planning the wedding.

I was looking forward to this stupid party nearly as much as I had the wedding.

Angie was so strung out, finally feeling the pressures of being a trophy wife. It wasn't all about looking pretty. She was damn determined to prove that she wasn't the gold digger she'd been labeled, that she had a right to socialize among them, even though not coming from any money herself.

She was scared to death.

And that meant she was on her second or third martini. *Who's counting?*

"What did I tell you?" she snapped at the middle-aged

woman. "I want the larger floral arrangements positioned in the front hall and going up the stairwells. Smaller arrangements go on the tables." She shook a handful of roses so hard, petals fell at her feet, while the florist only nodded and hurried away with her head down.

I couldn't help but sympathize with the florist.

Angie whirled on me, looking me over and I was surprised her eyes weren't glowing red. "Don't tell me you're wearing that." She waved a hand at me, tsking her tongue in disgust at my shorts and T-shirt.

"I'm wearing it right now." I looked down at myself, then up at her.

"Guests are arriving in less than an hour, Josie. Please, go change. I can't handle any additional stress." She sighed dramatically, picking up her martini. She stormed into the kitchen to yell at the cook and a small catering team she hired for the night.

I followed behind. "You don't really want me around tonight, do you?" I was asking sincerely, not to be a pain. I just didn't relish in the idea of spending my night with Elmwood's blue bloods.

She shot me a withering look before grumbling her approval over the hors d'oeuvres being prepared. "You're my daughter, and you're Steven's daughter."

"Stepdaughter," I corrected.

She ignored me. "Everyone will expect to see you here. Your brother will be there."

All the more reason for me not to be. I wanted to be nowhere near Carter. "I don't have a brother. I have a stepbrother. And frankly, I don't care if he's going or not."

She pressed a hand to her temple. "Don't do this to me. Not today."

"I don't see what the big deal is. None of these people care about me."

She slammed her glass down on the counter hard enough that I thought she might've broken it and cut herself. Alcohol sloshed over the rim. The wild rage in her eyes was a hurricane of anger building up inside. Hurricane Angie. She wanted to tear into me, to yell, but we weren't alone.

"Upstairs," she hissed through her teeth, marching out of the kitchen with her fists clenched at her sides. The witch actually forgot her drink. She must be pissed. I stared at the door she went through and then at the one on the other side of the kitchen. Two doors. Two choices. I wanted nothing more than to make my escape, but for some stupid reason, I followed Mom upstairs to my room.

Honestly, it wasn't just the people I was dreading, but the poofy dress as well.

The dress in question lay on my bed. I tried not to release the gagging sound that came up my throat. Flashy. Gaudy. And sparkly. Just like my mother.

No way in hell I was putting that on.

Not today.

Not tomorrow.

Never.

In my room, no one was around to hear or see us. Mom was quick to tell me of her displeasure. "Why do you always have to be so difficult? I am at my wit's end, Josephine. I had hoped this would be a fresh start for both of us. Do I need to send you away to boarding school?" she threatened.

"I'm not being difficult," I retorted, crossing my arms over my chest. "Would it really be that big of a deal if I hung out in my room?"

"It is a big deal to me and it would make me happy to have you there."

I snorted. "You don't want me there. You just want people to see me there. Your perfectly groomed daughter."

"You make it sound like that is a bad thing. I am proud of you. You can't fault a mother for wanting to show off her daughter."

It was pointless to deny I was still angry at her for everything. The move. The divorce. The new marriage. All of it still stung, and I didn't know how long I would go on feeling this burning anger. I didn't want her approval and couldn't care less how proud she was of me, even if it had been sincere.

But I didn't buy the act she was portraying.

I glared at her. "If you really cared then you would let me go live with dad." The words flew out of my mouth, hurtling across to my mother.

She blinked, her lips tightening and forming a hard line of disapproval. Fury leaped into her eyes. This might not have been the appropriate time to rehash this old argument, but I couldn't take it back now.

The next thing I knew, pain exploded along the side of my face. My head whipped to the side, strands of hair falling over my eyes. I breathed through the pain before turning back to face my bitch of a mother.

Right at that moment, I hated her. I trembled with the force of that hatred, my arms shaking at my sides, fingers curled into fists.

Still, I looked her dead in the eyes. If she thought I would break down or fall into place, she was sadly mistaken. This might be the first time she'd actually laid a hand on me, but I'd had plenty of practice at being hurt by her.

"Put on the dress, pull yourself together, get your ass downstairs, and smile," she seethed lowly, unable to hide the little tremor in her voice.

I said nothing, only lifted my chin in defiance. Nothing would ever be the same between us.

Spinning around, she left the room without another word. I listened to her heels clicking down the hall until the sound faded before exhaling. She had crossed the line today, one I wasn't likely ever to forget.

I pressed a hand to my cheek and winced. She'd hit me. The bitch actually hit me. Sitting down gingerly at my vanity, I checked out my face and was shocked to see a cherry handprint already forming on my cheek. Would it bruise?

Fucking wonderful.

Just one more thing for people to talk about at school on Monday. I was sure Carter would spin the rumors that I'd been beaten up. And probably deserved it too.

A grim smile tugged at my lips as I shook my head. No way in hell was I going to her fucking party now.

I had to get the hell out of here. I couldn't be at the house, not with all those people showing up. I couldn't pretend that we were some sort of happily blended family. I couldn't keep up the farce. Not today.

Grabbing my handbag off the dresser, I tiptoed downstairs, listening as Angie complained about the dust on the fireplace mantel. I hooked around the corner in the opposite direction and ducked into Steven's study to snatch a bottle of bourbon. What was it with rich people and bourbon?

It wasn't my drink of choice but would get the job done. That was all I cared about.

Getting out of the house was a cinch. No one looked twice at me or bothered to ask me what I was doing, the staff too busy with Angie's constant demands.

I contemplated taking the Lexus out for a spin, but with the bottle weighing heavy in my hand, I decided against it. Even as hurt and spitting mad as I was, I still wasn't stupid enough to drink and drive.

Besides, walking, along with the night air, might help clear my head. I had my pepper spray and cellphone in my purse. All my bases were covered.

I started the long trek down the driveway just as the first few cars started to arrive. Unscrewing the bottle, I took my first swing, letting the smooth and warm liquid coat my throat.

By eight o'clock, I had been wandering for two hours, the bottle half gone and me along with it. My new friend, bourbon, dulled the sting across my cheek, and I was feeling pretty good.

Stumbling down the path, I pulled out my phone, thinking about calling Ainsley. She was always up for a drink, but I remembered she had plans tonight. Without me.

That was a sobering thought and killed a bit of my happy

buzz. I took another pull from the bottle in an attempt to get back to that blissful place.

My thoughts drifted to Brock Taylor. *Wonder what he is doing this shitty Saturday?* His night had to be better than mine. I stared at my phone, scrolling through my contacts. There was no Brock Taylor in my phone. Nothing for Elite, either.

Thank God for small wonders.

The last thing I needed was to drunk text or call Brock.

That would end badly.

Like with me in his bed. *You are not booty calling Brock,* I lectured myself sternly.

But my drunk self really liked the idea of Brock in a bed. Would it be as mind-blowing as it had been the first time? Would his hands feel just like I remembered? Far too often my dreams were filled with the dark-haired god. Okay, god might have been an extreme description, but it wasn't that far off.

Sex with Brock had been damn near heavenly.

And in my current mood, I was capable of anything, which was exactly why I shoved my phone into my pocket and tipped the bottle back.

I closed my eyes for just a moment, a clear picture in my head of his face that night at the wedding. Those keen eyes, irresistible lips, and the way he looked at me as if I was someone special. Important. Worthwhile. Like he really saw me.

Firefly.

I could hear his voice in my head, rolling over the nickname like it was both a curse and prayer.

Yellow dots danced in the distance. Not fireflies. A pair of headlights shone down the street, approaching. I stared at the star pattern that hit the blacktop, memorized by the twinkling lights. They grew nearer, the car speeding down the road, hugging the curves. I lifted the bottle to my lips and tilted my head back, thinking it was probably time for me to make my way back to the Pattersons' mansion. My foot scuffled over the ground, catching the front of my shoe, and I tripped, bobbling the bottle in my hand. In an attempt to keep the bourbon in my grasp like a precious piece of glass, I stepped forward to regain my composure, and my foot landed in a pothole.

I went down.

I hit the hard surface, half sprawled across the road. Gravel pierced my palms, and I groaned. *Son of a bitch, that hurt.* And to top it off, I lost the damn bottle. I shoved myself into a sitting position, feeling the ground around me. Blinded by the impeding headlights, I lifted my hands in front of my eyes to ward off the glare.

Brakes shrieked, piercing my ears.

And in my sluggish brain, I had a second where my life flashed before my eyes.

Holy shit.

I'm going to die.

I squeezed my eyes shut, having no desire to watch the car hit me, and just waited for the impact. The high-pitched sound of metal grinding on metal finally ceased after the longest moments of my life. It took a few more before I could peel my eyes open.

I stared at a black bumper, headlights beaming on either side of me. The car was so close, I could have stuck out my tongue and licked it. *Oh. My. God. I'm not dead.*

In fact, I suffered not a scratch, other than the ones I sustained when I fell, but that was my fault and nothing to do with almost being hit by a car. The driver must have impeccable reflexes.

A bubble of hysteria left my lips, and I was two seconds away from either laughing or crying. My brain couldn't decide which. Through the darkness, I heard a car door open, followed by footsteps. Then a deep voice said, "You've got to be kidding me."

I wanted him to step in front of the light so I could see who it was.

"Why is it you are always stumbling into me drunk, Firefly?"

Shit. Shit. Shit.

Recognition ribboned inside.

No. It can't be.

But it was.

I lifted my eyes. Brock Taylor stared down at me, his lips pulled into a thin line, and a glint of some emotion in his aqua eyes.

Two silhouettes of the hottest guy I'd ever seen wavered in front of the headlights, his dark hair windblown like he'd been driving with the windows down. A soft beat of music drifted out of the car. "Brock?" I mumbled, thinking this had to be a hallucination. Or fate. I couldn't figure out which made more sense.

The devil or the angel.

I decided that Brock was both.

He leaned against the front bumper, crossing his arms over his broad chest. "What are you doing in the road?" he asked as if it wasn't the oddest question.

And to me in a buzzed state, it seemed a very responsible inquiry. "Looking for the bourbon," I replied. "I dropped it. After I tripped. Or was it before?" I let out a little giggle. "I can't remember."

His lips twisted. "Clearly."

I was still on the ground, banged up some and feeling woozy, but as I stared up into Brock's amused face, I didn't know if it was the alcohol or him that was making me feel so unstable. "Are you making fun of me?"

"I assure you there is nothing funny about this situation. I nearly killed you." His tone was so casual.

"Right. I had a bad day," I explained.

This seemed to pique his interest. "I can't imagine."

I snorted. "Bullshit." We stared at each other, and something passed between us that caused my lips to twitch. What was it about this guy that made me smile?

He shook his head and held out a hand for me. "Come on. I'll take you home."

I stared at his hand a brief moment before slipping mine into it. He pulled me to my feet and frowned as his gaze glanced over me.

Brock muttered something under his breath and then said, "You look like shit."

Normally, a comment like that would have pissed me off, but it was true. I shrugged. "Fitting, since I feel like it. Why do you care?"

"Who said I did?" He grabbed firmly onto my chin, but also with a gentleness that surprised me. Tilting my head to the side, his eyes took on a scary glint as he inspected my face. "Did someone hit you?"

I tried to jerk my chin away, but my movements were sloppy and weak. "It's nothing," I said, feeling color stain my cheeks, probably only deepening the imprint my mother had left. I didn't want to think about her or the problems I left at home.

Not when I was with Brock. I didn't know why, but I didn't want my family drama to bleed over into my time with him.

His lips pressed together. "Did Carter do this?" Cold violence simmered in his tone, and I shivered.

What made him jump to that conclusion?

For the first time, I might actually have pitied my step-brother, because Brock could kill him with that look alone. Why would he care what Carter did to me? They were teammates. A part of me wanted to tell Brock that it was Carter who had slapped me, just to see if he would do something about it, but as I stared into his eyes glittering with venom, I couldn't lie to him.

That was a problem.

I adverted my gaze and sighed. "No, it wasn't Carter."

He released my chin, shoving his hands into his front pockets as if he didn't trust himself. "Get in the car, Josie," he ordered. "Or I will put you over my shoulder and carry you home."

I bit the inside of my cheek. "I bet you could."

He lifted a brow.

"Carry me home," I said in answer to his silent question. "I bet you wouldn't even break out in a sweat." Sweet Jesus. I needed to stop my drunk rambling. *Someone put a cork or a sock in my mouth.*

The corner of his lip twitched. "As much as we might both enjoy that, I'd rather not leave my car on the side of the road. I'll take you home."

"Do you have to?"

He bent down and scooped up the bottle of bourbon before facing me. He took his fill of me like he was trying to figure out if I was serious or not before smirking. "I guess you won't find out unless you get into the car."

Damn it, why did my heart flutter? Probably a delayed reaction, right? It wasn't every day I nearly got hit by a car and ended up drunk once again with Brock Taylor. Though really, with the way my life went, it shouldn't have come as a surprise.

Ensnared by his eyes, I felt as if I was on the edge of some pivotal unseen cliff. Whether I decided to jump or not would change the course of my future.

I bit my lip as my body swayed toward Brock. What did I have to lose? Besides, wasn't I safer in the car with him than stumbling drunk at night back home? Hell, a car could actually hit me for real.

"Okay," I agreed, grabbing the bottle from his hands. "But I'll hang onto this." Shit. The bottle was empty, all the liquor had spilled out over the ground.

He grinned. "By all means."

Shaking my head, I walked around the front of the car to the passenger door and climbed inside. The seats were plush black leather and I sank into them, grateful to be off my feet. How long had I been walking for?

A quick glimpse at the car clock revealed that it was almost nine o'clock. Still early. No way was I going home.

Brock slid into the driver seat, and a thought occurred to me as he shut the door and the lights in the car dimmed. This was the first time we'd been alone since the night of the wedding. The air suddenly became thicker.

My hands clutched onto my knees and I wondered if I'd

made the wrong choice. Perhaps walking was the less dangerous option.

At least for my hormones.

And I wasn't sure if it was Brock I didn't trust or myself. My drunk self, that was. She was feeling all kinds of emotions toward Brock right now. The scent of him clung everywhere inside the car, driving my drunk self crazy.

"God, why does he have to smell so good?"

Shit. Did I say that out loud?

Brock shook his head, chuckling as he revved the car's engine. "Better buckle up, Firefly." He shifted the car into gear, waiting for me to fasten the seat belt.

"What are you doing out here?" I asked after I fumbled the buckle into place.

The car took off down the road. Brock drove like I expected him to.

Fast, without much regard for the speed limit.

"I was on my way to a party," he replied, his fingers wrapping around the leather steering wheel. "Your turn."

That explained why he looked and smelled divine, but then again, he pretty much always did. I glanced out the window, watching the night whiz by. "My mom's throwing some fucking party so she can wheedle her way into the rich women's club or some stupid shit."

His eyes turned from the road just long enough to give me a pitying look that I most definitely didn't want. "The bottle makes sense now."

"Like mother, like daughter," I mumbled. As soon as the words were out, I realized how close to the truth the statement was. The last thing I wanted to be was a miserable drunk like my mother, and yet… the first thing I'd done tonight was steal a bottle.

The liquid in my stomach churned, and I dropped my head to the back of the seat.

He slowed the car just enough to make a right turn. "Despite what others might think, I don't think you're like your mom."

I turned my head to the side, studying his profile. "You don't?" I said with surprise.

His thumb tapped on the wheel. "No."

Sighing, I forced my eyes off him. "You don't know me."

"I'm a damn good judge of people. Now, your mom, she is a money leech, but not you." An edge came into his voice. "This world, the money, the power, it doesn't faze you. It's not something you want."

He was right. I didn't want this world. His perceptiveness made me feel exposed. Fuck it. Plan or no plan, I needed to know the answer to the question that had plagued my mind since I found out who he was. "Why did you do it?"

A single brow rose. "Do what?"

Butterflies fluttered into my stomach, joining the warm bourbon sloshing around in there. I shifted my body in the seat, angling myself toward him. "Sleep with me?"

He looked over and held my gaze. "Are you really asking me that?"

"Only because I'm drunk." Tomorrow, if I remembered this conversation, I would be mortified, but tonight I was full of liquid courage and curiosity.

Brock chuckled, eyes back on the road.

I had a feeling I wasn't going to get a straight answer from him. "I'm told you have standby girls. Just so we're clear. I'm not a standby girl."

He frowned, a muscle in his jaw feathering. "Who have you been talking to?"

I snorted, not in the least bit intimidated by his serious face. "No one. No one talks to me."

"Not true. I'm talking to you."

I rolled my eyes. "Because you almost hit me." And presented me with the perfect opportunity to start working on the big plan Mads devised. Too bad I wasn't fucking sober.

His chest rumbled in a deep sound. "That isn't exactly my fault."

My fingers looped over the opening on the liquor bottle. "Blame the bourbon. You can't dodge all my questions."

His foot hit the brakes as he slowed the car down to a stop at a red light. "I didn't realize this was an interrogation. If I had, I would have left you on the side of the road." His tone hardened as if he was trying to prove a point.

But I wasn't buying it. Blame it on the alcohol, but there was something about this guy. He didn't give off the same vibes Carter did. There were assholes. And then there were *assholes*. I couldn't put my stepbrother in the same category as Brock, but there was plenty I didn't know about him. "I don't believe you," I said. "And I'm starting to believe your reputation as a bad guy is utter bullshit."

"I promise you it is very real. I don't have many redeeming

qualities. Don't look for something that isn't there, Firefly. I promise you, you'll be disappointed."

I gave him a wry glance. "You know that I never expected to see you again. Whether you believe me or not, I didn't know who you were."

The light turned green, and he hit the gas. "I'm not a nice guy."

"Says the guy who offered a drunk girl a ride. You're not going to kill me or anything?"

Something sparked in his eyes, and he grinned. "I said I wasn't a nice guy, not that I'm a serial killer." He made a turn, taking us into a gated community much like the one I lived in. The iron gate swung open, and the attendant in the gatehouse waved as we passed through.

In fact, I was pretty sure this community wasn't far from the Pattersons'. It was dark outside, but I could have sworn I drove past this place every day. "Then I'm not worried," I replied.

Guiding the car around a curve, Brock turned onto a long driveway before stopping and putting the car in park. He reached across my seat, and I turned my head to find his face so close to mine. "You should be, Firefly," he whispered, eyes locked onto mine.

Holy hell. I held my breath, my gaze shifting of its own accord from his eyes down to his lips. Fuck, I wanted to kiss him. The lips in question curled as if he knew exactly where my thoughts had gone.

All I had to do was close the tiny distance between our mouths and—

My seat belt clicked open.

I blinked as Brock leaned back into his seat, leaving me extremely disappointed. To cover my regret, I turned my head to the window. "Where are we?" I asked, glad that my voice remained level.

It was a sad day in my book when I started to grow desensitized to the sight of gorgeous houses. We were parked in front of another impressive mansion with unique angles that pulled your gaze. The exterior was a deep, dusty blue trimmed in cedarwood.

"My house," he stated simply, killing the engine on the Range Rover.

I whirled to face him. "The party you were going to is at your house?"

His lips curved into a make-your-knees-weak grin. "My parents are out of town." As if that was enough of an explanation, then added, "Beer run."

I was no longer sure I wanted to get out of the car. Perhaps it was best if I sucked up my pride and went home. Surely someone was looking for me by now.

Who was I kidding?

No one at home actually gave a damn about me.

"Last chance. Do you want me to take you home?" Brock asked, picking up on my hesitation to get out of the car. I picked up a hidden warning in his offer. He was giving me an out, because once I walked through those glass doors, everything would change. I might not be an Elite, but Brock bringing me here, it set a precedent.

Why would he do that?

I glanced at the massive house, the trimmed hedges and softly glowing windows. Shaking my head, I replied, "No."

When word got out Monday that I was seen in Brock's car, that I arrived at a party with him, shit was going to hit the fan.

And I couldn't wait. Mads would be ecstatic that our plan was rolling into motion.

CHAPTER TEN

I walked through a set of glass doors alongside Brock, wondering what kind of trouble I was in store for. The attraction I felt in the car faded into nerves. From the sounds filtering from the other room, it wasn't a large party, not like Grayson's had been. This was tame in comparison.

Less than a dozen or so people were lounging in the family room, including Micah, Fynn, and Grayson. The TV was on low, bottles of liquor and cans of beer scattered over the tables. My eyes swept through the rest of the room, scanning the faces. I recognized a few but knew only one other person by name. The bitch queen herself, Ava Whitmore.

Brock leaned close to my ear and murmured, "If you're not in the mood to deal with people, you can crash upstairs."

A stab of desire flared inside me. Inclining my head slightly to the side, I aligned our lips and arched a brow. "Am I going to find a girl in your bed... or two?"

"Probably," he admitted, smirking, the arm holding a case of beer brushing against mine.

A deliberate move, one that had my stomach kicking up a notch. "I'll pass." I was attracted to Brock, there was no doubt about it, but that didn't mean I had to act upon what my body was feeling. I had more willpower than that. Well, when I was sober, I did.

Right now, I couldn't stop thinking about kissing him.

Not happening.

Micah's eyes skimmed over me from where he sat on the massive sectional sofa, and he grinned. "Hey, new girl."

There was a girl in between Grayson and Micah. Grayson sneered when his cognac eyes landed on me, disdain shining in them. "Since when do you pick up stray dogs?" he asked Brock.

I stiffened beside Brock, two seconds away from bolting. My foot shifted as a hand lightly pressed to my back. The warmth of his solid body flooded into mine.

"I took you in," he retorted gruffly, moving into the room and setting the case of beer onto the floor. He grabbed himself one before dropping into an oversized chair.

Micah and Fynn snickered. Fynn had a girl on his lap who had her fingers in his chestnut hair. They looked cozy and comfortable with each other, and if I hadn't known better, I would have thought she was his girlfriend, but the Elite didn't date exclusively.

Grayson continued to frown at me. "Seriously. What is she doing here?" he demanded.

There weren't any seats open, so I just stood awkwardly in

the room, feeling so out of place and unsure of myself. The empty bottle of bourbon feeling light in my hand.

Brock slammed back a drink of his beer, eyeing me. "I don't know yet."

That made two of us. Just what the fuck was I doing here? In Brock's house? Alone? With the Elite?

"Ohmygod. Is this a joke? *Right?*" Ava snapped as she twirled a strand of red hair around her finger. She glared at me like I'd just dumpster dived in a back alley.

I probably did look atrocious, but for good reason, and I really didn't give a shit what I looked like. I glared back at the bitch, daring her to start shit with me. "You got a problem with me?" I was in a goddamn mood and would love nothing more than to take out my anger on her.

Brock leaned back in his chair, his expression unchanged as he said, "If you don't like it, Ava, get the fuck out. My house. My booze. My rules."

Ava glared at me, and I was pretty sure she was plotting the numerous ways she would make my life a living hell. Hostility and jealousy came off her in waves. I could all but taste the hate in the air.

I grinned back at her with equal contempt radiating from my eyes and triumph on my lips. Ava already claimed me as an enemy before even meeting me, just because I had slept with Brock.

Her smug smile slipped. "Your parties used to be fun. *You* used to be fun," she said to Brock, pouting.

He barely blinked. "Yeah, well, I'm not here for your entertainment. You're here for ours."

If I didn't already despise Ava, I might have felt a shred of sympathy for her, but I was beginning to suspect there was something wrong with this chick. It was as if the crueler Brock was to her, the more desperate she became for his attention.

Undeterred, Ava got up from her seat, flashing everyone in the room a view of her ample breasts, and sauntered behind Brock's chair. She leaned down, running her hands along his wide shoulders to his chest, whispering something in his ear.

"Clingy much?"

Multiple eyes swung in my direction, and there might have been a gasp or two. I realized I had done it again, spoken my thoughts out loud. I needed to get that shit under control.

Micah's lopsided grin widened as he laughed. "I call dibs on the new girl." He patted the vacated seat at the end of the couch beside him where Ava had been.

I rolled my eyes but wove around all the outstretched legs and feet to take a seat next to Micah who handed me a drink. He seemed harmless enough, and at least I was no longer subjected to Grayson's glares. They were lethal.

Brock scowled at me as I glanced over at him. Our eyes locked. He knocked Ava's hands off him and sighed heavily. "Ava, go do something else with your mouth other than complain."

"I got something she can do with it," Micah said, unbuttoning the front of his jeans.

I almost spat a mouthful of beer all over Micah. It would probably be wise to cut myself off, but I needed something to dull the throbbing ache for Brock that wouldn't go away. Even his fucking frown turned me on. But it was the damn eyes that would be my downfall.

"What do you have here?" Micah asked, snatching the empty bottle from my hands. "Oh, shit. Bourbon. The good stuff. I approve, new girl. But next time, save me a swig." He swung an arm around my shoulder.

I remembered what Mads said about Micah. He was the playboy of the group, but for reasons I didn't understand, I felt safer with the platinum blond Elite than I did with any of the other three. I risked another glance in Brock's direction and found his eyes still on me, his face unreadable. I got the sense he wasn't thrilled about something.

Ava, having given up on gaining any attention from Brock, moved on to Grayson, who pulled her down into his lap. She seemed all too comfortable being passed from one Elite to the other, and I remembered the girl in Brock's bed at his party. Was Ava a standby girl?

"You just missed your brother," she said, so sickly sweet it gave me a toothache.

"Step," I corrected, taking my bottle back from Micah. "Carter was here?"

Micah nodded. "Yeah, for five minutes before we threw his ass out."

That would piss Carter off. But why would they toss him out? And wasn't he supposed to be at Mom's party? Or had he escaped as well?

I didn't care, as long as the prick didn't show back up here.

"He had a lot to say about you before he left," one of Ava's friends chimed in. Izzy, I thought. She was blonde, tanned, and gorgeous. Definitely a standby girl.

"I just bet," I grumbled.

"He said your mom's a bitch."

I let out a short laugh. "My *step*brother needs to come up with new material." I wasn't going to deny that for once, I agreed with Carter. My mother was a bitch.

"He mentioned that she's having a party. So why aren't you there?" Izzy asked as she traced a nail around the rim of her drink.

I stared at her, wondering if I could sew her plump lips shut. I'd grown tired of the questions—of being on display. "Stuffy parties aren't my idea of a good time, and I didn't want to hang around while her guests laughed behind her back," I admitted, a slight hardness moving into my voice. It was the truth. These girls were as fake as they came, but I refused to stoop to their level. I wanted them to understand that I knew who my mother was—I acknowledged her ambitions and the methods she used to get what she wanted. I didn't agree with them, but I wanted Ava and her crew of mean girls to know they couldn't hurt me by pointing out the obvious. Yes, my mother was a gold digger. Get over it.

"But sleeping around is your thing?" Ava chimed in, wiggling on Grayson's lap, who definitely didn't seem to mind.

"Enough with the girl bullshit," Grayson interrupted, grabbing the beer someone handed him. "I'm sick of listening to your catty jealousy. Take it somewhere else."

Another guy whose name I didn't know pulled out a deck of cards. His buddy beside him started to clear off the long rectangular coffee table in front of the sectional. I took another drink of my beer, trying not to make a face. Beer wasn't my choice of liquor.

Micah leaned forward closer to the table. "Do you play?" he asked, a playful excitement sparkling in his light blue eyes.

I eyed him cautiously. This guy was trouble. I could see how Mads had fallen for his charm. "Play what?"

Micah's smile was pure wickedness. "Strip poker."

I had to admit, there was something about Micah that was utterly captivating. My lips twitched in response to him. "Why does that not surprise me."

He lifted a cocky brow, taking the deck and shuffling the cards in his large hands. "So are you in, new girl?"

I flashed him a smile. "Only if you want to find yourself completely naked by the end of the night," I boasted. Poker was my game. Dad taught me. When I was little, I used to stay up late during his Friday poker nights. Eventually, I joined in, hanging out with the guys at my dad's mechanic shop. The cards always smelled like grease and gasoline, just like Dad.

I shook my head, clearing the memories and the sadness that accompanied them. Now was not the time to go there.

Micah laughed, a boisterous, rich sound, but everyone else in the room groaned. Obviously, I'd stepped into an inside joke that was over my head. "I've been wondering what color bra is under that shirt since you walked into the room. It is now my mission to find out."

"I'm sure she'd take it off," Ava bit out.

Grayson dumped Ava onto the couch and groaned. "You have no idea what you've done."

"This fool loses on purpose," Fynn chimed in. "If I have to spend another night looking at Micah's bare ass, I'm fucking going home," he said, but there was humor in his words, green eyes sparkling with it.

"I'm out of here." Grayson stood up, grabbing a girl who was not Ava. I could guess where they were going. As he sauntered out of the room, he shot me a sidelong glare. Something told me Grayson didn't like me much. Not that anyone here really did, but his went deeper than the other guys'. Why? What had I done to him?

There ended up being about eight players, including Micah, Ava, Fynn, Izzy, Brock, and myself. The first few rounds were painless, with Ava and Izzy both losing their shirts, seeing as they didn't have many clothes on to begin with. Neither wore socks or shoes.

Micah lost the third round. And much like Fynn predicted, I swore it was deliberate. He flashed me his hand and winked before moving straight for the pants. I rolled my eyes as he stood up, unbuttoning them. With a holler and a few whistles around the room, Micah did a little hip action before sinking down beside me in his boxers.

I laughed, shaking my head at him. "You're crazy," I said.

He flopped an arm around my shoulders. "And don't you forget it." He smelled like beer and cologne. It wasn't a bad combination.

The rounds were dealt, the clothes came off, and the drinks kept coming. It was just the distraction I needed, and for a few hours, I didn't think about Angie or the party. Even Ava was semi-tolerable, and it made me wonder. Perhaps the Elite weren't as bad as everyone made them out to be. Were they just misunderstood like I was? Or had they actually earned every negative mark on their rap sheet?

When the game ended, Brock and I were the ones who were mostly still dressed. Micah did get to see what color my bra was, to his delight.

"Pink, huh?" He tugged a strand of my hair. "I should have guessed. It fits you, new girl."

Fynn unfortunately did in fact have to bear witness to Micah's ass, which he proudly paraded around the room. I never met anyone who was so damn comfortable naked before, especially with a crowd, but I had to admit, Micah was impressive in all departments.

I wasn't a nun.

Of course I looked.

My head rested on Micah's shoulder, who'd begrudgingly tossed his pants back on, but no shirt. I had to text Ains and Mads. Later. When my head stopped spinning. They were going to freak out. Phase one of our plan was in motion. It had been completely accidental, but I didn't think either of them would care. The outcome was better than we could have hoped for. Not only did I cross paths with Brock (throwing myself in front of his car totally had to count), I was inside the house, hanging out with the Elite.

Who was I?

Sure, I wasn't supposed to put myself in danger, and almost getting run over definitely constituted as dangerous, but it had been worth it.

I snuggled against Micah, letting out a yawn, the night

finally catching up to me. From across the room, my eyes got hung up on Brock's. He was watching me, a frown on his lips. I didn't look away but stared back at him. Despite the seriousness of his expression, heat burned in the center of his breathtaking aqua eyes. I all but felt myself go up in flames from the intensity of them. I might have been curled up next to the playboy, but it was the bad boy I wanted. A shiver went through me, and the corner of Brock's mouth lifted. He knew exactly what my body was feeling.

What would he do if I wandered over and climbed into his lap?

Would he discard me as he had Ava?

The thought was mortifying and enough to keep my ass planted on the couch.

I lost track of how long we watched each other, but eventually, my eyes became too heavy to keep open, and I let them drift shut, not caring that I was half-dressed. My body relaxed into the couch as I listened to the lingering group laugh and bullshit, but it was Brock's magnetic eyes that followed me into my dreams.

I woke up to a dark, silent room—an unfamiliar room. My head was throbbing, but it was the least of my immediate concerns. Rubbing the sleep from my eyes, I rolled over in the bed, unsure if I would find someone else besides me. A rush of air expelled from my lungs. I was alone, thank God. *But where the hell am I? What time is it? And where the fuck is my shirt?*

Digging my phone out of my pocket, I checked the time and groaned at the number of missed calls and texts. It was all too fresh a reminder of the mess that waited for me at home.

I swung my legs over the bed, taking stock of the room. The blackout blinds were closed, explaining the utter darkness despite it being ten in the morning. It was a stunning room with vaulted ceilings, exposed wood beams, and a king-size bed. A lantern-style light fitting hung in the center of the ceiling, and nestled under the three large windows was a sitting area. The room was so inviting.

I was tempted to curl up and go back to bed, but my damn phone buzzed. Another text from my mother.

"Shit," I mumbled, raking my fingers through my hair. I searched the ground for my shirt and shoes. When I couldn't immediately find them, I flipped on a light. "Shit," I swore again, not seeing either of them in the room. Looked like I would be sneaking out shirtless and barefoot. That should make an interesting trip home.

Of course, I could just borrow a shirt from Brock, a thought that I found too appealing.

Then I needed to figure out how I was getting home.

I mentally flipped through my options. I could call Angie. Hell, no. I could text Ainsley. I could walk. Or request an Uber.

Damn bourbon. Never again.

Quickly rummaging through the dresser for a shirt, I grabbed the first one I found and tugged it over my head. I straightened the bed (because in good conscience I couldn't leave it a mess) and made use of the attached bathroom before peeking out into the long hallway. A new problem arose. *Son of a bitch.* I stood in the hall, looking left and right. *I have no idea which way to go.*

I found a flight of winding stairs and tiptoed down, praying I wouldn't run into anyone, particularly Brock's parents. I did remember he'd said they were out of town, but for how long? For all I knew, they could be due back any second. Come to think of it, I doubted seeing a girl sneak out of their house would be a shock.

Once on the main floor, it wasn't so difficult to weave my way toward the front of the house. I passed by the room where we had played cards, and lo and behold, strewn inside a potted palm was my shirt. I wasn't even going to question how it got there. As I slipped the borrowed shirt over my head and reached for mine, a husky chuckle sounded behind me, sending goose bumps over my exposed skin. I whirled around, knowing it was Brock.

Leaning against the wall in a pair of dark gray sweats and an Academy football T-shirt that hugged his chest, his dark hair was messy in a way that made me itch to run my fingers through it. "Not going to lie, Firefly. I like you better without it."

Rolling my eyes, I slipped the shirt over my head and pulled it down past my pink bra. I shook out my hair. "And I liked you better before I knew your name."

He put a hand to his heart in a mock wounded gesture as he walked toward me. "Ouch." His eyes locked on mine. "Were you thinking of leaving without saying goodbye?"

I shoved my hands into my pockets before I did something reckless. Those lusty feelings I wanted to blame on the alcohol were coming back. And they were stronger than ever. "It crossed my mind," I admitted. "I need to get home before my mom calls in the National Guard."

"Come on. I'll give you a lift." His voice brushed against the back of my neck as he moved to open the front door.

Grabbing my shoes, which I found by the door, I followed out after him.

My eyes adjusted to the light as we rounded his Ranger Rover. No sooner had I shut the car door than Brock had us driving down his driveway and through the gates. The ride was quiet and short. I couldn't tell if it was his driving that made the trip less than three minutes or if we lived that close to each other. But something changed the second we got in his car. Brock's guard was back up, and his face clouded.

I couldn't figure this guy out. Not before coffee.

"Thanks for... not running me over. And the other stuff too," I said as I opened the door and climbed out.

He said nothing, sunglasses hiding his eyes from me, the one part of him I wanted to see. I got a stiff nod. That was it.

Confused, I shut the door and watched as the black Range Rover peeled down my driveway.

WTF?

CHAPTER ELEVEN

I made a shitty attempt at sneaking into my house. The party was over, but the evidence was still strewn about the backyard and inside. Empty wineglasses. Twinkle lights still lit in the trees. Used napkins wadded up on the tables. I entered through the patio, wanting to avoid everyone, but the staff was already hard at work, cleaning up the mess. As I headed straight for the stairs, dying for a hot shower, someone cleared their throat, alerting me I'd been busted.

I paused, feeling the anger vibrate off Angie. I didn't have to turn around to know she was standing behind me, mad as hell.

Regrettably, I faced her.

Cheeks white, mouth pinched, and eyes dark, my mother gripped the mug in her hands tighter. "Do you have any idea what time it is? Where have you been all night?" she clipped out.

I ran a hand over my face, remembering all too clearly why I had left in the first place. My mother had slapped me, and the memory brought on a sharp sting to my cheek. "Does it matter?" I snapped bitterly.

"Josephine."

I tipped my chin up. "I was out."

"With *that boy*," she said in disgust, eyes shimmering in anger.

So she had seen me come home. My annoyance reared its head. "Are you spying on me now? And yes, I was with *that boy*. The one I fucked on your wedding night." I braced myself for another slap, hands clenched at my sides.

She blinked, sucking in a sharp breath. "You are not to see him again. Is that clear?"

"I'm confused. Isn't this what you wanted? For me to make influential connections, date the rich boys. Besides, it will be kind of hard to avoid him since we go to school together," I pointed out, being a smartass. "Or are you sending me back to Public?"

Waving a dismissive hand in the air, she walked toward me, heels clicking on the hallway floor. "Don't be ridiculous. I meant outside of school. I've heard things about him."

My eyes fell flat. "Why do you care who I hang out with?"

Her mouth tightened in a thin line. "I will not have you sleeping around."

I snorted. "So you think I'm a slut. Thanks, Mom."

"I wouldn't think it if your behavior suggested otherwise."

"You've made your point. Can I go now? It's been a long night, and I need to shower."

"You missed the dinner party," she said, reaching to smooth a stray strand of my hair.

I flinched. "Don't touch me," I replied coolly. "Don't ever touch me."

Hurt fractured through her eyes. "Josephine, darling. You're being absurd. You're my daughter. It might not seem like it, but I'm looking out for you. I only want the best for you, and *that boy*, he is not it."

"I find that hard to believe giving the amount of money his family has."

"It isn't his money I object to. It's his reputation. Steven has told me all about him and his friends. If you had been at the dinner last night, you would have gotten the opportunity to meet some of the most influential heirs."

I rolled my eyes. "Here we go again. I do not want or need you to set me up on a date. Is that clear?"

"Do you always have to be so problematic?" She sighed, her fingers trembling as they clutched her coffee cup.

"Don't worry. I won't be your problem for long. The moment I turn eighteen, I'm out of here." It was something I'd thought about all summer, but I convinced myself I could at least make it until the end of the school year. It became clear after last night, I had to leave as soon as possible. For my sanity.

Her eyes widened, a wildness creeping in that frightened me. "You're not eighteen yet. So until then, you follow my rules."

I wanted to say fuck her rules. Gritting my teeth, I narrowed my eyes. "I'm going to take a shower. Is that okay with you, or is that against the rules?" I snapped mockingly.

She blinked at me, shaking her head like I was the crazy one, and that was all the response I needed.

Swiveling on my heels, I headed up the stairs to my room. I didn't see her for the rest of the day. I didn't see anyone, in fact, which was goddamn perfect, except for Shelly, one of the day maids who brought up my dinner that night. She gave me a sad smile of sympathy that almost broke me. And although I needed to cry, needed to release all these pent-up emotions inside me, the tears never came. Nothing but numbness coated me inside.

On Monday morning, I was up early and eager to get the hell out of this house, making a stop in the kitchen for my ritual latte the cook had taken to making me. It was better than any Starbucks, and I adored her for it.

I found the to-go cup waiting for me on the counter, but that wasn't the only thing waiting for me.

Carter leaned against the center island, stuffing a bowl of cereal in his mouth. I had managed to avoid him entirely on Sunday, but my luck just ran out. "Heard you were at Taylor's party, *sis*," he said, chomping on his Frosted Flakes. The smug smile on his lips looked like he had a secret he was refusing to share.

"I heard you got kicked out," I retorted, wrapping my fingers around my latte. The warmth seeped into my hand.

He scraped his spoon along the bottom of the bowl. "I had better things to do."

My ass. I just rolled my eyes.

"Everyone is speculating on who you slept with this time. My money is on Bradford."

His words caused warning bells to go off inside me. "Just one? Huh? Don't underestimate me."

His stupid, arrogant grin brightened as he held up his phone for me to see. A picture of me in my pink bra passed out on Micah was splashed across Carter's phone.

The coffee nearly slipped out of my hand. "Where did you get that?" I demanded.

Carter clicked the screen closed and shoved the phone in his pocket. "There are more. Videos too. Do you want to see?"

I wanted to wrestle his phone from him and smash it on the ground. "Fuck off," I spat and marched out of the kitchen, Carter's stupid ass laugh following me.

My foot slammed onto the Lexus's gas pedal as I shot down the driveway. I wanted speed and rash danger, something to take the edge off of my anger. If Carter had pictures, they would already be all over school. I didn't know how, but a name came to mind. Ava.

That little bitch.

It had to be her, but what I didn't understand was why Brock let it happen. Surely he had seen her take the photos with her phone—the other guys too. And not one of them did anything to stop her.

Assholes.

How foolish I was to think that for even a night I'd been accepted.

I banged my hands against the steering wheel, letting out a string of F-bombs.

Whipping the car into a parking spot, I came to a screeching halt, not caring that I was parked slightly crooked. The Academy could bite my ass. My fingers were shaking as I killed the engine and I reached for my cold, untouched latte. I took a swig, hoping the caffeine would calm my nerves. "Shit," I swore at the coffee.

My gaze went to the school. Did I really want to go in there? I tapped the side of the cup as I bit my lower lip. I could back out right now, go wherever I wanted, skip my classes and not look back. I'd never blown off school before, but there was always a first for everything.

Knock. Knock. Knock. Knuckles rapped on my window. "Josie."

I jumped at the sound of my name and turned. Mads peered in at me, both her hands up in question. "What are you doing?"

Instead of yelling through the window, I grabbed my stuff and opened the door. "Deciding if I want to make a run for it," I said, slumping against the car.

Her hair was braided on both sides of her head. "Do you want to explain what the hell happened this weekend?" she asked.

My shoulders lifted and dropped in a sigh. "I'm guessing you've heard."

"What I want to know is why the hell you didn't text me and why I had to find out about it from Chelsea Walker."

"Who?"

Mads shook her head. "That is beside the point. How the

fuck did you end up at Brock Taylor's on Saturday night in just a bra?"

"It was an accident."

She lifted a brow. "Your shirt accidentally came off?"

It shouldn't have been funny, not when the horror of what awaited me inside the school had yet to pass, but my lips twitched. "No," I dragged out dramatically. "Like an actual accident. Brock almost hit me with his car, but to be fair, it was more or less my fault. I was drunk and fell onto the road." I filled her in on all the details as fast as I could.

A grave expression dropped over her eyes. "There are pictures."

I rubbed at the tension building at the back of my neck. "So I've been informed. Carter was all too happy to share this morning over a bowl of Frosted Flakes. How bad are they?"

"Asshole," she muttered. "It could be worse. Your bra could have been off. I wouldn't be surprised if he isn't behind this whole thing. We need to talk at lunch."

I nodded.

Her eyes flicked to the brick building and then back to me as she readjusted the laptop in her arms. "So have you decided yet?"

"About?"

A grin lit up her face. "Whether or not we are blowing off classes?"

Mads was a true friend, a partner in crime. I tapped my shoulder against hers and started walking toward the school. "Come on, let's go before I change my mind."

We separated after crossing through the front doors. I

headed toward my locker and Mads to the west wing. She had first period auto mechanics. I didn't know if it she was serious about the class or something she took as rebellion. Who the hell wanted to get greasy this early in the morning? No, thank you.

The murmuring and snickers were expected as I went down the hallway. So the entire school saw me in my bra. How was it any different than a bikini? It wasn't. I turned the corner to my locker and stumbled. Dread dropped like an anchor in my stomach. I drew closer, seeing what all the fuss was about, all the hushed whispers, the secret giggles, and the snotty glances. It all made sense now.

S-L-U-T was written boldly across my locker in what looked like pink lipstick. But the horror didn't end there. Pictures of me at Brock's were plastered around the word like wallpaper. My eyes darted from photo to photo. Behind me, a few girls snickered as they passed by, but I barely heard them over the roaring in my head.

I had a damn good idea who was behind the stunt.

Ava.

This screamed jealous girlfriend, except she wasn't anyone's actual girlfriend, just a standby girl. Perhaps the same rules of possessiveness applied?

Honestly, I didn't give a flying fuck.

Did Brock know about this? Was he in on it? Was it all part of their plan to embarrass me, run me out of the Academy?

Tears stung at the back of my eyes.

"Don't give them the satisfaction." Fynn Dupree stood behind me, scowling at my locker. His green eyes didn't hold any of the gloating I expected to see. He looked... irritated.

I quickly smeared the wet spots away from my eyes. "What do you want?" I demanded, hardening my voice.

"Nothing. Just giving some unsolicited advice." Fynn ripped one of the pics of my locker. "This isn't a bad shot."

I didn't bother to look at the picture. They were all tasteless in my book. "I'm glad someone finds this funny." Turning away from my locker, I strolled down the hall. Fynn followed. I glared at him from the corner of my eye. "What are you doing?"

The big linebacker shrugged. "Walking to class."

Fynn was an intimidating guy when he wanted to be. People gave him a wide berth as we walked by, stepping out of his way. It was almost like having the red carpet rolled out in front of us. I snuck a glance at him. "Do you even have class in this wing?"

His eyes bounced over the brick walls. "What wing is this?"

That was answer enough, but still, I replied, "The east."

"Nah, I have Intro to Architecture with Mr. Schue."

Specials were usually in the west wing. "Are you going to be late?"

He shrugged. "Mr. Schue is cool."

I eyed him carefully, trying to figure out what his angle was. "You don't have to do this. In fact, I'm trying to figure out why you are walking me to class. I can get there all on my own, you know. I wore my big girl pants today."

Fynn's lips lifted at the corners, eyes sparkling with humor. "They look good on you, the pants."

"Thanks," I drawled.

Fynn ran a hand through his curly locks. "You still haven't

figured it out. When Brock gives an order, you obey, no questions asked."

I laughed, but then stopped when I realized he wasn't joking. "You're not kidding."

He gave me an unblinking stare.

I paused outside the door to my English class. "Okay, that is the most absurd thing I've ever heard. Let me guess, if he told you to walk into oncoming traffic, you'd do it without thinking."

Fynn opened the door for me as he said, "I trust him."

Fine. Whatever. He was the leader of their little group. "So this is Brock's idea. Got it." Now I knew who to yell at. "Thanks for the unnecessary escort," I said, walking into class with a wave over my shoulder.

After each of my morning classes, one of the Elite was waiting for me. Brock appeared to have given them all the same orders. I just didn't understand why. It couldn't possibly have anything to do with the pictures, but I meant to find out.

"Where is he?" I asked Grayson.

I had yet to see Brock today, but I'd had enough of being tailed or watched, whatever his damn order was.

Grayson's scowl looked painful. "I'm not his babysitter."

No. He was just mine. At least Grayson didn't play dumb. He didn't want to be here any more than I wanted him here, and yet, he came because Brock ordered it. "This borders on stalking, you know." I shoved my laptop into my locker.

He gave an obscene snort. "Let's get one thing straight. I'm not interested in you in any way, so don't flatter yourself."

Ouch. I winced. "Got it. You hate me. Join the club." Between the slut coughs and obscene gestures I'd gotten today, I wouldn't have been surprised to find a Facebook group dedicated to hating me.

His big brown eyes showed no remorse, and I wondered if Grayson had a heart.

Meandering around the unmovable Grayson boulder, I went to track down Brock without his help. It was my lunch period, the only time during school that the Elite and I were all together. I had a class or two with Micah, Grayson, and Fynn, but none with Brock.

Grayson shadowed me into the cafeteria until both our gazes landed on Brock. He let out a sigh of relief like he was finally relieved of Josie babysitting duties and went to sit down at the Elite table. My focus was zeroed in on one person or I might have made a snarky comment at Grayson's swift departure.

I marched right up to Brock, put my hands on his chest, and pushed him back a step or two before he could sit down. "We need to talk, Taylor," I hissed between my teeth.

The green hues in Brock's eyes were more prominent than the blues as he glared down at me.

Not waiting for a response, I grabbed his hand and pulled him outside into the courtyard. I was shocked he didn't resist as I dragged him. Brock gave a group of kids who were hanging by the gazebo a single glance, and they migrated back inside without a complaint.

Who was this guy?

Why did everyone treat him like he was on a damn pedestal?

Were they afraid of him?

Some, I admitted, but I'd seen just as much respect in their eyes as I had genuine fear.

I whirled to face him. "What the hell gives? Why are Micah, Fynn, and Grayson following me around like lost puppies?" His lips twitched at the idea of his friends being compared to something as innocent and harmless as puppies, but I carried on, despite the quickening of my pulse at the sight of that crooked grin. "And why the fuck did you take those photos and pass them around? I don't understand you."

His brows furrowed together. "I didn't take the photos."

"But you were there," I pointed out. "You let it happen. And you didn't answer my other question. Why are your friends following me?"

A gleam of anger glittered in his eyes. "It's for your protection."

"Protection? From who? Ava? Carter? The entire school?"

"Yes," was his only reply.

God, he made me want to scream. "Are they going to protect me from you?"

His jaw worked. "If necessary, yes."

What did that even mean? I wasn't safe with him? I didn't know why I was so angry. This was exactly what I wanted, what Ainsley, Mads, and I discussed. The Elite were shielding me. Then why was I so upset? Why didn't it feel like they were keeping a close eye on me for more than just my safety?

I put a finger into his hard chest. "Look, I don't need or want your protection. Just back off, okay?" Screw the plan.

Those dreamy eyes that still kept me up at night drifted over my face, lingering a tad too long on my lips. His hand wrapped around my wrist, and with one quick tug, I was plastered against him. "I give the orders around here."

My chest heaved against his as I met his stare. "So I've heard. But I don't take orders from you or from anyone."

The hand around my wrist loosened but neither of us moved. "Why does that not surprise me, Firefly?"

"Don't call me that. I'm not a bug. We don't have cute nick-names for each other. That would imply that something is going on between us, which clearly there isn't."

"Is that so?" He arched a dark brow, calling me out on my lies. "Do I need to prove just how wrong you are, *Firefly*?" he rebutted, purposefully using the nickname to piss me off.

Which, of course, it did.

He leaned forward so his breath tickled the side of my cheek, and I struggled to keep my eyes open. *You have more willpower than this*, I scolded myself. "A demonstration would only embarrass you," I said plainly. "I want *nothing* from you."

He chuckled, a warm brush of air over my face. "You're going to get yourself hurt."

If he wanted to play games, so could I. Tilting my face toward his, I aligned our lips so we were so close I could almost taste his on mine. Our gazes connected, and I was pleased to see the storminess working its way into his eyes. "Are you threat-ening me?"

"Would it do any good if I did?" His hand found its way

under my shirt, and his fingers trailed over my lower back, sending an electric current singing through my blood. *Holy. Shit.*

I sucked in a sharp breath of shock and something else. I wanted him to touch me in places that weren't appropriate for the school courtyard. My insides clenched as my heart beat faster. "No," I answered honestly.

Is he going to kiss me?

If he did, would I kiss him back? Or just combust from all the waves of heat pouring off us?

I never got to find out. Brock pulled away, releasing his hold on me, and said with a shake of his head, "Try and stay out of trouble, *Firefly*." He left me in the middle of the courtyard, striding back inside to join the other guys.

I sunk into a nearby bench. "Fuck." I exhaled, dropping my face into my hands.

CHAPTER TWELVE

My week more or less dragged on. Thanks to the janitorial staff, my locker had been scrubbed clean and painted. The murmurs and musings over the pictures died down, replaced by the excitement for this year's first football game against none other than Elmwood Public. It was a welcome distraction, mostly because it took the spotlight off me and put it on the football players.

They could keep it.

In true Academy fashion, there was always a party after the game to celebrate the school's victory, assuming they won. Their record spoke for itself. All one had to do was look at the multiple cabinets of trophies that lined the walls outside of the main office. The players were confident in a win for a reason. They didn't lose.

What a bunch of pompous assholes.

No, I wasn't attending the game, no matter how much Mads

pleaded. The fact that she wanted to go at all shocked me. She didn't strike me as a girl who sat in the stands, face painted, screaming "go team." But she argued it was a perfect opportunity to implant myself into the Elite's world, which prompted me to tell her we needed to talk.

Mads and Ainsley were coming over after the game for a debriefing. I had just finished texting them both and was lounging by the pool when I heard a voice that made me cringe. My asshole stepbrother wheeled a keg into the backyard, dropping it off near the outside bar area. We hadn't talked much since our run-in Monday morning. I'd been avoiding him.

He was dressed in basketball shorts and a tee, his sandy hair blown messily to one side. "Don't tell me you're going to the game dressed like that," he sneered, giving me a once-over that lasted too long. Sometimes, I swore he looked at me like he was seeing a dead girlfriend. It gave me the creeps, which when I thought about it, kind of made sense since Carter was creepy as fuck.

I clicked off my phone screen and glared up at him. "Please. Like I'd ever lower myself to rooting for the enemy." My fingers clutched my phone. I was about two seconds away from hurling it at his head, but then I'd need a new phone.

He sauntered over and sat down at the end of my wooden recliner. I quickly pulled my feet out of the way before they were crushed by his hundred and eighty pounds. "I thought you'd want to support your boys," he sneered, forking a hand through his windblown locks.

"They are not *my boys*," I said dryly, contemplating kicking him.

"Then why do they follow you around at school like your pussy is a drug?"

I choked at the idea of Brock, Fynn, Micah, and Grayson being addicted to my vagina. "I'd like to see you say that to their faces."

The smug smile vanished from his lips, and I knew I hit a sore spot. Carter might be teammates with the Elite, but he was not part of their inner circle. That burned his ass.

"What's the keg for?" I asked, diverting the conversation.

His frown morphed back into a grin, an evil grin. Carter was basically a walking, talking horror movie villain. "Haven't you heard? We're having a party tonight."

I groaned internally. "The party is here?" Of course, the after-game party would be here. Angie and Steven were out of town today and through the weekend, which left me alone with dickhead. Thank God, Ainsley and Mads were coming over.

Carter nodded, tiptoeing his fingers up my bare leg. "If you knew what was best, you'd stay out of my way tonight."

I gave in to the urge and kicked his arm. "Don't touch me, you creep."

His hand lashed out, wrapping around my ankle, and with one swift tug, he pulled me toward him at the end of the lounger. "Don't pretend like you're an innocent virgin, sis. You can spread your legs for them." His hand went to my inner thigh and squeezed roughly. "It's not like we're blood-related."

Still. Ew. The idea had my stomach recoiling. I reacted, grabbing his balls and squeezing, making sure he felt the imprint of my nails. "Touch me again and I'll rip these off. Got it?"

Carter made a squealing sound like a pig. I released his balls and jumped off the recliner. "You crazy bitch," he hissed.

I turned around, walking backward as I threw him a not-so-nice smile. "That's the nicest thing you've said to me. Don't forget it. Oh, and Carter. I thought they'd be bigger than that. I barely felt anything at all."

"Wrong move, bitch," he seethed, still clutching his junk on the chair.

I flipped him off, hightailing it back into the house.

Carter left shortly after our incident, slamming all the doors on his way out to the football game. It was a home game. So far all I've learned about this side of Elmwood was the people were jackasses and they liked to party.

Despite refusing to go to the game, a part of me couldn't help but be curious about the Elite. When I was at Public, I never went to any games, because football meant nothing to me then. And now... I still didn't like football, but I was starting to like the Elite. God help me. If I were smart, I'd give up this plan and do as Brock suggested. Stay far away from them.

But... I couldn't.

Regardless of what happened, of what part they might have played in harassing me, I found I was drawn to them and curious. Not just Brock, but all four of the guys. I didn't know what that said about me, but I probably needed a shrink on speed dial for times like this.

I waited for Mads and Ainsley to show up, pacing up and

down the entryway and biting on my chipped pink nails. The doorbell rang, chiming a melody throughout the house, and I jumped. Two seconds later, I threw open the door. "About time, bishes. Get in here. We need to talk." I dragged them both through the front door and up to my bedroom.

Ainsley stood in the middle of the room, her mossy green eyes taking everything in. "Your room is fucking huge." This was the first time she'd been here. I'd forgotten. "Not your style, but still. You have your own bathroom."

Mads made herself at home on my bed. "What's going on? You sounded frantic on the phone, which is understandable considering the week you had."

Ainsley joined Mads on the bed. "Shouldn't you be getting ready for the game?" she asked, eyeing my clothes as I turned my desk chair around and sat down.

"I don't think I can do this," I announced, ignoring her. My clothes weren't the problem here. Nor was my messy hair.

Mads kicked off her shoes and pulled up her legs, crossing them like a pretzel on the bed. "Did something happen? Because from what I can see, the plan is working beautifully."

I rolled my eyes. "It might seem that way, but something is going on, something they're hiding."

"Have you heard anything?" Ainsley asked Mads.

Mads shook her head. "Nothing more. Grayson swears he didn't have anything to do with the pictures or them being leaked out."

Ainsley plucked one of many decorative pillows and stuffed it in her lap to lean on. "And you believe him?"

"Hell no," Mads replied. "They all lie through their teeth, especially to protect each other."

My foot tapped on the floor. "So you think they're hiding something too?"

Mads shrugged. "Honestly, I don't know. They've never acted this way before. It is not like them to single a girl out. You can't quit now." A flash of something sprang into her eyes, but then it was gone.

I thought about Carter and his wandering hands earlier by the pool. I thought about all the other girls he might have harassed, about how far he might have taken things with them. Had they been too afraid to speak up? And I thought about the girls Carter had not yet set his eyes on. No one else should be subjected to my stepbrother's shit.

And since neither his father nor Angie would do anything about his actions, it was up to me.

"You should go to the game," Mads said, seeing the wheels in my brain turning.

Ainsley cast me a furtive glance. "She has a point."

I frowned. "Are you the two of you ganging up on me?"

Mads hopped off the bed, strolling toward my closet. "We're looking out for you," she said over her shoulder. "And you need to be wherever the Elite is. You need to be at the game."

An hour later I sat in the football stands, flanked by Ainsley and Mads. Not how I pictured my Friday night, but I'd learned that when my two friends paired up against me, I was doomed to give in.

Bright lights lit up the field, highlighting the main event. Cars were jammed into the school parking lot. It was expected though, considering who we were playing. The long-standing rivalry between Public and Academy continued.

Fall was in full bloom tonight, and although the air was scented with bonfires, leaves, and grilled food from the tailgaters, a crispness bit the air that made me glad I'd worn a hoodie.

"Come on, let's grab some drinks," Ainsley said cheerfully, slipping a hand through mine as if she was afraid I'd bolt at the first opportunity.

She wasn't wrong.

I didn't want to be here.

But then as we weaved our way through the crowd past the school locker room doors, I caught a glimpse of someone standing in the doorway. Micah. His eyes locked with mine, lips curling into a cocksure grin. Dressed in his blue-and-black uniform, he swung his helmet in his hand. The pads made him look bigger, more muscular everywhere.

Mads's nose wrinkled when she saw who had captured my attention. "Be careful with that one. Playboy, remember?"

Micah winked before I dragged my gaze away from him.

At the concession stand, I grabbed a soda and a hotdog. My stomach rumbled the second I sniffed out food. It had been hours since I'd eaten, and I didn't think a single hotdog would do it, but it would hold me over until after the game.

It proved to be a challenge finding an empty spot on the bleachers to sit. That's what we get for coming minutes before kickoff. As we zigzagged through the rows, Mads filled Ainsley in on all the Academy gossip, pointing out who was who. And Ainsley did the same, waving across the field to a few of our friends from Public. I realized that we were sitting in enemy territory, and I hoped Ains wouldn't get too much shit for being on the wrong side of the field.

We had just planted our asses down and I'd managed to take a single bit out of my hotdog before the crowd suddenly jumped to their feet in an uproar. Ugh. The players made their way out onto the field, introduced over the loudspeaker. I stood up with everyone else, awkwardly balancing my hotdog while pretending to give a shit about football.

I told myself I wasn't looking for anyone in particular. I didn't care about the game, and yet my eyes scanned each player in blue and black, listening intently for a name. They were the last on the field, and they strutted in one after the other as if they owned the place. And perhaps they did.

The crowd went nuts, but when Brock's name was announced, I swore the earth shook as the onlookers went wild, stomping on the bleachers as they chanted his name.

"That's your boy," Mads whispered into my ear.

I rolled my eyes. "He is not mine." Not by a long shot, but I couldn't deny the little patter I felt in my heart when I heard his name. Seeing him run onto the field turned the patter into a sprint.

The whistle blew, and the ball was kicked. I tried my best to follow along, but my attention repeatedly was drawn to number four. TAYLOR scrolled across the back of his jersey.

Micah scored the first touchdown, and I jumped out of my seat with everyone else, a stupid grin on my lips as I screamed. Micah glanced to the stands, spinning the ball in a victory cele-bration. The crowd ate him up.

Even Mads smirked, shaking her head at him. "Showoff," she muttered.

I spent the rest of the game laughing and smiling with my friends. Though Carter played, his name was rarely called over the speaker. It was the Elite that dominated the field, just like they dominated the school.

No surprise.

People loved them, and I had yet to figure out why. The obvious was because they were beyond good-looking, they had money, and buckets of confidence. But was there more to it?

The game ended with a final touchdown by Public, but it wasn't enough to pull a win. Academy had blown them away, crushing Public once again.

Mads looped an arm around my shoulder as we climbed down the bleachers. "You had fun, didn't you? Admit it, Josie, you liked seeing them in their tight little uniforms?"

"She'd have to be dead not to," Ainsley added.

"Whatever. It wasn't half as bad as I imagined, but there is no way in hell I am becoming one of those Elite groupies," I informed them. Apparently, Brock, Micah, Grayson, and Fynn had their own personal cheerleading section made up entirely of some of the Academy's most popular girls. They cheered, chanted their names and numbers, giggled, and bounced in the stands until their boobs nearly fell out. I wanted to shove their scrunchies down their throats.

"Aw, yes," Mads nodded. "Each one dying for the chance to be a standby girl."

I snorted.

"At least we won," Mads noted, and then turned to Ainsley

apologetically. "Sorry, I know you were rooting for Public, but we are pretty hard to beat."

"They're fucking gods," Ainsley said, tucking her rainbow-streaked hair behind her ears. The wind had picked up and blew recklessly as we strolled into the parking lot.

Mads groaned. "Don't ever say that to their faces. It's bad enough they think they're invincible."

We had hung around in our seats, waiting for most of the crowd to leave so we wouldn't get caught in the bulk of traffic leaving. Plenty of cars still lined the parking lot, most of them probably players and coaches.

Since we had gotten to the game late, Mads's car was on the far side of the lot. I was weaving between a pair of SUVs, following Mads and Ainsley, when a pair of arms came out of nowhere, wrapping around my stomach and lifting me off my feet. I started to shriek until I heard a voice near my ear.

"Hey, sis. Aren't you going to congratulate me?" Carter asked. His chuckle washed over the side of my face, causing my blood to freeze.

"Put me down, you prick." I struggled in his arms, but Carter's hold remained steadfast. You would think after a game like that he would be tired.

Adrenaline pumped through my veins as two of Carter's friends stepped to either side of my friends. They had spun around to see what the commotion was about, and before either one of them could rush forward, Shawn and Porter grabbed them around the waist, locking them into a bear hug. My friends squealed, fighting against the football players, but they didn't stand a chance.

"Let me go, you asshole," Mads swore, kicking and scratching.

"Just chill, Clarke. We won't hurt you. We just want to have a little fun," Porter told her. "The celebration party has already begun."

Mads wasn't convinced. "I swear to God, if you don't put me down, I will sue the shit out of you."

Ainsley had stopped fighting, her smoky eyes locked onto Carter, who finally set me down, only to spin me around to face him. "What is the fucking point of this?" I asked Carter in disgust.

His hands were locked onto my wrists, keeping me from scratching his eyeballs out. He lowered his head until our noses were almost touching. I tried to turn my face away, but he yanked me forward. "You and I have unfinished business," he grunted. He reeked of beer and sweat, making me gag. "That stunt you pulled today, well, this is payback."

Fuck.

I wanted to shove him away, but I couldn't get my arms between us. He was too close, pressing me up against an SUV, the door handle digging into my lower back. "Oh, did I hurt your poor little balls?"

"You want to play rough, sis?" He pinned me in place with his body. I tried to free my hands but the bastard was strong.

"Let her go!" Mads screamed.

Ainsley still looked shocked, like she couldn't believe this was happening. Shit like this didn't go down at Public, or if it did, we didn't know about it. But at the Academy...

The lights in the parking lot weren't as bright as the field, and Carter had chosen one of the darker corners to grab me, but still, someone should have heard us, someone should be coming to check out what was going on.

Right?

Carter wedged his knee between my legs, spreading them. Terror kicked inside of me, but my fight was far from gone I wouldn't make this easy for him. Hell no. He would have to work for each inch he touched me. I spat in his face.

Carter laughed, pressing his hips into me as he wiped the side of his face on his shoulder. "I figured you'd like it dirty."

"Get. The. Fuck. Off. Me," I growled, but he pressed into me harder, grinding his hips against mine. Nausea rolled up in me.

Was he really going to rape me in the parking lot while his friends watched? While my friends were forced to witness? He couldn't be that evil, could he? But at the sound of fabric tearing, I suddenly wasn't certain of anything, other than I had to get away from him.

Carter lowered his head to my neck and started to suck painfully hard. I yelped, bucking my hips to try and dislodge him, but it only seemed to encourage the sick prick. He nipped me, hard, and I swear he drew blood. "The fun's just beginning, sis."

My God, such malice lingered in his voice. I shuddered, the taste of fear strong on my tongue.

He released my wrists, only to shove his fingers into my hair, tangling the strands as he yanked my head back to look at him. His eyes brimmed with dark desire and so much violent anger. I was truly afraid.

"Carter, don't do this—"

Carter was suddenly jerked off me. My limbs buckled, and yet I managed to stay on my feet. No, someone was holding me up. Gentle hands were at my elbows. Wildly, I spun, claws out. A sob left me as I stared up into Micah's face. His normal playful light blue eyes were cloudy and stormy. He didn't say a word to me, just pulled me into his arms and out of the way.

I gulped in air, breathing deeply the scent of Micah and fresh air.

"What the hell, Taylor!" I heard Carter roar.

I lifted my head off Micah's protective chest. Brock, Grayson, and Fynn had Carter surrounded.

"This is family business. Back off," Carter warned, trying to step around the wall of Elite. That wasn't happening.

"We are not family," I gritted out, refusing to admit how relieved I was to see Brock's deadly calm face.

"Go home, Patterson," Grayson ordered, his voice trembling with the dark promise of pain if Carter didn't do as he was told.

Fynn cracked his knuckles beside Grayson.

I glanced around, searching for Mads and Ainsley, needing to know they were safe. They were huddled together, no sign of Shawn or Porter. They must have taken off when the Elite showed up. Smart.

Carter was a fool—an idiot with a death wish. "I'm sick of you thinking you can boss me around. You might be the quarterback on the field, but off the field, you don't own me." His chest puffed out, boasting a bravado that was going to get his ass beat.

Not that I felt a shred of sympathy for him. Carter earned every inch of the beat down that was coming.

Brock stepped closer, Flynn and Grayson following suit. I felt Micah behind me stiffen. "Don't I?" Brock challenged, his voice low.

Carter clenched his fists at his sides. "This is bullshit. She's nobody."

Brock grabbed him by the front of his shirt. "Then there is no reason for you to be here, is there?"

The uncertainty that sprang into Carter's eyes proved he wasn't confident about standing up to the Elite. "What? She is good enough for you to fuck, but not the rest of us?"

Brock's hand shot out so fast that I wasn't sure what was happening until I heard the crunch of fist on flesh. Carter's head snapped back, and my stepbrother groaned in agony. "What the fuck, Taylor!" Then the idiot lunged, dropping his shoulder to tackle Brock to the ground.

He never touched him.

Fynn and Grayson stepped in. They slammed Carter to the ground. One of them kicked my stepbrother in the ribs, the other looming over him to make sure he didn't get back up. "Stay down," Grayson ordered.

All I could do was stand there, stunned, with my legs shaking hard enough that if it hadn't been for Micah, I'd been a mess on the ground.

Brock turned to me, eyes so dark. "Get out of here. Now," he growled.

I didn't know how I found my voice, but it was weak as I asked, "What are you going to do?"

His entire body tensed, and his voice was strained as he said, "Don't worry about it."

"It's best you don't know," Micah added, steering me away and toward my friends. He kept an arm around my waist, supporting me.

I wanted to argue, wanted to ask what they were going to do to him—not that I cared. I shouldn't give a fuck what they did to Carter. It would be no more than he deserved, as long as they didn't kill him. It was on the tip of my tongue to tell Brock not to kill him, but Mads put a hand on my arm.

"Let's go, Josie," she said gently.

Micah handed me off to my two best friends, and I let them pull me away.

CHAPTER THIRTEEN

"Are you okay?" Mads asked as soon as we were inside her car. She hit the start button, turning on the heat.

The shaking wouldn't stop. "I think so," I replied, my teeth clanging together.

Ainsley clicked her seat belt in place in the back seat as Mads hit the gas, guiding the car into the line leaving the lot. "Ohmygod. I can't believe that happened," she gasped, her voice breathless.

Me neither.

I didn't want to look over my shoulder, didn't want to see what Brock and the others were doing, but my eyes seemed to have a mind of their own. It was too dark to see anything other than the shadow of five guys.

"You're staying with me tonight," Mads declared, glancing at me. "There is no way I am leaving you alone in that house with that psycho."

That sounded like exactly what I needed. I couldn't be in that house with him. Not now. Not ever. "Thanks," I chattered, arms wrapping around myself.

"That was seriously messed up, Josie. What are you going to do?" Ainsley asked.

"I don't know," I muttered, staring out the window.

Ainsley touched my shoulder lightly. "You have to tell your mom."

"Yeah," I agreed, but deep down, I knew it would be pointless. Perhaps it was time I phoned Dad. I didn't know what else to do.

I spent the weekend with Mads, sending a text to my mom, letting her know where I was. Not that she truly cared. Ainsley stayed Friday, but had to leave early in the morning to get to work. A girls' night was just what I'd needed. I didn't know how I would have made it through the night without them.

Mads's parents were amazing and normal for Elmwood high society. On Saturday morning, her dad made blueberry pancakes. Her dad, not the cook. I didn't know what she told her parents, if anything, and I didn't ask. Truthfully, I wanted to forget last night ever happened, but that was going to take some time, or so I found out in the shower. Every time I closed my eyes, Carter was there. The shower did little to erase the stain he'd left behind. It wasn't the bruising, but the memories that haunted me.

Mads let me borrow some clothes, nothing fancy, just comfy

shorts and a T-shirt. I padded down the stairs in search of my friend and heard the voices. Male voices. I paused on the stairs, listening. Yes, it was totally wrong to eavesdrop, but that wasn't what I was doing. I was trying to figure out who was here and if it was safe for me to go downstairs.

"How is she?" a gruff voice asked, and I sucked in a breath. That was Brock.

"Okay, considering," Mads replied as I descended the remaining stairs.

I turned the corner into the kitchen, immediately locating Brock. He was leaning against the island next to Grayson, who shoveled leftover pancakes into his mouth.

Brock's eyes lifted to mine. He didn't smile. His expression remained the same, a mask of indifference as if I was no one, and yet, he was standing in Mads's kitchen asking about me.

WTF gives?

"What are you doing here?" I asked, moving into the room.

Mads's head turned toward me, finally noticing me. "Grayson's mom asked him to stop by and grab some papers from my mom," she quickly explained. Her cheeks reddened as if she was uncomfortable being caught fraternizing with the Elite.

Grayson and she were cousins. I knew that. But still, it was odd seeing her talk so casually with them. At school, they didn't even acknowledge each other. "Oh," I replied, stopping a few feet from Brock.

I should thank him or something, shouldn't I? But the idea of bringing up last night made my stomach churn. The last thing I wanted was to toss up breakfast all over Mads's kitchen.

"I also came to check on my cousin," Grayson added, scowling at me like he wanted to stick his syrup-covered fork in me. The look he gave me was one of mistrust, as if I was the one who might hurt Mads. It didn't make sense. Another day, I might have called him out on it, demanded to know why he disliked me so much, but today, I didn't have the strength.

Mads cleared her throat. "As I told these two Neanderthals, we're fine."

Brock forked a hand through his hair, and that was when I noticed his knuckles. They were red and swollen, and his right knuckles had a nasty cut. "You're hurt," I gasped, moving forward to inspect his hand before I realized what I was doing. It looked worse than it was.

Jerking his hand from my fingers, he shoved them into his pockets, and I raised my eyes to his. "I'm fine," he said briskly Those aqua eyes became glaciers, cold and untouchable.

An awkward silence descended. I took a step back, regretting my impulsive action to touch him. "Sorry," I muttered.

"You don't have anything to be sorry for," Brock said. "He's right," Mads added gently, trying to take some of the edge off Brock's tone. "This is not your fault."

Perhaps I should have inquired what happened after I left, if Carter was alive, but I didn't. I couldn't. And I really did care that much. I shrugged, adopting my blasé attitude, which was a total front. "Still doesn't make it suck any less."

Grayson finished his pancakes and stood uprinsing the plate off in the sink. "We should go," he said to Brock. I couldn't help feeling like Grayson was rushing to get away from me. Brock nodded.

Shifting my weight, I leaned against the counter and brushed my slightly damp hair off to one side. I'd forgotten about the mark on my neck until Brock's gaze darkened. His hand reached for my chin, and I didn't stop him as he angled my head slightly, exposing my neck where there was a bright cherry-red mark and bruising from Carter's teeth.

His thumb brushed softly over the skin, the line of his jaw hardening. "He never should have touched you."

I couldn't help sensing there was a warning in that statement, as if Brock wasn't done with Carter. His fingers slipped away from my neck, taking his warmth with him. I tipped my chin to look at him, but Brock was already walking away, right behind Grayson. I just stared at his back and swallowed.

The rest of the day was chill and far less exciting than the last twenty-four hours had been. It was just Mads and me hanging out, binging trashy TV, and eating everything in sight. I never wanted the weekend to end, but of course, Sunday rolled around. I would have to go home eventually, and I debated whether I should call Dad. After mulling it over, I decided this was a conversation I needed to have in person. Mads refused to let me take an Uber to my old neighborhood despite my arguing and demanded I let her drop me off. I begrudgingly agreed.

So here I was, late Sunday morning, staring at the house I grew up in.

It was a white ranch with black shutters and a wraparound porch. At the end of the driveway was a two-car garage Dad used as his shop. We never parked our cars inside. There wasn't room with all his tools and workbenches. Not to mention the car lift he had installed a few years back. I'd spent countless hours in that garage, watching him work under a car, handing him tools and listening to old eighties rock.

A wave of nostalgia hit me as I just stood in front of the house staring. Tears blurred my eyes. I missed everything about this little house, from its creaking floors to the leaking faucets. It was home.

Dad's truck was parked out front, and as I walked past, I let my finger trail along the metal trim. I had learned to drive in this car. Sniffing back the surge of emotions, I wiped at my eyes and walked onto the porch. It felt so strange ringing the doorbell to my own house, but since he wasn't expecting me, I didn't just want to barge in.

God forbid if he wasn't alone. I didn't think my dad was dating, but it had been a while since we talked.

From the other side of the door, I heard him shuffling and fumbling with the lock. He blinked at me after opening the door, staring at me as if he was dreaming. "Josie?"

"Hey, Dad," I said with a wobbly smile.

His face was covered in stubble, like he hadn't shaved for a day or two. But other than the tired lines under his eyes, he looked the same. He ran a hand through his black hair that only had a dusting of gray at the temples. "Are you okay? What's wrong?" His brown eyes grew concerned as he took a good look at me.

I let out a watery laugh, trying to keep myself together, but it was hard. Seeing him in person, I suddenly felt five again and longed to have her dad make everything better—take away the pain. "Still wearing those silly band T-shirts, I see."

He let out a gruff chuckle, glancing down at his shirt. "Yeah, well, they pissed your mom off."

That was a good enough reason for me.

Letting the door swing wider open, he stepped to the side. "Come in, kiddo. I was just having a cup of coffee."

I nodded and walked over the threshold. My eyes swept over the room, and I swallowed back a sob. Nothing had changed. Every piece of furniture was exactly where it had been before Mom and I left.

Following him into the kitchen, I sat down at our second-hand table. A moment later he placed a mug in front of me, taking the seat directly across from me. "Are you going to tell me what is going on, Josie?"

I wrapped my hands around the cup, letting the heat warm my hands as I brought it up to my face and inhaled. No one made coffee like Dad. I took a sip and savored the sweet and creamy brew before answering. "I can't stay with Mom. It's not safe for me," I said, dropping the bomb—at least, that was how it felt.

The kitchen fell silent. "You know it's not that simple, kiddo."

"Nothing ever is," I mumbled, staring into my cup.

He cleared his throat. "I know you, and I can see that something is wrong. Did you and your mother have a fight?"

If only it was that simple. "Mom and I fight all the time."

"So if it isn't your mother, then is it Steven? Did he do something?" His jaw hardened a fraction.

"No." I sighed, suddenly having a hard time finding the words to tell him what happened with Carter. I was embarrassed when I had no reason to be. None of this was my fault. And what could my dad do? He would confront my mother and Steven, which would cause problems.

Dad tapped the side of his coffee, watching me carefully. "You know you can talk to me."

I gave him a small, reassuring smile that was for me as much as it was for him. "Yeah, Dad, I know. I just really needed to see you."

His hand reached across the table to cover mine, squeezing it. "Well, I'm glad you're here."

The pressure clamping down on my chest since Friday night eased. "Is it okay if I stay for a while?"

He grinned, leaning back in his chair. "I'd like that. I can order us pizza from down the street, and we can watch movies all day, if you'd like."

Just like old times. I desperately needed the familiarity of my old life. It gave me comfort I couldn't find anywhere else. I nodded, trying not to get emotional. "Sounds perfect."

If he heard the hitch in my voice, he ignored it. "You do have to go back though, Josie. As much as I want you here, we have to abide by the judge's ruling, just until my lawyer can get it amended. I haven't given up."

It was costing him money he didn't have to fight the arrangement, my mother's highly paid lawyers bulldozing him. "Dad, you don't have to do that. Really. It's only a few months until I'm eighteen." What was the point? I'd be free to make my own choices then.

"I know. Still, you're my little girl. You'll always be my little girl. I've missed you so much, Josie."

"Me too," I said, smiling, and sipped my coffee.

* * *

It was after dinner when Dad dropped me off at the end of the Pattersons' driveway. I waved him off and punched the code into the security gate. Full on pizza and hours of *Lord of the Rings* movies, I dragged my feet down the driveway like I was awaiting my own execution. All that lightness I'd felt being with Dad disappeared, and the weight in my chest returned.

Angie was waiting on the porch for me, sitting on one of the rockers with a big glass of, surprise, wine. "Was that your father's car I saw?"

I'd been dreading this moment, but I couldn't avoid this house or my mother any longer. I sat down in the chair beside her and replied, "Yes."

She lifted the sunglasses off her eyes, placing them on top of her head. It was too dark for sunglasses, which meant she was attempting to hide her bloodshot eyes. "Is that where you've been all weekend? With him?" Bitterness eked from her voice.

"No, I was staying with a friend. I just saw Dad for a few hours today. What's going on?" Something was up. She had that look on her face, the one that said I had done something to displease her.

Lifting the glass to her lips, she took a long drink. "Carter is in the hospital."

This was the first I was hearing of it. If the Elite beat Carter that bad, why hadn't I heard about it? Did Mads keep it from me, knowing I would be upset? It wasn't that I was concerned for Carter, but I was afraid of what he would do to me when he came home. Carter would blame this on me.

She saw the startled expression on my face. "You didn't know. Hmm." She pressed her lips together. "He was attacked Friday night after the game. Steven and I had to cut our trip short when we got the call."

That explained the sour attitude. It had nothing to do with her concern for her stepson, but the fact that her precious trip with her husband had been interrupted. "Is he okay?"

"He got banged up pretty good. A few fractured ribs, but he will recover. The doctors say he won't be able to play football for at least two months."

I made a noise of disgust in the back of my throat that had my mother arching a brow at me.

"Do you know anything about what happened? Carter refuses to tell his father anything. He claims he didn't see who attacked him."

My brows furrowed in confusion. Why would he do that?

"If you know anything, Josephine, I expect you to speak up. This is your brother. Steven is understandably upset, not just about his son's safety, but what this will cost Carter's future. He is to be scouted this year."

Unbelievable. Was that all they cared about? Football? I almost felt sorry for Carter. Almost, but then I remembered what the bastard had done to me. He didn't deserve my sympathy.

My face must have been given me away. Under Angie's scrutiny, she guessed who might be involved. "If *that boy* had anything to do with this..."

I clamped my mouth shut, refusing to say anything on the matter. Perhaps that was the wrong way to handle the situation, but I didn't want to outright lie to my mother. Instead, I asked, "When will he be home?"

Angie rocked her chair, turning her eyes to the setting sun. "They are keeping him one more night for observation at Steven's insistence. Most of his teachers will be emailing his homework while he recovers at home, but I need you to check in with the office at the end of each week."

Joy.

I'd rather burn all his assignments.

CHAPTER FOURTEEN

I was lying in my bed staring at the ceiling when my phone buzzed beside me. Groaning, I let it vibrate a few more times before grabbing it and swiping the answer button. "Hey, Ains. What's up?"

"First, how are you doing?" she asked, genuine concern in her voice.

"I'm a mess," I answered honestly. "But I'll be okay. You don't have to worry about me."

"Don't be stupid. Of course, I'm worried."

A flood of warmth filled me. Ainsley would always be on my side. "Well, Carter is in the hospital. He has a few cracked ribs and won't be feeling up to physically assaulting me anytime soon. The doctors are saying it will take six weeks until he is fully healed. Maybe more." Crossing my fingers. Too bad it wasn't closer to my birthday, then I wouldn't have to worry so much about what Carter planned to do to me next. He would have six weeks to plan his retribution.

"I heard," Ains said. "That's why I'm calling. I'm sending you something." From the other side of the phone, I heard her tapping away. A second later, I received a text.

"Hang on, I just got it." I flipped from my phone app to my text messages and stared at the screen.

It was a video.

A large lump formed in my throat. I was afraid I knew precisely what the video would show.

"Is that what I think it is?" I said, switching the audio to speaker and turning the volume down so as not to be overheard. Carter wasn't home yet, but I didn't want the staff, or worse, Angie, to hear.

"It's from Friday night," Ainsley confirmed. "You're on the video."

Jesus, Mary, and Joseph. There's a video?

I let out a breath. "Where did you get this?"

"It's everywhere, Josie."

Fuck. Which meant everyone had seen it. Everyone but me, that was.

"It shows Carter harassing you and then getting the living shit beat out of him. The camera was strategically placed so you never see the attackers' faces. Convenient, huh?" she said with a twist of respect.

Those Elite boys were smart. I'd give them that. "Yeah," I agreed, staring at the thumbnail. It was dark, showing someone's back—that someone being Brock. "How did I not know about this?"

"It just popped up today. I'm guessing whoever made the video didn't release it until this morning."

Why would they release their own video? It had to be the Elite, right? But it didn't make sense to me. Was it a message? A threat?

I frowned. "I've got to text Mads."

"She's seen it."

"You talked to her?" I asked, surprised.

"Yeah, we've been texting all weekend. I was worried about you."

"I'm sorry you got mixed up in this." It wasn't fair to her. She had only been at that game because of me. If something had happened to her... I wouldn't have been able to live with myself.

"Stop it right now. I know what you're doing. You can't blame yourself, Josie."

"So everyone keeps telling me," I grumbled, picking at a loose thread on a pillow.

"Well, listen for once in your life. Look, my mom's calling me. Text me later?" I could hear her mom in the background yelling her name.

"Yeah, okay." Disconnecting the call with a push of my finger, I stared at the video and bit my lip. Did I want to see this?

A part of me said yes, thinking maybe it would give me some sort of justice. But the other part of me had seen enough that night. Dredging it back up would only make getting over what happened harder. What I should do was delete the video off my phone.

And yet I hit the play button.

There was no sound, which I knew had been deliberate. Voices could be recognized. The first few seconds of the video made me feel like I had jumped into an icy pool. It threw me right back into that moment with all paralyzing fear and utter helplessness. I wanted to escape even now, scream out for help.

Then I saw Brock—well, the back of Brock. Carter was already on the ground, and Brock delivered a kick to Carter's ribs. Someone else put a foot into Carter's back. Another punch to the face. It kept going.

I gasped, putting a hand over my mouth. They were downright brutal, absolutely merciless.

In the end, Grayson and Fynn had to pull Brock off Carter. I couldn't hear their voices or see their faces, but I imagined them telling Brock to stop, that he'd had enough. Any more and they risked killing Carter.

The video stopped on a picture of Carter's bloody face as he curled himself up into a fetal position. I stared at the image, knowing I should feel something, but all I felt was nothing.

What did that say about me?

I didn't care about Carter.

It was amazing, the things I'd tell myself to make sense of my stupid decisions. For instance, Monday morning there was a car idling at the end of my driveway, just outside the gate—a black Range Rover.

I had a choice. Get in the car with Brock or drive myself to school. It might not have seemed like a big deal, but once I got into the car, everything would change. To be honest, it already had. I just didn't realize as I walked down the driveway and slid into Brock's SUV just how much my life would alter. Hindsight was a bitch.

"What are you doing here?" I asked, shutting the door behind me. His scent clung everywhere, teasing my nostrils and other parts of my body. The damn smell of him was like a drug.

Brock rubbed at the back of his neck. "Driving you to school."

I rolled my eyes. "That's the best you can come up with? I'm capable of driving myself."

"Just put on the damn seat belt, Josie." His voice glided over me.

My stomach flipped. Hearing him say my name, even in exasperation, caused a flutter inside me. I clutched my bag, needing to do something with my fingers that didn't involve running them through his hair.

He put the car into drive as I snapped the belt into place. "Why are you doing this?" I asked when he turned off my street, heading toward the Academy.

"I have my reasons," he replied, leveling me with a stare. He had his white button-down shirt rolled up to the elbows, one of his tattoos peeking underneath the material.

I lifted a single brow. "Would you care to share them with me?"

"No," he said flatly.

"Asshole," I muttered.

His lips curled into the most wickedly delicious grin. I was spellbound.

"Don't do that again," I said, shaking the lust from my head, but it didn't work, since my entire body hummed. Not even a cold shower would help cool what I was feeling for Brock. How could a single smile make me so weak?

And why him?

My taste in guys completely sucked.

Then again, as I stared at him, I rethought that statement.

Brock Taylor was fucking gorgeous. Arrogant. Aloof. An asshole. And a thousand other different adjectives that started with an *A*. But he was gorgeous.

That deviously charming grin widened. "What?"

"That!" I replied. "Don't smile at me. It's like a weapon of female destruction."

He chuckled. "I'll try to remember that."

"Can you be serious for just a minute?" It was sort of a stupid question, considering Brock was the epitome of seriousness, at least when he was around me.

"Depends." He glanced at me for a moment before returning his gaze to the road.

My fingers fumbled with the strap on my bag. "I don't get you. Why would you release those pictures of me but then turn around and put Carter in the hospital? I'm trying to make sense of it all, but I can't."

"We didn't release those pictures," he told me, eyes flashing with danger. How quick he could go from playful to dickmood. "Trust me, if I had known beforehand, it would have been dealt with before being circulated all over school."

So he said before. "Then who did?"

His fingers clenched and unclenched against the steering wheel. "Carter and Ava."

The idea of the two of them teaming up spiked a ribbon of dread inside me.

"Ava took the pictures. She was really sneaky about it. We assumed she was just texting her friends for a ride home," he explained.

"Okay, what did I do to make this girl hate me so much?" I spluttered.

He gave me a knowing look and arched a brow.

Shit. "Oh, right. That." How could I have forgotten? I had sex with him. Apparently, that made most of the female population at the Academy hate me. My cheeks warmed, and I cracked my window. "And Carter, how does he play into this?"

Brock turned his stormy eyes on me. "Ava made the stupid mistake of showing the pictures to your stepbrother. He was the one who distributed them, texting them to the football team and printing them out."

"He texted the pictures to you." I shook my head. "What a fucking idiot."

The corner of Brock's lips curled. He swung the Range Rover into the school lot, getting in the line of cars hustling to find spots to park.

It was the first time I'd been back since Friday night, and I had expected this sense of panic to press down upon me. I stared straight ahead, my fingers clenching the side of the seat. That whole night came rushing back. I could feel Carter's hands pinning my wrists, smell his breath on my face, and hear his eager and callous voice in my ear.

"Firefly," Brock whispered.

I closed my eyes to drown out the memories, but it only made them worse.

It was the warmth of Brock's hand along the side of my cheek that shook me out of my terror. The pad of his thumb ran just under my lower lip. "I didn't ask for this shit," I bit out. The tension in my muscles slowly relaxed.

His eyes darkened, lips pulled into a thin line. "No, you didn't, but you're not alone."

God, I was a basket case. Why was he even here? Helping me? Any other guy would run for the hills. My life was a fucking mess, a big, sloppy mess. I took a deep breath and nodded, steeling myself. *You're not alone,* I repeated Brock's words to myself as I gathered my stuff and opened the door.

The lot was crowded with students, more than usual. They were hanging around their cars; others were out in front of the building, but it seemed as if everyone was holding off going inside, waiting for something. Or someone, I soon realized. I just didn't know if it was Brock or me that had them gathered like a flock of geese.

I swore all conversation stopped as I hopped out of Brock's SUV, hundreds of eyes glued to us. Brock came around to my side of the car. Something in the way he strode toward me with purpose in his eyes made me wary. I watched him, securing my bag over my shoulder. His fingers tangled into my hair while his other hand went to my hip.

"What the hell are you doing?" I hissed, blinking up at him.

Eyes locked on mine, he held me prisoner. "Making a statement," he murmured right before his lips crushed over mine.

What the—

My brain short-circuited at the first touch of his lips, and for a long moment, I stood there, completely unsure of what was happening and of myself. Then his tongue touched my lips and a floodgate opened, emotion pouring through me. I no longer cared why Brock was kissing me, just that he never stopped.

The bag on my shoulder fell to the ground as I wound my hands around his neck, fitting our bodies together. His hand at my hip pushed me back until my ass hit the car. I parted my lips on a gasp, and his tongue swept in. It was a kiss meant to make an impression—to brand me. It was a kiss that made me forget the horror of Friday night.

He unsealed our lips as abruptly as he had dived in. Dark lashes fanned over guarded eyes, but I was lost in the depths of them.

"Why did you stop?" I whispered breathlessly.

His husky laugh glazed over my swollen lips. "If there weren't a parking lot of people right now, I would take you in the back of my car."

A whimpering noise purred in my throat, and my fingers tightened in his hair. Not to mention what his words did to my insides. People? What people? I lifted on my toes, taking his lower lip between my teeth, needing his lips again, needing him to make me forget. His kiss made me realize the only time I felt alive, the only time I felt safe was when his lips were on mine. I didn't want the feeling to end. Not yet. Not when I'd just found it again.

"Firefly, I swear to God—"

I pressed my lips to his again, silencing his protest before he finished. This time when he broke off the kiss, he backed away, keeping me at arm's length. My body sank against the side of the SUV. His eyes were an unbridled turmoil of passion and caution, as if he didn't trust me. "If you do that thing with your tongue one more time, we're both going to end up in detention."

My lips curved. "What thing?" I said, feigning innocence. Something told me he was no stranger to the principal's office.

"Stay there," he warned, raking a hand through his hair. "Shit," he swore under his breath. "That wasn't supposed to happen."

I angled my head to the side, no longer caring about school or being late. "Which part? You kissing me? Or you enjoying it?" Feeling stronger and encouraged by his reaction, I took a step toward him.

He held out a hand, warding me off like I was some sort of temptress. "God, I don't know what it is about your lips."

Clarity broke through. "Why did you kiss me then?"

Now it was Brock who was smirking, like a cat who caught the canary. "Because you're ours."

Ours. Not mine. The high I'd been riding dissipated at Brock's declaration, extinguishing the burning flame inside me. He had stamped me property of the Elite in front of the entire school. And those who didn't see our very public kiss would hear about it by the end of the day. Everyone would know.

CHAPTER FIFTEEN

I felt myself get riled up. It was amazing how quick need could flip to anger. "Newsflash, Taylor. No one owns me," I hissed. "Not you. Not your friends. And certainly not this school." Each phrase was punctuated with my finger in his chest. And afterward, I didn't want to admit it, but my fucking finger hurt.

His lips twitched, and the asshole Brock was back. "Good. That's better. You'll need that fight. It's the only way to survive here."

WTH.

This whole thing was a ploy, a way to mark me so no one would mess with me. Perhaps I should be grateful for whatever reason Brock extended his protection. The problem was, I didn't want to be *owned*. "Kiss my ass, Taylor," I said, spinning on my heels and stalking off toward the school.

And thanks to Brock, his stunt, and the video I started

another week being the hot topic. It wasn't just the girls that looked at me differently—the guys did too. Unlike the girls, who glared at me with equal parts envy and hatred, the guys were wary, keeping their distance as if they were afraid to so much as say hi to me.

Great. Brock had labeled me a fucking pariah.

By lunch, I was ready to wring Brock Taylor's neck. That rage only doubled when I strolled into the cafeteria and saw some floozy on his lap. I swore, steam blew out of my ears. It wasn't so much that a few hours ago his lips had been locked on mine as it was who was on his lap.

Fucking. Ava.

The same bitch who was doing everything possible to make my senior year hell.

"Are you seeing this shit?" Mads said in disgust beside me. "He is goddamn shameless. Elmwood Academy's manwhore. That will be his yearbook caption."

Mads really was a good friend. "I couldn't care less who he hooks up with. Any of them," I said, tightening my jaw.

"Uh-huh," she said, clearly as unconvinced as I felt.

A body wormed its way between Mads and me, and Micah threw his arms around our shoulders. "You're sitting with us now, new girl." He began guiding us toward the Elite table.

Like hell I was. I dug my heels in, refusing to take another step. I didn't freaking care if I made a scene. Everyone should be used to it by now, considering it was all I had done since school started. "As long as she is there, I'm not going anywhere near your table." My gaze pinned Ava.

Micah rolled his eyes. "Fine. I'll get rid of her. Now stop

being difficult or I will throw you over my shoulder. Don't test me, James."

I couldn't decide if I was more curious to see Micah get rid of Ava or if he would actually haul my ass across the cafeteria. "You win," I replied.

The devil winked at me. "I always win." He squeezed Mads's neck. "Come on, little Maddy. You're coming too."

"Oh, goodie." Her fake enthusiasm made me smile, and I momentarily forgot that I was pissed off.

Micah flashed her a thousand-watt grin, and my poor friend scowled at him, but I saw through her farce. She totally was still hung up on Micah Bradford and his dimples.

When we got to the table, Micah hauled Ava off Brock's lap, who didn't seem to care one way or the other. "Get lost," Micah said, dismissing Ava.

She flipped her glossy red hair over her shoulder, shooting daggers at Micah. "You can't tell me what to do."

The playfulness vanished from his features. "You want to bet?"

"Leave," Brock told her, not bothering to even look up at her when he gave the order. If he had, he would have seen the hurt flash through her big hazel eyes, but he was too busy staring at me. Ava's cheeks grew as bright as her hair right before she whirled on her Jimmy Choos and stormed off.

"Why was she here?" I demanded as I sat down as far from Brock as I could manage. Mads took the seat next to me. Of course, the entire cafeteria was watching us. Mads and I changed the dynamic at the Elite table, and they were all waiting to see what would happen next.

So was I.

Mads leaned forward on the table, setting her bottle of water in front of her. "Seriously. Everyone saw you kissing Josie this morning, and now you have Ava throwing herself at you," she pointed out. "What the fuck, Brock."

She took the words right out of my mouth. I flipping loved her.

His narrowed eyes flipped from mine to Mads. "You know how things work. What I do is my business."

Mads snorted. "I don't buy into your bullshit, remember? Why do you let her hang around? That bitch is imbalanced. She needs to be committed."

Micah and Fynn chuckled. "She has you there, Brock. That bitch does belong in a psycho ward," Fynn agreed.

Grayson frowned at me, and I scowled back. "Is anyone going to tell me why I'm here, sitting with the four of you?"

All eyes turned to Brock. "Carter gets out of the hospital today, isn't that right?" He completely ignored my question, and distracting me with my stepbrother was a dirty trick. "Unfortunately," I groused, a rock of dread dropping into my empty stomach.

"Grayson, Micah, and I have practice after school, so you're going to ride with Fynn," Brock informed me in his no questions asked tone.

I smoothed my suddenly clammy palms down the sides of my plaid skirt. "Since when do you dictate with whom I go home? Or anywhere, for that matter?"

"You might as well just accept defeat now," Mads said beside me. "He's got that look. He won't take no for an answer, and if you don't do things the simple way when Brock asks—"

"You'll find out just what an asshole I really can be," Brock interrupted, a sinister grin on his lips that made me think he might just be capable of bad things.

So this did have something to do with Carter.

My face must have shown my displeasure, because Brock lifted a brow at me, daring me to challenge him. I actually believed he half hoped I would so he could throw his dominance around us lesser mortals.

I picked at the corner of my sandwich and blew out a breath. "Why can't Mads drive me home?"

The table fell silent, as if none of them could fathom my ability to negotiate with Brock. "Because you aren't going home, not immediately," he added, the muscles around his mouth tight.

"Where am I going?" He had another thing coming if he thought I would just blindly go wherever. I barely knew these guys, despite how intimately I might know Brock. A blush stole over my cheeks.

"Fynn's."

I slid a glance to the golden, green-eyed god-like football player. He flashed me a teasing grin.

Wonderful. What the hell was I going to do alone with Fynn?

I spent the rest of lunch coming up with ways I could ditch Fynn. It wasn't that I didn't like the guy, but I wasn't sure how I felt hanging out with him. Alone. Surely it wouldn't be too hard to sneak out of school without him knowing.

My mind was full of crap as I walked to History class. Fynn. Carter. Brock. Grayson. My mother. It was a never-ending Ferris wheel of hell that I couldn't get off. Since Carter wasn't at school today, my shadows backed off. I hadn't expected to feel a sense of loss at not having one of them pop up after each class.

What is wrong with me?

The halls around me filled up fast as kids spilled into the hallways, either on their way to the next lunch period or to class. I wove through the crowd, heading to the stairwell that led to the main floor. My feet descended the first few steps as I clutched my laptop to my chest, doing my best to clear the memory of Brock's kiss from my brain. It wasn't working.

Why did that bastard have to kiss me?

I was doing just fine forgetting the night we hooked up.

Lies. But they were my lies to tell myself.

Someone brushed up behind me, and I didn't think anything of it until I was fucking flying.

No. Not flying. Falling.

For a split second, I had this moment of perfect clarity—someone had shoved me—and then it was all drowned out by the thundering of my heart and the terror racing through my veins. Someone screamed. Someone else cursed. One of them might have been me, but I wasn't sure which. Blurred images scrambled to get out of the way as I frantically attempted to reach for the railing, but it slipped out of my hand, along with my laptop.

Metal crashed, tumbling down the stairs, with me right behind it.

Motherfuckerrrrrrr.

I couldn't stop myself. So I did the next best thing. I braced for an epic crash.

"What the hell?" A girl jumped out of the way when I finally stopped on the bottom landing. "What's wrong with you? Did you just learn how to walk yesterday?" She dusted at her skirt in disgust and stalked off.

Fuck you very much.

I didn't have it in me to give her a dirty look, not when I had the wind knocked out of me and the world was spinning. My body begged me not to move. Of course, I didn't listen.

Groaning, I peeled myself off the ground and sat up, a sea of people swarming around me. It hadn't been a horrible fall—jarring, to say the least, but it could have been much worse. I could have broken my neck. Luckily, the only thing broken was my laptop. My body seemed to be more or less intact.

But that didn't mean I wasn't hurting everywhere. My wrists. My hands. My ass. My knees. Shit, even my boobs throbbed.

Waiting a minute for my vision to steady itself, I gulped air. *Breathe. Just breathe, Josie.*

"Are you okay?" someone asked as they walked by.

I nodded and waved them on, unsure if I was going to pass out or puke. Maybe both.

A pair of shoes stopped in front of me. "What the hell did you do now?" a gruff voice demanded, sounding irritated.

What does he have to be annoyed about?

I'm the one who is on the ground.

I craned my neck back, regretting the movement. Grayson

glared down at me. Go figure. The last Elite I wanted to see. "Someone pushed me down the stairs," I rasped.

He blinked, an expression of disbelief in his eyes. "You're kidding?"

"Would I be on the floor if I was kidding?"

He seemed to think it over before offering me a hand. "Here, let me help you up before you get trampled to death."

"Gee, thanks." I put my hand in his. "Are you being nice to me?"

He pulled me to my feet, the edges of his lips twitching and his cynical brown eyes softening a tad. "Don't let it go to your head. We are not friends."

There was something familiar about the way he looked at me. It tugged at my mind, but I couldn't place what it was. "Duly noted. Why, again, do you hate me?" I winced, sucking in a breath of air against the pain that shot through my ankle. "Holy crap, that hurts." I immediately took the weight off my right foot.

His lips pressed together, eyes darting down to the ankle in question. Before I could protest or tell him not to touch it, Grayson crouched down and prodded the tender spot with his fingers.

"Ouch," I grated out between clenched teeth.

"You should probably have the nurse look at that," he said seriously, all semblance of someone capable of compassion gone in just a flick of the eye.

"Yeah. So much for History."

He bent down and picked up my smashed laptop. "This thing is toast."

I glanced at the cracked computer, the screen nothing but splintered glass, and sighed. "Any chance the school replaces those for free?" Then I remembered this was the Academy.

Grayson shoved the laptop into his bag, which he secured on his back before slipping an arm around my waist. I leaned into him, grateful for the support, and wobbled alongside him. It was strange. This was the closest I'd ever been to Grayson, and I couldn't shake the feeling that he was itching to put distance between us. Did he find me that repulsive? Or was it some sort of bro code because Brock had seen me first?

But that didn't make sense.

I knew they often hooked up with the same girls. And Micah literally flirted with me every chance he got.

So what gave?

I glanced sideways at him, taking a moment to study Grayson. On the rare occasions I had seen Grayson not scowling, he seemed friendly. Dare I say even approachable, but that was all the vibes I got from him. I never had to worry about Grayson hitting on me, and somehow that was okay with me. Don't get me wrong, he was an extremely attractive guy, but he wasn't my type. And I surely wasn't his.

Perhaps it was the scorn that usually poured off him when I was around that turned me off. I didn't know what it was, but there was no chance of Grayson and me ever hooking up. Ever.

Hell, I didn't even know if we could ever be friends.

A mystery I was determined to uncover. There was a reason this particular Elite member didn't trust me, and I meant to find out why.

After I had some painkillers.

"Do you want me to carry you?" he suddenly asked, breaking me out of my stupor.

I couldn't tell if he was serious, because the expression on his face said he'd rather jump into a pool of poisonous spiders than have to carry me down the hall. I grinned. "Don't worry, I've got it. Just go slow," I suggested.

He let out an exasperated breath. "It would be quicker if you let me carry you. I'm not sure you should be walking on that ankle."

"You sound so thrilled. How could I possibly say no?" I grumbled back, trying my best not to roll my eyes as I so wanted to do. "Look, I'm sorry," I apologized after an agonizing bout of silence. "Pain makes me bitchy. I know you are only trying to help, and I appreciate it, even if it doesn't seem like it. Are you going to get in trouble for missing class?"

The idea made him laugh. Like actually laugh. "You do know who I am, right?"

I thumped myself on the head. "Oh, right. Elite. No rules. How exactly does that work anyway?"

"Our parents run the school board," he answered with a nonchalant shrug.

"Of course they do." It made perfect sense. I winced at the pain in my ankle as we drew closer to the nurse's office.

His expression was deadpan as he glanced sidelong at me. "Wait until Brock hears about this." His voice suggested Brock would raise hell when he found out.

My head started to pound, and I wondered if it was wise to give up figuring out just why Brock had taken an interest in me. There was always tomorrow. "I have a brilliant idea. How about we don't tell him," I suggested, pasting on a false smile of hope.

Grayson adjusted his hold on me as we turned the corner, the door to the nurse's office in sight. Despite my protest about being carried, he was all but lifting me off my feet. "No, fucking way, Li'l J. You can lie to Brock if you want to, but I will not be the one he loses his temper at."

"What is his deal? Why would he care?" So much for being patient. Headache be damned.

"You're not the only one who is trying figure shit out," he replied disconcertingly, darkness edging into his eyes.

"Well, let me know when you do. I'd like to know."

He shook his head, a partial smile on his lips. Opening the door with his free hand, Grayson helped me into the office, and I slumped with relief into a chair next to the door, keeping my injured leg extended. I stared at my foot, knowing it was swollen under my boot and sock, unable to believe how I got here.

Had someone really shoved me down half a flight of stairs?

FML.

Fuck Elmwood Academy.

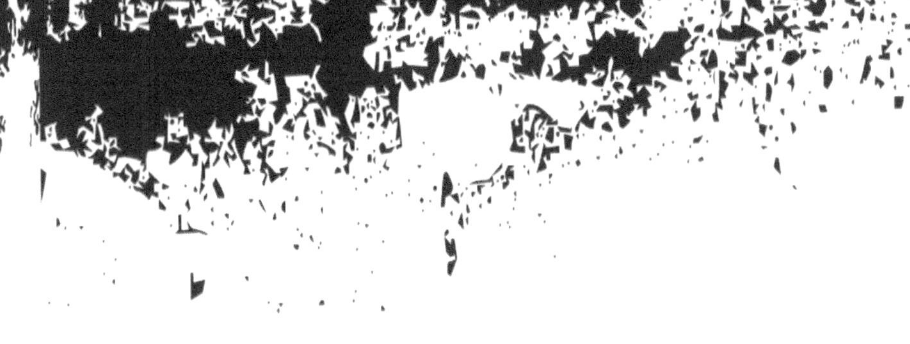

CHAPTER SIXTEEN

To my surprise, Grayson stayed with me while Nurse Shelly examined my ankle, asking questions while she poked and prodded. I nearly kicked the woman more than once, and if she pushed down on my ankle one more time, I would do more than kick her. Was it necessary to use so much pressure? Just looking at the red and puffy area, it was clear to see something was wrong. I'd be sporting one wicked bruise over the next week or so.

"Well, I don't think it is broken." Nurse Shelly told me what I already expected. "Most likely a bad sprain, but you will want to probably get X-rays to make sure there isn't a fracture." Her eyes darted to Grayson every now and then in a mistrusting manner.

My fingers clenched tight against the edge of the hard seat, Grayson scowling over at me. I understood her uneasiness. He was like a dark, foreboding cloud hanging over the room.

"I'm going to wrap it up. I want you to elevate the foot for this period and put ice on it. I can give you something mild for the pain," she offered.

"I would appreciate it." I'd take anything until I got the chance to raid my mother's medicine stash for the good stuff when I got home. Maybe mix it with a shot of vodka.

Grayson's lips twitched as if he could read my mind.

"It is going to bruise over the next few days." She set my foot gently down to inspect my elbow and tsked her tongue. "Did you hit your head?" she asked, scanning for any other unknown cuts or bruises.

Tomorrow, I was positive there would be all kinds of aches popping up. "No. I don't think so."

"At least not today," Grayson added. "She could have been dropped as a baby. It's still a topic of debate."

I scowled up at him and flipped him off when the nurse went to get the pills, ice pack, and wrappings.

He chuckled, if you could call it that.

She came back minutes later with her supplies. Grayson helped me stand up, and I hobbled on one foot over to the recovery chair where Nurse Shelly wrapped up the ankle and gave me a glass of water and two little white pills, which I gladly took and swallowed.

"Can I call someone to pick you up?" she asked when she was finished. "I'm not sure you should be driving."

I shook my head, staring miserably at my foot. "No, I have a ride." I was not calling my mother. Not only did I not want to explain what happened, but she was probably at the hospital with Steven to pick up Carter. They didn't need extra stress, and knowing Carter, any attention taken away from him would come back to haunt me. It wasn't worth it.

"Well, you can stay here for the remainder of the day, icing your foot, but you, Mr. Edwards, need to get to class." She glanced at Grayson sternly through her wire-framed glasses.

Grayson didn't budge from his lounging position against the wall. His long legs stretched out as he tapped away on his phone. "Sorry, Ms. Shelly. No can do."

"Grayson," she said more firmly. "Ms. James does not need a guard dog."

His intense brown eyes lifted. "I'm not leaving. Call Principal Wallis if you must, but I'm not leaving Josie's side. I can make up my classes later."

I shifted uncomfortably on the recovery chair at the sudden tension that dropped into the room. I couldn't believe he'd talked to her like that. I'd been told that rules didn't apply to the Elite, that they did and said whatever they wanted, but there was a difference between being told and seeing it firsthand.

Grayson had on his scary face, and for once, I was glad it wasn't pointed at me.

Nurse Shelly was not happy about being undermined, and for a second, I thought she might actually dial the principal's extension. "Fine," she reluctantly sighed. "Have it your way, but this isn't a free pass. I expect you to use this time as a study hall."

Grayson pulled up one of the spare chairs beside me and made himself comfortable.

"What the hell was that?" I whisper-hissed to Grayson.

His bag with his laptop and mine stayed against the wall. "That was me reminding her who I am."

Grayson played on his phone while I closed my eyes, my body grateful for the rest and the quiet. He seemed to understand what I needed and left me alone, but even that had its drawbacks, because it gave my mind too much time to think—to dwell on what happened. And once the pain relievers kicked in, the throbbing of my ankle no longer distracted me.

Grayson nudged my shoulder, stirring me awake. I must have fallen asleep. "The final bell is going to ring in about ten minutes. Fynn is on his way here to pick you up."

"He is?" I yawned, stretching my arms out, careful not to move my ankle too much.

He shoved his phone into his back pocket. "Yeah, I texted him while you were snoring."

"I don't snore," I argued, wrinkling my nose.

"Uh-huh. Do you want to see the video?" His hand went back to his pocket as if he was going to pull out his phone again.

I was wide awake now. "So help me God, Grayson. You better not have taken a video of me sleeping."

A single dark brown brow lifted. "And if I did?"

"I'll string you up by your balls."

Grayson snorted, as if the idea was absurd. The door opened just then, and Fynn strolled in, offering me a sympathetic grin. "She's your problem now," Grayson told Fynn as he stood up, gathering his things. "You might want to get yourself a new laptop."

My smile was slow. "Thanks, Grayson. For everything. I

mean it." He might not be the warmest and cuddliest of the bunch, but under the scowls and suspicion was a decent guy... I thought.

He had been for the last few hours, and that had to count for something, even if it was just a temporary thing.

Clearing his throat, Grayson shoved a hand into his messy auburn hair. "Don't mention it. Seriously, don't ever mention it again." He gave Fynn some kind of guy fist bump and pat on the back before leaving.

Fynn's sparkling green eyes ran over me, and he let out a low whistle. "Wow, you took quite the spill. That looks like it hurts."

"Ugh. Don't remind me," I groaned, sitting up and swinging my legs over the side of the chair.

"You ready to spring this joint?" he asked, an aura of restlessness vibrating off him.

He wasn't the only one eager to get out of here. "God, yes."

Fynn helped me to my feet, keeping his arm around me. He was a few inches taller than Grayson, making me feel short. "Good, because we need to get out of here before Brock comes tearing through the halls. He will be furious, and I don't want to stick around to watch his wrath be unleashed."

"He doesn't know?"

"Oh, I'm sure he has heard by now, and once that bell rings, he will come straight here, which is why we need to be gone. You ready?"

I nodded, doing my best to disguise the pain. I couldn't have him thinking I was a wuss.

We made it through the halls, into the parking lot, and to his car before the bell rang. He shut his door and grinned at me. "Will your mom flip when she finds out what happened?"

"Only if I tell her," I said with fair warning.

He pressed the start button on the Infiniti, the engine purred to life, and he put the car into reverse. "You don't plan to?"

"I haven't decided," I answered truthfully, resting my head on the back of the cushioned seat. This car took luxury to a new level. The ride was so smooth, it was like driving on a cloud. "Nice car," I complimented as Fynn turned out of the school parking lot with effortless ease.

"You into cars?" he asked.

"Not really, but my dad is. He's a mechanic," I explained.

"No shit. Huh," he said like something suddenly made sense. It was lost on me. "Grayson is the car buff in our group. He has a garage full of some of the most badass cars, races them when he gets the chance."

"He races?" I didn't know why this surprised me, but it did. Grayson seemed far too serious to participate in something as reckless as racing.

"Yeah. And he is damn good at it. You should come to a race sometime." His offer seemed genuine, and it made me wonder how long they planned to keep me around.

I wasn't foolish enough to believe we were becoming friends. Not with these guys. I had to be tested or some shit before I'd even get a foot inside their circle of trust. "Maybe."

His house was empty when we walked in and stupidly huge. His parents were both high-profile professionals, and it showed in the sophisticated décor. His house wasn't far from Grayson's, a few blocks at most. We hung out in his media room, which was by far my favorite space in his house. Also, other than the bathroom and hallway, it was really the only room I'd seen, but I didn't see how it could get better than this.

After he fussed over my foot and made sure I was comfortable, Fynn offered me a drink. How could I refuse? "I'm never leaving this spot," I informed, taking the glass of... I wasn't sure what it was, maybe rum and orange juice with a splash of something else, but it was strong enough to make me feel super relaxed.

He laughed, sinking onto the other couch. "Enjoy the quiet while you can, because when my little sister gets home, it is nonstop chaos."

"You have a younger sister?" I didn't know why the idea astonished me, but for some reason, I'd assumed he was an only child like Brock. Now that I thought about it, I didn't know much about the Elite's family life, other than what their parents did.

A goofy smile came over his face as he nodded and made me believe he had a soft spot for his sister. "Avery. She's six and is going to freak out when she sees you."

I took a long sip of my drink and set it on the side table. "Why is that?"

Soberness descended on his features. "Because I don't bring home girls. Ever."

"Oh. Is that one of Brock's rules?" I asked, twisting the ends of my pink hair.

"No, I just haven't met someone worthy of meeting my family."

He valued his family, and I found that surprising and admirable. "Thanks for breaking your rule for me. Not that I had a choice," I added.

"No, you didn't," Fynn agreed, grinning. "Brock always gets what he wants."

"Are you implying he wants me?" That came out a bit more provocative than I meant it to, and my cheeks burned at the smirk on Fynn's lips.

He reached for the TV remote, clicking the on button. "Or something from you."

I couldn't imagine anything Brock would want from me. My brows furrowed. "What does he want?"

His eyes that had been almost been trusting shifted into green chips of stone. "Can't say. It's not my place."

"Oh, no. I'm not letting you back out now." I was almost out of my seat, but the spear of pain at my ankle stopped me and I slumped back down.

"Sorry, JJ, my lips are sealed." Those lips turned into a lopsided grin that would have been almost adorable if it wasn't for his stubbornness.

"Fynn," I groaned.

He began scrolling through the movie options on the TV, ignoring my protest. "Tell me you like scary movies."

My fucking life was a scary movie. I didn't need to watch one to know everyone but the main character died. "You suck, you know that? And to think I thought you were the nice one."

"That's your first mistake. None of us are nice."

"And why is that? Are you telling me you were born assholes?"

His eyes locked on mine, and I swore regret shone in them. "I'm not sure we have enough time."

If any of the Elite would crack, it seemed as if it would be Fynn. He was the only one who had a semi-conscience.

He hit play on a movie, filling the room with the opening scene spooky music. We drank, he ordered pizza, and as we watched the movie, I strategically asked a million questions, digging up any information I could get on the Elite. Fynn was easy to talk to. The best way to decipher what it was Brock wanted from me was to learn everything I could about him, including his friends.

Fynn told me about his family and how tough his dad was on him to be perfect—the best wide receiver, the obedient son, the ideal student. It all seemed like too much pressure for one person, and impossible to live up to.

Was I feeling sorry for him?

I began to understand more about the Elite. They weren't just football gods on and off the field. Two years ago, they had gotten into some trouble. Fynn's mom had to call in some favors, use her lawyer connections to bail them out of the mess, but it had come close to ruining their lives. "We were lucky the four of us didn't land our asses in jail or juvie," Fynn said, helping himself to another slice of sausage pizza.

That one mistake had changed them, hardened their outlook on life and who they trusted. I could see that now. It was the four of them against the world and that was what made the bond between them so strong.

I wanted to press him for details, but the hard set of his jaw and haunted shadows in his eyes stopped me. Whatever happened still troubled him, even two years later, which only piqued my interest more. There were other ways to learn what had happened, and I knew just where to start.

Mads.

I learned stuff about Fynn's family, but the other guys as well. Some I knew from Mads, like how Micah hated his father and suspected he was cheating on his mom, who Micah was very protective of.

A classic case of money doesn't buy happiness… unless you were my mom.

It seemed they each had their roles. Micah the playboy. Fynn the all-star. Grayson the aloof asshole. And Brock the leader.

Halfway through the movie, his sister, Avery, burst into the house at full speed. Her little feet padded down the hall, followed by fingers wrestling with the doorknob until it sprang open. "Fynn!" a cute and excited voice cried as she bounded into the room and jumped onto the couch beside him. She had the same mocha skin coloring as Fynn and those same sparkling green eyes. Her hair was a shade or two lighter than his.

"Hey, Bitsy. How was school?" he asked, tugging on the end of a braided pigtails.

She gave me a toothless grin, plopping down beside Fynn. "There's a girl here," she whispered to him, too interested in me to answer his question.

Avery was so adorable, and I couldn't help but smile back at her.

"Where? Are you sure there is a girl here?" he teased her, looking around the room.

If there hadn't been a little person in the room, I would have flipped him off. "I'm Josie," I said to Avery, ignoring Fynn's chuckle.

"You're pretty," she stated, kicking her shoes off.

"So are you," I told her. She was as cute as a button, and that old familiar longing for a little sister snuck up on me.

Fynn flicked the end of her nose, and Avery swatted at his hand. A girl after my own heart. "Why don't you go to the kitchen and get started on your homework," he suggested.

"Will you help me?" she asked. I didn't think there was a person alive with a heart who could have resisted her request.

"In a little bit," he assured. And just like that, the little ball of energy hopped out of the room, but not before sneaking me another toothless grin.

I waited until I heard her skipping down the hall before I asked, "Are you sure it's okay that I'm here?" If Avery was home, that meant at least one of his parents was as well. I wasn't sure how he felt about that, and since Fynn was more or less being nice to me, I didn't want to overstep.

The dramatic lighting from the movie flashed over his face. "Honestly, my parents will be thrilled. Don't be surprised if my mom gets you to stay for dinner. You don't have any siblings?"

I adjusted the ice pack on my ankle, which was pretty numb at the moment. "No. I always wanted a little sister."

He frowned slightly. "What about a brother?"

Shrugging, I replied, "I would have been happy with either. It would have been nice to have someone there to talk to. Guess I'll just have to steal yours for the day. If you ever need a babysitter, call me. Seriously."

Fynn gave me a polite smile. "Don't let my mom hear you say that. Your parents never wanted more kids?"

I snorted. "My mother isn't the maternal type."

"Does she hurt you?" he asked, suddenly serious. His eyes had darkened, and with the eerie music playing in the movie, he looked kind of frightening.

I swallowed. "Depends on your definition of hurt." I couldn't believe I was opening up to him. This could come back and bite me in the ass. They could use this information against me, and yet, something about Fynn told me I could trust him. He didn't mess with family.

"Josie," he prompted, his voice low. He wanted a straight answer.

I sighed. "My mom prefers to use her words than her fists. She only hit me once. And honestly, if she tries to slap me again, I'll probably hit her back."

The color of his eyes morphed into a dozen shades of green. "If you ever need to get away, call me. This has nothing to do with Brock or the Elite. Got it?"

My lips curved. We were having a moment, and it was nice, even if it didn't last. "I'll keep that in mind."

My afternoon with Fynn turned out not to be a complete waste and surprisingly fun. Stuffed on pizza, liquor, and painkillers, the mention of my mother made me realize how much I wasn't looking forward to going home. Especially since

Carter would be there. He'd been released from the hospital today.

But my time had run out.

It was just around six o'clock when Brock darkened the doorway. "It's time to go, Firefly," he said, his tumultuous blue eyes pinned to mine.

CHAPTER SEVENTEEN

I took in the impressive sight of him and told myself that my heart wasn't beating faster. So what if he was hotter than most guys? He also had a bad attitude and an unchecked ego. Did I really need that in my life?

He bit his lower lip, his eyes never straying from mine, and the answer was clear.

Hell yes!

Ugh. It was hopeless.

What was the point in pretending I didn't have a thing for this guy? I was just fooling myself. From the moment I saw him at the wedding, I wanted him, and that want hadn't dulled in the slightest. If anything, knowing who he was only made me want him more.

Fucked-up.

"Where is your posse?" I asked, breaking the tension mounting between us.

Brock leaned a shoulder against the doorframe, damp, dark hair falling messily to one side, as if he'd recently showered. "I sent them home after practice."

Fynn turned on the couch, resting his arm over the back of it. "You want backup?"

He shook his head. "Nah. I can handle this."

I didn't understand the exchange between them. Handle what? Me? How absurd. "What's going on?"

Fynn and Brock shared a look, but Brock responded, "Nothing. I'm taking you home."

I wasn't so easily brushed off. "Okay. It doesn't feel like nothing." And what was the point of all of this?

"How's the ankle?" Brock asked, his gaze shifting to my foot as I glared at him.

"Gah. You are so frustrating."

He shoved off the doorframe and stalked toward me. "You just attract trouble, don't you?"

"Only since I met you," I mumbled, carefully swinging my legs over the side of the chair.

"Somehow I don't believe you."

I stood up on my own, but it only took the slightest pressure on my ankle and I was wincing. Brock swore under his breath. Unlike Fynn or Grayson, Brock didn't give me an option, instead just swept me into his arms.

"As independent as you are, I don't have all night. And knowing you, you'll wind up injuring yourself further," he scolded as he moved toward the door.

"Whatever," I grumbled, trying to figure out where I should look. Being in his arms made it so our faces were close. Too close. I glanced over Brock's shoulder at Fynn, who just smirked at me. Nothing was preventing me this time from flipping him off, so I did. My fingers still worked just fine, but I softened it with a smile of thanks.

Brock had us through the house and in his car in less than a minute. I didn't see what the rush was. Perhaps he had somewhere else to be.

My fingers lightly ran over the base of his neck where the ends of hair curled.

I told myself it was accidental.

But it was a lie.

I wanted to touch him. To test myself. To test him.

I had to know if this thing between us was just one-sided. I needed to know if he was as affected by me as I was by him.

"What are you doing?" he asked gruffly, turning his face toward mine. That was his mistake, but I took advantage of the situation, banking on his reaction to be just that.

My face was in direct line with his jaw and brushed over the area, bringing our lips a fraction apart. Our breaths mingled. His eyes darkened.

I continued to play with the damp ends of his hair. "Nothing. I was just curious."

With a growl, he stared hard at me. "You don't want to toy with me, Firefly."

"Aren't you the one who is toying with me?" I countered in a voice just over a whisper.

He set me down on the passenger seat, but he didn't pull away. Instead, his arms caged me in on either side. "Why can't I get you out of my fucking head?"

The rum was definitely impairing my better judgment. My gaze dropped to his lips, and I lifted my hand, running the tip of my nail across his chin. The urge to touch him kept pestering me. It was too strong to ignore. "Let me know when you figure it out, because I'd really like to forget you."

"Liar." Something flashed in his eyes, beyond the sparkle of desire. Anger. Scary anger, and he was looking for someone to punish.

I didn't know why I did it. Perhaps I understood that kind of rage that simmered just under the surface, building and building until you exploded with it. That sort of anger could be a prison of its own, it could be poisonous. He needed an outlet, somewhere to release all that violence swimming inside him before he hurt someone.

That's what I offered him when I crushed my lips to his. I'd gladly absorb the storm brewing inside him. It gave me a reason to lose myself, to escape my demons.

What a fucking pair we were.

He didn't push me away, but he also wasn't giving me what I wanted, that reckless heat. I wanted to lose control, even for just a minute. So I grew bolder, running my tongue along his bottom lip before I took it between my teeth. I smiled as he sucked in a breath, his lips parting as he cursed against my mouth.

Then he consumed me, his tongue invading my mouth, tangling with my mine. Something happened each time our lips touched. We exploded. Nothing mattered—nothing but the taste of him inside my mouth. His fingers moved to my thighs, grabbing them as he turned me in the seat, tugging me toward him. I wrapped my legs around his waist, securing him to me.

It seemed like a lifetime since he kissed me this morning, but my mind hadn't forgotten. It also didn't care about his reasons for kissing me. Later, when I wasn't buzzing from his lips and the rum, I might remember why kissing Brock Taylor was a bad idea.

His fingers dove into my hair, gripping a handful before yanking my head back. It was just rough enough to incite a flare of lust between my legs. "You don't know what you're doing," he said, and then ground his lips against mine again, his words fluttering over me like paper flying in the wind.

He had that right.

I also didn't care.

He pulled away a second time, pressing his forehead against mine. "This isn't supposed to happen," he rasped.

"Me kissing you?" My voice came out breathless. I traced the edge of his face, pleased to see that some of the tension had left his body. His eyes were clearer as well, less destructive, but they were dark with hunger now.

He was beautiful.

Shaking his head, he exhaled and unwrapped my legs from around him, careful of my ankle. "You can't keep doing that."

Chills broke over me at the loss of his body. "I'll try to remember that the next time your lips assault me in the school parking lot."

My eyes drifted shut as the door closed and Brock got in on the other side. The Range Rover's engine purred, and I tried to bank the ache at my core. Why did it have to be him?

Why couldn't it have been Fynn?

That nagging urge to climb into Brock's lap remained the entire drive to my house. Neither of us spoke as he drove, and by the time he pulled into my driveway, I was ready to run from the car... or lock the fucking doors and finish what I started.

He killed the engine and declared, "I'm coming in. I need to see Carter."

A ribbon of hesitation tangled inside me. I remembered the anger I'd sensed from him and the reason. Carter was released from the hospital today. "I'm not sure that's smart."

"Look, I won't do anything stupid," he proclaimed. "If that is what you're worried about. I just want to apologize. I never meant to lose control like that."

I wasn't buying it, but what did I care? "Okay, but it's your funeral. Apparently, my mother has it out for you."

A grin broke out over his lips. "Don't most mothers?"

Before he could try to carry me, because I couldn't deal with being that close to him again, I exited the car and hobbled my way to the front door. He caught up with me quickly. The house was dark and quiet as we entered, leaving me to wonder if anyone was home. I gestured for him to follow me up the stairs.

I knocked on Carter's bedroom door, glancing over my shoulder to make sure no one was coming. If Angie or Steven found Brock in the house... I refused to even think about what that scenario would look like.

From the other side of the door, a voice grumbled something that sounded like "what." I rolled my eyes and cracked the door. "Carter?"

"What the fuck do you want?" my lovely stepbrother groused.

"I brought you a visitor," I replied smugly, no longer feeling guilty about Brock being in the house.

Brock shoved open the door and brushed past me, going straight for the bed. The look on Carter's face was absolutely terrified when Brock approached him, and I instantly regretted agreeing to this.

He is going to kill him.

Carter must have had the same thought, because he shifted uncomfortably on his bed like he was searching for something. His phone maybe? But Brock got there first, and Carter froze. Brock hovered over his bed like Death waiting to take Carter's soul. "I'm only going to tell you this once. Stay away from Josie," he warned, his voice so dark and dangerous it sent a shiver down my spine.

I blinked, unable to believe what I was hearing. Brock threatening my stepbrother on my behalf. Why?

Brock leaned forward and whispered something to Carter as my fingers tightened on the doorknob. What was he saying? I strained to hear, but I couldn't make out a single word. Then Brock straightened, Carter watching his every movement like a hawk.

For the first time, my stepbrother went tongue-tied and pale. He looked as if he had gotten a glimpse of death.

Brock sauntered from the room, never looking back, his face a cold mask as he took my hand, pulling me away. With long strides, he ate up the hallway, shoulders rigid. I felt the tension from him in the air around us.

"Wait," I panted, tugging back on his arm just as we reached the top of the stairs. The obvious pain in my voice halted him in his tracks.

"Shit, I forgot," he cursed, running a hand over his face.

I frowned, leaning all my weight on my good foot. "What was that all about?"

Something darted over his eyes but was gone the next second. "Just some unfinished business," he clipped out.

"Okay, so you're not going to tell me." The harsh reality that he was still keeping secrets splashed over me like a cold shower.

He didn't respond.

"You lied to me. God, you're such an asshole." The words ripped from me, and I hated the hurt I heard in them. I didn't want Brock to have the power to cause me pain. I had enough people in my life who disappointed and hurt me, and I sure as hell didn't need another.

He held out his hand and demanded, "Give me your phone."

I stared at him, locking our eyes. "What do you want from me?"

"Right now, just your phone," he stated flatly. He was all business, unyielding and arrogant.

Annoyed, I dug it out of my pocket and slipped it into his open palm.

His fingers brushed over my hand as they closed over the phone and tingles flared between us, a spark neither of us wanted.

My heart pounded as he tapped on the screen, a scowl

marring his lips. "If he so much as looks at you the wrong way, I want you to text me. Got it? I'm not screwing around."

"Yeah, fine," I agreed, but I wasn't sure it was a promise I'd keep. Brock was itching for another chance to sink his fists into Carter, but I wouldn't be the cause of Brock ending up behind bars. Carter might have kept his mouth shut this time, but if Brock touched him again, Carter would find a way to get revenge.

My stepbrother was a snake. He was just waiting for the opportunity to strike. Carter wouldn't forget what Brock had done or what he had prevented him from having.

For now, I had to handle my stepbrother myself, and luckily, for a few weeks he wouldn't be much of a threat.

Brock returned my phone. He trotted down the stairs, pausing at the bottom to glance back up at me. "I'll pick you up in the morning. Don't make me wait."

I was about to roll my eyes when I heard my mother hiss from the bottom landing. "What is he doing here?" She stepped into view wearing a black silk robe and high heels. Who the fuck actually walks around the house like that?

Brock must have had the same thought as he glanced my mother over and made a sound in the back of his throat.

Shit. Shit. Shit. I felt like I just got caught in the middle of the night sneaking a boy out of my room. Except he hadn't been in my room and this wasn't just any boy. My cheeks flushed. "He drove me home. It's not a big deal," I said nonchalantly. *Please don't make this a big deal. Please don't fucking embarrass me. Not now.*

She noticed for the first time my limp as I hobbled down a

step or two, clutching the banister like it was my lifeline. "What happened to you?" Most mothers would sound concerned when asking such a question. Not my mother. It came out more like an accusation.

My eyes bounced from Angie to Brock, pleading with him not to say anything. "I had an accident at school. It's nothing, just a sprained ankle."

"Which you might want to get looked at," Brock added, leveling Angie with a disapproving glower. He towered a good foot over her. "There could be a hairline fracture."

Angie's black smudged eyes narrowed. "I think I can take care of my daughter," she spat.

I gasped. She was such a deliberate bitch to Brock. Mom had definitely hit the bottle tonight—not that she needed liquor to be a raging bitch.

Brock wasn't intimidated. "Let's cut the bullshit. We both know you're not winning any mother of the year awards. Don't we?" His tone was savage.

My mouth dropped open. But once I got over the shock of hearing him speak to my mother with such disdain, the words registered. My fucking head was spinning, and I just wanted to get into bed.

She sucked in a breath. "How dare you. Get out before I call the cops." Her finger pointed down the hall as hostile darts shot from her eyes.

"Gladly," he said icily. He turned and left without a good-bye, the front door slamming behind him seconds later.

I stared down disbelievingly at my toxic mother.

She whirled on me, eyes wild, chin lifted in the air. My

mother could be stunning when she wanted to be, and men found her attractive. She knew how to use an alluring smile and a flirty bat of her lashes to get what she wanted. But she could also be downright pathetic and a loose cannon just waiting to detonate. "Your boyfriend is not to step foot inside this house again," she said in a sharp voice that cut through me like glass.

My heart sank, and I was suddenly too damn tired for this. I didn't have the energy in me to fight with her. Not tonight. "Brock is not my boyfriend."

"I don't care what you call him. He is to stay away from this house, from this family. Is that clear? The next time he shows up, I will call the police," she threatened as a light down the main floor hallway flipped on.

"Is everything okay?" I heard Steven's concerned voice.

"Fuck this," I mumbled, turning to limp off to my bedroom.

"You will not speak to me with such disrespect. Don't you walk away. Josephine!" she cried after me.

Darkness cloaked my room, and the only sound was the ringing from my phone. My ankle elevated on a pillow, I snuggled under the bedcovers. The clock on my phone had read just past ten o'clock when I hit Maddy's number. Locked in my room, I spent the last three hours trying to calm down. When reading or watching YouTube didn't work, I turned to a friend.

"Hello?" Her voice filtered from the other end of the phone.

"What are you doing right now? Can you talk?" I asked, biting on my lip as I waited for her to respond.

A series of wrestling noises came through, as if she was searching for something. "Sure. Is this about what happened at school? Rumor is someone pushed you. Are you okay? Grayson was pissed. More than usual," she rambled. This was the first we'd talked since my fall.

I frowned. "You talked to Grayson?"

"Yeah, I called him after practice."

As much as I wanted to ask her what she and Grayson talked about, I had another matter on my mind. "That's actually not why I called. What do you know about what happened two years ago?"

Silence greeted me from the other end of the phone.

"Mads?" I prompted, glancing at my screen to see if we'd been disconnected.

"I'm coming over," she proclaimed.

"Now?"

"Do you want to know or not? It isn't something I feel comfortable talking about over the phone," she explained.

I stared at the ceiling. Yes, I was bone-tired, but something told me this was important. "Come around to the back of the house to the stairs that lead to my balcony," I told her.

"I'll be there in ten," she replied, ending the call promptly.

Rolling out of bed, I flipped on my balcony light and unlocked the door. I was already in my pajamas and didn't have it in me to change. My hair was still damp from the bath I'd managed, so I just slipped on some fuzzy socks and wrapped my ankle in an ice pack one of the kitchen staff brought up to me. As much as I protested living in this house, the staff was a fucking godsend. Particularly since I couldn't rely on my mother to take care of me. They would all be getting Christmas gifts from me this year.

I sat impatiently on the bed, when what I really wanted to do was pace as I waited for Mads. So instead, I tapped my thumb over my phone.

Almost ten minutes later, a small knock rapped on my glass

sliding doors and they slid open, a head poking in. "Hello?" a soft voice whispered into the dimly lit room.

"Over here," I whispered from the bed, waving her in.

Mads stepped over the threshold, closing the door quietly behind her. Kicking off her shoes, she padded over to the bed and climbed into the other side. Her gaze went to my wrapped ankle perched on top of a pillow. "I can't believe that bitch had the balls to push you."

The venom in her voice caused me to blink. "You know who did it?"

In a pair of yoga pants and a T-shirt, Mads leaned back against a pile of pillows, her gray eyes gleaming. "Of course, she can't keep her big mouth shut about it. Ava is going around telling everyone that you fell into her hand. I swear she has an empty hourglass for brains. Why the fuck would you brag about something like that? It's like she is begging to be caught."

Perhaps, or she is hoping that I would tattle on her so she'd have another reason to despise me. Banging Brock wasn't enough for her little hateful heart. "I'll deal with Ava eventually, but Fynn mentioned something that happened two years ago. I want to know what it was."

The expression on her face shifted. She'd been annoyed on my behalf a second ago, but now she was guarded, watching me with careful eyes. Then she sighed, her shoulders dropping. "I'm not surprised it was Fynn. He has a soft spot for you. Micah too, but I suspect Micah is just hoping you'll sleep with him."

I snorted. "Do I need to put out a bulletin that says I don't sleep around? If either of them had a soft spot for me, they have a funny way of showing it."

"Maybe," she agreed, her lips in a thin, thoughtful line. "But it might be the same reason they all feel protective when it comes to you."

She had my interest now. "And what reason is that?"

"Because you remind them of Kenna," she stated in a voice that almost sounded pained, but then she forced a smile, tucking her legs underneath her on the bed. "It's more than your resemblance. There's something else. Something in your smile and your personality too."

"Who is Kenna?" I was afraid I already knew, but I didn't want it to be true. It was obvious from the way Mads spoke that they all cared about this girl, so did that mean she was a standby girl? No. She was definitely something more. A girlfriend? A lump of emotion clumped in my throat. Brock's girlfriend?

Mads gaze met mine. "She's Grayson's sister. Twin sister, actually."

I swallowed, relief allaying my fears. Not a girlfriend. "His twin sister?" I echoed. "No one mentioned he had a sister." Let alone that she was his twin.

"And they wouldn't. They don't talk about her. Ever." She averted her eyes, but not before I caught a glimpse of sadness, and unless my ears were deceiving me, her voice had cracked as well. "Kind of like Sawyer. It is too painful."

"Okay," I said, taking a moment to make heads or tails out of what she was telling me. If I'd never heard of Kenna after attending the Academy for nearly a month, something was up. "Where is she?" I asked, doing my best to be sensitive because this seemed like a difficult subject for her. My first thought was she had an accident like Sawyer.

"It's a long story, and before you jump down my throat, I need your word this stays between us," her eyes implored mine. "I don't like to meddle in Elite business, and if Brock found out I told you, he would fucking have my head. He went to a lot of trouble to keep Kenna safe, and talking about her here, well, let's just say it's a really stupid and risky move."

"I don't understand."

"You don't. Not yet, but you will. Is Carter here?" Her gaze went to my closed door before returning to my face.

I nodded. "But he is asleep. The pain meds knock him out," I assured. "And he is basically bound to the bed for as long as the staff will dote on him."

She scooted in closer to me, folding her legs pretzel style on the bed. "Promise me that no matter what, we'll still be friends."

A chill went down my back. I didn't like this. "Mads, you're starting to freak me out."

"I'm serious. Promise me."

"I promise." And I meant it. How the hell would I survive the Academy without her as my friend? I'd be stuck eating lunch outside behind a bush.

"God, I could really use a cigarette." She pulled out a piece of gum from the side pocket on her yoga pants and popped it in her mouth. "Grayson and Kenna were close, really close. After Sawyer died, their whole family fell apart. It was bad. Sawyer loved to make people laugh. He was naturally a fun guy, someone you always wanted around. He was popular. After the accident, Kenna took it hard. She pretended otherwise, and only

Grayson and I really knew how messed up she was inside. She began partying too much, hanging out with the wrong crowd, basically shutting out everyone who cared for her. That was two years ago." Mads took a breath as if preparing herself.

I stayed silent and patient, giving her all the time she needed. Had Kenna died? Had Grayson lost both his brother and sister? Dread sank inside me. No wonder he was so angry all the time.

"I know what you're thinking. Kenna isn't dead, at least not literally. She suffers from depression and has for a long time. It was something she battled every day, but she never gave up. And because I can see the question in your eyes, she was... close to Brock. They weren't exclusive, not yet, but they might have been if Carter hadn't gotten in the way."

Carter? What did he have to do with Kenna?

My mind whirled. Just how did Grayson feel about one of his best friends messing around with his sister? Grayson didn't strike me as a guy who would make it easy for anyone to date his sister, even more so if it was a friend.

The glittering emotion in Mads's eyes tugged at my heart. It also diminished the arrow of jealousy spearing through me at the thought of Brock with another girl, especially one who looked like me. I didn't know how I felt about that. Was that the reason he was so hot and cold with me? Was I some sort of warped replacement for Kenna?

I was going to be sick.

"After the homecoming game, Grayson threw one of his legendary parties," she continued, lost in her memories. "The entire football team was there, including Carter. Like Brock,

Carter was popular, on the football team, and had a reputation with the girls. I don't know why, but Kenna caught his eye. He started to flirt with her. She liked the attention, something she desperately wanted. And Carter didn't have the entire female population at school trying to get into his pants. Not like Brock did. There were always girls hanging around Brock. Kenna wasn't good with the competition."

I didn't like where this story was going and wasn't sure I could stomach the rest.

"Everyone was drinking, dancing, and having a good time. At least I thought we were having a good time. I got so wasted that night and passed out in Grayson's room." Her voice hitched, and I could see that there was such guilt in her eyes. I reached over and put my hand over hers, squeezing it. She took another long breath and went on. "But Kenna, her night wasn't as fun as the rest of ours. Carter had slipped her something in her drink. No one saw him do it, but football players talk, and someone like Carter likes to brag about his conquests."

"Oh God," I gasped, my hand flying to my mouth. He didn't. But even as the thought fluttered through my mind, I knew damn well that Carter was capable of doing something so seedy and invasive. It turned my blood cold.

Mads was in a trance, swept back to the horror of two years ago. "He took advantage of her, left her passed out and alone. She swears he didn't rape her, but afterward, Kenna was so ashamed. It sent her spiraling into a dark place. Things only got worse. The bastard took pictures of her and sent them around the school, saying how she was a sloppy lay or if you wanted a good time to call Kenna, stupid juvenile shit like that."

I never expected to have sympathy for a girl who was possibly in love with Brock, but how could I not? Carter had violated her. Someone I knew to be capable of doing such heinous things. He was lower than scum. I couldn't think of a word to describe just how deplorable he was.

And he was my stepbrother.

I felt dirty, and I had done nothing wrong, but it didn't change the fact that I wanted to shower and scrub myself clean of him.

Mads clung to my hand as if she needed me to anchor her to the present. "As you can imagine, once the guys found out, they went apeshit. That was the incident that almost landed them in jail. Grayson wanted to kill Carter for what he'd done to Kenna and might have if the other guys hadn't stopped him. They were able to talk sense into him with a promise that they would get Carter back without getting caught."

"What happened to Kenna?" I softly asked.

"She never pressed charges against Carter. She was too embarrassed to go to the police, too fragile, which is exactly the kind of girl Carter preys on. He knew she wouldn't want the negative attention. Kenna was popular. And that acceptance, however misplaced, was all she had. No one wanted to push her over the edge. So she left, transferred schools and went to live with a relative. No one at school knows where."

I understood what she was silently telling me with her gaze. "You don't have to tell me. In fact, don't tell me. I don't want any chance of Carter ever finding out where she is."

Relief breezed through her body. "I'm sure he believes that he got away with what he did, which only makes him more dangerous. You have to be careful around him, Josie. I know you already know that, especially with what happened to you after the game. I never should have made you go." Her voice was heavy with regret.

I squeezed her hand, bringing her bright gaze back to mine. "You didn't. I won't have you blaming yourself for Carter's fucked-up actions."

"I was so scared when I saw him grab you. It was like Kenna all over again. I couldn't do anything to save you and I imagined her feeling that way. She was on suicide watch for months after a failed attempt." She choked on the last part, tears welling up in her eyes.

"Oh, Mads," I cried, wrapping my arms around her. Her shoulders shook as the tears fell. I held her, letting her cry until she was spent. My own eyes filled with water. I cried with my friend and for the girl I'd never met but felt a kinship with. "Jesus. No wonder they hate him so much," I said as we both wiped at our eyes. "Are you okay?"

She nodded. "I didn't realize how much I needed to tell you her story."

"I'm glad you did," I said softly and soothingly. "I needed to hear it, needed to know just how dangerous Carter really is."

"Just be careful. I don't have to say it, but the guys have been waiting for the right opportunity to get revenge. They are going to make Carter pay without getting any of the blowback."

"How do they plan to do that?"

She shook her head, gray eyes wide and shining. "I don't know. Believe it or not, they don't tell me shit. I was cut out of the loop the second Kenna left. I thought they were trying to protect me, but I'm not so sure. The four of them are smart, cunning, and too fucking patient. They've gotten Carter to let his guard down and think everything is back to normal. Until you."

"How could I possibly have anything to do with their plan?" I was trying to make sense of all this information and how I fit in. Then to top it off, I had Ava and her crazy ass trying to kill me. It was all too much.

"I think seeing you shook everything up, including Carter. You not only scare him but probably also thrill him. You're a living reminder of that night. And I wouldn't doubt the sick fuck would love another chance to recreate that night. What happened after the homecoming game was proof enough for me. The guys must have come to the same conclusion."

My fingers dug into my palms. "Is that why they suddenly became all alpha around me?"

Her lips cracked into a weak smile. "Most likely. Before you came, I thought they had given up on destroying Carter, but when I saw you and how much you look like her, I knew they were up to something. You do really have an uncanny resemblance to Kenna. It took *me* by surprise. I had to do a double take. For a split second, I thought Kenna had come back, but then I noticed little differences. The way you dressed and held yourself. Your eyes are different colors, and Kenna has a beauty mark just below her right eye."

"Ohmygod. She's your cousin," I proclaimed, suddenly just making the connection.

Mads nodded. "And my best friend." She chewed on her lip, watching my reaction. "Don't be mad at me. I swear, the plan, it was to protect you. I know how evil Carter can be. The idea of you in this house with him…" She shuddered. "It fucking gives me nightmares. This was the best idea I could come up with."

Holy. Shit.

The plan. It made more sense now why she would suggest I become part of the Elite. "And what about the guys? Do they know about your plan?"

She shook her head. "God, no. They'd kill me for interfering, but when I talked to you that first day, everything came flooding back. I know you don't want to hear it, but I looked at you and I saw Kenna. I couldn't bear the thought of you becoming Carter's next victim."

"This shit is seriously messed up. What am I supposed to do?"

"Let the Elite protect you," she stated like it was the most obvious answer, and maybe it was.

"But that means I let them use me to get to Carter." Did that also mean that Brock was in a way using me as a substitute for the girl cared about, loved even? The girl he had failed to protect? When he was kissing me, was he actually kissing her?

Fuck.

Was that why he always seemed so torn up about kissing me? Was it his guilt?

"Yeah, but I'm telling you, Josie, it's worth it. You don't want to be involved with someone like Carter. The Elite, believe it or not, is the lesser of two evils."

A wild statement, but she was probably right. I hoped.

CHAPTER NINETEEN

I skipped school the next day. And the next.

It had nothing to do with letting my ankle heal and everything to do with avoiding Brock. He was pissed when I sent him the text on Tuesday telling him not to pick me up, that I wasn't going to school. I half expected him to show up outside my bedroom door, banging on the glass, demanding I get my ass up.

He didn't.

And I wasn't sure if I was disappointed or relieved.

Both, perhaps.

By Thursday, I'd run out of excuses and knew I couldn't continue to evade him. Or anyone else, for that matter, but I'd needed those last few days to myself.

Brock picked me up for school Thursday and Friday, and I did my best to act cool, naturally. I failed miserably, because he kept staring at me oddly and asking what was wrong, to which I replied with a too-high-pitched "nothing." I'd never seen someone scowl so much in forty-eight hours. It had to be a world record. The other guys didn't seem to suspect anything about my quiet nature, but that could be because none of them watched me as intently as Brock did.

Mads noticed. She was the only one who knew what was going on inside my head, and I planned to keep it that way, just like I promised.

If Brock wanted me to know about Kenna, then he was going to have to tell me himself, which seemed unlikely.

The two days of rest had helped the pain and swelling in my ankle, but it still bothered me, and I kept it wrapped. The guys returned to taking turns helping me to class, including Brock. With Carter still recovering at home, I wasn't sure who they were protecting me from.

Ava?

The queen bitch and I were going to have words when I figured out how to ditch my shadows. I didn't want them stepping in, or worse, preventing me from putting this bitch in her place. I wasn't someone she could bully, especially over a fucking guy.

I currently sat in the cafeteria surrounded by the Elite—more like dwarfed by them. They had this presence that made me feel cocooned in muscles. Mads was retaking a math test, so it was just the guys and me. I'd checked out of the conversation the moment they started talking football. There was a home game tonight, and I absolutely was not attending. My plans tonight included a gallon of mint ice cream, a bag of cheese popcorn, and a Harry Potter marathon. Nowhere in my agenda did it say anything about football or four overbearing, hot jerks.

It was my name from Fynn's lips that had my attention refocusing from Ben and Jerry's to what the four of them were scheming up now.

"Just have her stay with you," Micah said to Brock. "Your parents are out of town, right?" The playboy's lips curved in a lopsided grin as he winked at me. He was wearing a light blue shirt, which intensified the color of his eyes.

What the—?

He couldn't possibly be talking about me. I glanced at Brock beside me.

Scowl three hundred and fifty-two graced Brock's lips. "Yeah. They won't be back until Monday night."

God, even when those fucking lips were turned down, I still found myself wanting to kiss them. My body didn't care that I looked like Kenna, but my brain couldn't forget. A war brewed inside me, and I didn't know which side would win.

"That will totally get under his skin," Fynn agreed. The sleeves of white shirt were rolled, hugging his defined arms.

Seniors or not, the four of them didn't exactly look like typical high school boys.

Brock's leg pressed against mine under the table as he leaned forward, and my mouth watered. "What are you talking about?" I interrupted, ignoring the heat that transferred from his body to mine. I swore he had moved closer to me on purpose, and it drove me to distraction.

Micah's glittering eyes found mine as he shook his head in

amusement. "Haven't you been listening? Stop staring at Brock's lips."

"I was not staring at his lips," I protested in a whispered hiss.

"If you say so." Micah grinned and leaned back in his chair, folding his arms over his chest. "I bet if I was inside your head right now, you'd be thinking about where he could put his lips."

Gah. Micah was such a damn troublemaker.

I gave him a menacing grin, wishing I had something to throw at his head, like a fork or a bottle of water. "So you're jealous of the way my mind works, huh?"

Micah laughed. "It's too damn bad I didn't see you first. We'd be so good together."

I rolled my eyes.

"You're staying with me for the weekend," Brock announced harshly.

I sat up straighter in the chair, my attention snapping to full force. "Why the hell would I do that?"

"Do you remember what happened at the last game?" he said bluntly.

How the hell could I forget? "I'm not going to the game. And Carter won't be there either," I reminded him.

"No, but his friends will be," Grayson replied, his expression colder than normal.

Fynn tapped his thumb on the table. "Let's just say they aren't happy we interfered with their fun."

My chest tightened. "Fuck that. I'm no one's *fun*."

"No one but Brock's," Micah mumbled under his breath.

Four pairs of eyes glowered at him, and I kicked his shin

under the table with my good foot, which only caused him to grin. Unbelievable.

Then Fynn thumped him on the back of the head, becoming my new favorite Elite, and it was my turn to grin.

"Hey," Micah grumbled.

"Nice one, man," Grayson said, displaying a rare smile for Fynn.

But Brock was all business. "They know that your parents are gone again this weekend. Do you really want to be home alone with Carter?" he asked, already knowing damn well what my answer was.

Shit. Goddammit.

Steven had to return to the city to finish his business from last weekend. He'd been pulled away when the hospital called about Carter. My mom was going with him after she had lectured me about not getting any more emergency phone calls.

"No," I admitted softly, hating that I wasn't safe in my own home.

Brock's gaze seared mine. "Just tell your mom you are staying with Mads."

"Can't I just stay with Mads?" Anywhere but Brock's house. How would I survive the weekend? We'd either kill each other or... I couldn't even entertain the other possibility. Common sense told me it was a mistake to spend an hour alone with Brock, let alone the whole fucking weekend. No way. I would only get myself into trouble, like fall deeper for the asshole. Was I doomed to fall for a guy who was hung up on another? How could I compete with a girl who wasn't even here?

"Not happening," Grayson said. "She's my cousin. I don't want her put in danger."

Shit. I also didn't want Mads to be hurt, remembering how Carter's friends had held her back. I glanced around the table, looking at the four menacing guys staring at me. "You're not giving me much of a choice, are you?"

Brock's laugh was weak and raspy. "No. This is just us trying to be polite. If we have to, one of us will lock you in our house. We have rooms for that." The guys exchanged looks.

My eyes narrowed. Most people might think they were kidding. I didn't. "You wouldn't."

"He would," Fynn said. "Just don't let her hurt herself more," he said to Brock.

Brock nodded at Fynn. "Good point."

Fuck it. Maybe I deserved a weekend free from Angie and Carter. Maybe I deserved a weekend in bed with the hottest guy in school, regardless of his reasons for wanting me. It was for one weekend. I'd suffer the consequences later, just file it somewhere deep in my head with all the other shit I couldn't deal with.

"Fine." I gave in, sighing. "But I need to grab some things from my house, and I have to be back Sunday night." Angie was having a family dinner.

* * *

Brock drove me home after school and waited as I dashed inside to gather an overnight bag. He drove me to Mads's where he instructed me to stay until he came to get me after the game. I rolled my eyes and shut the door in his face.

"So, you're spending the weekend with Brock Taylor. Interesting," Mads said when we were alone, a wicked grin teasing her lips.

I picked at the bowl of peanuts on the table, popping one into my mouth. "Don't start. I didn't have a choice."

"Hmm," she hummed, gray eyes sparkling as she pulled out a cigarette. "I did warn you. When the four of them gang up on you, it's best to nod and agree."

We sat in her screened-in porch, listening to the sounds of the football game in the distance. Mads lived the closest to the Academy, but it was far away enough that all we heard was the occasional cheer of the crowd or the muffled announcer. Her parents were in the kitchen, and her mom's laugh floated out through the screen doors. Mads had a good life—a life I dreamed about. It wasn't the big house or the expensive furnishings I desired. It was her parents, the way they looked at each other and the way they looked at her.

That's what I wanted—a family that loved one another unconditionally.

Mads had an older brother who was in college, Jason. Photos of the two of them were plastered all over the walls, and I couldn't stop the pang in my chest. We didn't have a single family photo hanging in my house. "I still don't understand why they care," I said.

She took a long drag on her smoke, gazing out at the setting sun. "They have their reasons."

And that was what frightened me.

Almost as much as Carter did.

It was dark when Brock showed up after the game to collect me. "You ready?" he asked from the doorway, sweaty and still in his football uniform, his hair messy.

I swallowed.

Jocks were not my type. Then why did my heart do a series of backflips each time I laid eyes on Brock fucking Taylor? My last boyfriend had been a skateboarder who didn't actually know how to skateboard.

"Don't do anything I wouldn't do. Oh, wait, you already have," Mads called after us as we left.

I flipped her off but smiled as her laugh echoed behind me. "Did you win?" I asked Brock as we walked to his Range Rover. I didn't really give a shit about football, but I was trying to make small talk so I would stop thinking about how his ass looked in those fucking tight pants.

He flashed me a grin, and I wished I hadn't asked. "What kind of question is that? Of course we won."

It was only a five-minute drive from Maddy's to Brock's, but the ride seemed so much longer when I was caged inside a box with him, his sweaty yet delicious scent filling up the car and wreaking havoc on my willpower.

He keyed in the code, engaging the alarm once we were inside his house. "I need to shower. Make yourself at home," he said, dropping his key fob on the entryway table. He disappeared up the stairs, leaving me to wander his house.

I'd been here before, the night Ava took those photos of me. It was eerie how much Kenna and I had in common. But I didn't want to think about her. Not tonight. I banished her from my thoughts and moved past the family room, exploring the lower level. It was almost sad that I'd grown used to these impressive houses that belonged on the covers of magazines.

I roamed through the kitchen, then into the rec room equipped with a badass TV, pool table, wine cabinet, and bar. On the other side of the house was an enclosed pool and sauna. I walked through the glass doors, inhaling the chlorine and balmy air. Crouching down, I dipped my hand into the water, testing the temperature. It was perfect, and I was half tempted to go for a swim. I didn't have my bathing suit, but something told me Brock wouldn't care if I went in buck-ass naked. He'd probably join me.

And it was that thought that had me promptly leaving the pool area. An exercise room was connected off to the right. I kept walking until I stumbled onto the library. As I flipped on a small table lamp, casting the room in a soft yellow glow, my heart rejoiced.

Holy shit. Look at all these books.

I wondered if Brock spent any time here. Running my hand along the spines, I plucked one from the shelf and sank into an oversized circular chair. My eyes scanned over the rest of the room as I spun the chair in a circle. Only one wall wasn't covered from floor-to-ceiling with books, and that was because a rich mahogany-and-brick fireplace filled the space. Half-burned logs sat on top of the grate, and I picked up faint traces of smoke lingering in the air.

I tipped my head back and laughed. My burst of happiness turned into awe. Through the glass-domed ceiling, millions of stars twinkled above me like fireflies. Nothing like reading under the dazzling star-strewn sky.

This room was my dream.

I was still gazing at the night, searching for constellations, when an amused voice said, "Why am I not surprised to find you in here?"

My eyes closed for a moment, savoring the sound of his voice. I'd lost track of time. Reluctantly, I pulled my gaze from the stars and looked toward the doorway where Brock was leaning against a bookshelf in nothing but a pair of gray sweatpants. He was barefoot and shirtless, his dark hair damp. His scent reached me, and my heart skipped. I knew I was staring, but it couldn't be helped.

My. God. He was gorgeous. Every fucking lickable inch of him. My eyes traced over the ink tattooed on his shoulder.

"I think you forgot something," I said.

A single brow arched.

"Your shirt?" I told him, my voice sounding huskier than I intended. Completely his fault.

He glanced down and then back at me. "Does my chest make you uncomfortable?"

"Yes! No. Maybe. Does it matter?" My cheeks flamed.

One corner of his mouth twitched, tugging upward, and I really wished he wouldn't do that. I wished he didn't look at me that way, because it was almost too much to resist. The angel and devil on my shoulders were having a helluva time fighting it out.

"This isn't going to work," I declared, dropping the book in my hands onto the little side table.

He moved into the room, going to a built-in cabinet that framed the fireplace, and took out a decanter and two glasses. "Why is that?" he asked, pouring the amber liquid into each lowball. He turned to me, lifting one of the glasses to his lips.

My brow shot up, eyes flickering to his chest, then back to his mischievous eyes. This playful side of Brock was dangerous. *Be careful, Josie. Or you might fall for him.* No. Definitely no. Falling in love with a guy who was in love with someone else was not on my senior year bucket list. "You know why."

He offered me the other drink, which I gladly took, but he didn't let it go immediately. Our fingers touched. "Because you can't be alone with me without jumping my bones?"

I snorted. "You're an asshole."

Releasing the glass, he grinned down at me. A smile like Brock's should have been outlawed. The things it did me... I was sure I had stopped breathing, and I wasn't imagining the ache between my legs. "And I own it," he said, clinking the top of his glass against mine.

"But you don't own me," I replied, taking a sip of the liquor, hints of smokiness hitting my tongue. Bourbon. I hated that it brought a grin to my lips as I thought back to the night he almost ran me over with his SUV. Surely that had been his intention.

He angled his head to the side, male confidence pouring off him. "Not yet, Firefly."

"Ever," I stated firmly, glowering. "Let's get one thing straight. I'm not, nor will I ever be a standby girl."

"I always get what I want." He sank his other hand into a pocket with a grin that made my insides light up.

Fuck. What was it about him? He was so arrogant, a self-proclaimed asshole who acted as if the world was his playground. "And you've decided that you want me? Is that it?"

His smirk was smug. "Perhaps."

Because I look like her? The thought should have been enough to sober this irrational desire building inside me. It wasn't. In fact, I could feel my resolve crumbling. I wanted him. "If we have sex, it will be on my terms."

"When," he corrected with a devilish look.

Need throbbed between my legs. It was unbearable because I knew exactly what I was denying myself. I blinked. "What?"

"*When* we have sex, Firefly. Not *if*, because you and I, it's inevitable."

Cocky son of a bitch. He was so fucking sure of himself. "Is this whole thing some elaborate ploy to have sex with me?"

The playfulness vanished from his eyes as if I'd just slapped him across the face. His irises were dark and grim. The swift change in them took me by surprise. "I don't need to trick a girl into sleeping with me," he stated.

I realized what I had implied and how sore of a nerve that must have hit for him. No, Brock was not Carter. Not even fucking close. They weren't even on the same playing field, and I wanted to tell him that, but I couldn't, not without risking the secret I'd sworn to keep. I wouldn't betray my promise to Mads, even to soothe the churning storm in Brock's eyes.

But I knew another way to calm the turmoil within him.

Taking a long swig from my drink, I set it aside next to the forgotten book. I couldn't even remember its title. I stood up. "No, you don't," I agreed, my gaze fastened to his.

His aqua eyes were cloudy as I walked to him. I didn't know

how I knew, but I just felt it. He needed me as much as I needed him. We were both suffering, and for one goddamn night, we both could lose ourselves. It was one night. I wouldn't lose my soul or my heart in one single night.

This meant nothing.

One night.

That's what I told myself.

But as I stopped just inches from him, my fingers reaching out to take the glass from his hand, I knew once wouldn't be enough. Not for either of us. We wouldn't be leaving his room the entire weekend... if we made it there at all.

"So, what do you want to do?"

The sound of his husky voice nearly was my undoing. Instant lust. I might not have a thing for jocks, but I did have a thing for troubled guys. The more fucked-up they were, the more I wanted them.

And I wanted the ever-loving shit out of Brock Taylor. Right now.

I dipped two of my fingers into the glass, swirling the liquid before lifting them to run along his lips. His mouth parted as he licked my fingers, tasting the bourbon there, and then he took them between his teeth.

Desire flared throughout me.

I lost all rationality. I was caught up in him, and there was no turning back.

Setting the glass on the fireplace mantel, I removed my fingers from his mouth, letting my hand fall to his bare chest. My eyes never left his as I ran my nails down the length of muscle to the flatness of his stomach. He sucked in a sharp breath when I skimmed over the low waistband. I tilted my head to the side, enraptured by the whirlwind of need gleaming in his eyes.

Screw it.

Or screw him was more appropriate.

One night. Then, after the weekend, my resolve would be rock hard.

Kind of like his abs.

Dear God, what was he made of?

My heart pounded as he caught my wrist.

I smirked.

CHAPTER TWENTY

Brock pressed into me, capturing my body between him and a wall of books as he nuzzled against my cheek, his breath hot near my ear. "Is this what you want, Firefly?"

The nickname coming from his lips sounded like a curse and a prayer. I arched my neck closer to his mouth. "Yes," I breathed, lacing my fingers into his hair, desperate to feel his mouth on me.

"I won't hold back," he warned, his fingers moving to my chin and tipping my head back. The intensity in his eyes stole my breath. "Not this time."

The implication that he had held back the first time caused my blood to race. What would it feel like to be completely at his mercy? It was both a thrilling and terrifying thought, and I wanted to find out just as much as I wanted him to surrender to me.

The pad of his thumb traced over my lips. "I'm giving you the chance to stop this now. To walk away, because once I kiss you, I won't be able to stop."

Slipping my fingers down his bare back to his ass, I tightened my hold, pressing him deeper against me. I felt the hardness of him through his sweats and grinned into his neck. "I don't want you to stop," I whispered, pressing a kiss to the column of his throat. "And before you ask..." One of my hands moved between our bodies, and he allowed just enough space between us for my fingers to wrap around him.

"Josie," he groaned as I squeezed him, moving my hand down and then slowly back up.

He wanted me.

But it went both ways.

"...yes, I'm still on the pill."

His chuckle was raspy, remembering how he had asked the question the first time we found ourselves in a similar position before I knew who the fuck he was. "I always use my own protection, but it's a good thing no one is home, because I am going to make you scream, Firefly."

Our lips finally collided, and my blood soared. A tremor wracked through me, and I was blinded by my need for him. His tongue coaxed my lips open, and I happily obliged. He nipped, slid, sampled, devoured, and basically consumed me.

My body responded and answered his every demand— relished in it. I was powerless to do anything else.

But he wasn't the only making demands.

My fingers stroked every long inch of him, then flicked over the tip, and he shuddered against me. Realizing the power I had over him caused an addiction I couldn't sate.

"Jesus," he hissed, his lips tearing from mine. He grabbed my wrist again, this time pinning it to the bookshelf behind me. "If you keep doing that, this is going to end far too quickly for both of us."

"Is that a problem?"

His eyes brimmed with hunger and grew darker as he stared at me. "Yeah, it is." He bent and kissed my neck and murmured, "I have every intention of taking my time, unlike before." He released his hold on my hand and moved his so they cupped my ass, lifting up. My legs instinctually wrapped around him.

Ah, yes. The wedding, when my mom walked in on us. That had been all wild and reckless emotions, built from anger and hurt.

His muscles shifted against me as he walked us to the couch, sitting down so I was straddling him. It gave me the control I sought, and I realized he was letting me lead. I leaned back slightly in his lap, my fingers fastening on the ends of my shirt as I lifted it over my head, leveling the playing field.

Those aqua eyes ran over my body in an appreciative glance that left me longing. A second later, the clasp on my bra flicked open and the white lace was discarded on the floor with my shirt. My head fell back as he cupped my breasts, and I gasped as his thumb brushed the hard tip. Pleasure rocketed through me.

"Look at me," he commanded. "I want to see you."

I did as he asked, dragging my eyes open and gazing into the depths of his. It was like drowning in the sea. He was beautiful, but more importantly, he made *me* feel beautiful. There was something almost vulnerable about the way he stared at me, more exposed than being naked before him. I sealed our lips in another kiss, my fingers exploring over his shoulders, down his chest, reveling in each tremor.

He intoxicated me—with the feelings he enticed.

Brock's head dipped, enclosing around a nipple. His tongue swirled over the little bud, flicking and teasing me. I squirmed in his lap, my hips grinding against his to find some kind of relief for the building pressure between my legs.

A guttural groan pulled from him, and he flipped me so I was on my back. His fingers made swift use of the buttons on my jeans, tugging them down my hips. After tossing my pants aside, he slipped off his sweatpants and moved to climb on top of me, but I shook my head. "Those too," I said, indicating his boxer briefs. The impressive length of him strained against the material, begging to be set free.

He grinned slyly, dropping them to the floor before he came to kneel on the couch, spreading my legs apart. The lacy white thong was brushed aside with a skillful finger. He glided it inside me, and my muscles clenched around him, welcoming the invasion. He groaned as I tightened, enclosing his finger in my wet warmth. "This isn't supposed to happen."

My back arched off the couch. "What are you talking about?" I murmured, not really wanting to talk at all, my mind too cloudy with desire to think straight.

His finger moved, sliding in and out of me in lazy strokes. "This. You and me. No one takes me by surprise. Not until you." His voice was gruff and needy.

"Brock," I begged, biting down hard on my lip. "Stop talking and fuck me."

The soft chuckle was a caress against my inner thigh. He slid the last tiny bit of material down my legs, and I watched as he bent over me, lowering his body to mine. The contact of skin against skin sent a wave of lust to every molecule I possessed.

A crinkle of a wrapper sounded, and then he poised to enter me, the tip of him teasing my opening, and I lifted my hips up in encouragement and impatience. Slowly and deliberately, he sank inside me, only to pull out with the same languid stroke. I bit my lip, drowning in that glorious feel of him. Then with one quick thrust, he was buried deep inside me. His eyes never left mine as he watched me while he moved. Pleasure increased with each stroke, and I could no longer keep my eyes open. They drifted shut, basking me in the glory of his body joining with mine.

I rolled my hips in rhythm with his, but the bastard took his sweet time torturing me, keeping me right on the edge of tumbling over the cliff. That didn't work for me. My legs clamped around him as my thighs rose high, thrusting him deeper inside.

A curse fell from his sexy lips. His hands attached to my wrists, holding them prisoner over my head as he thrust into me hard and fast. This was exactly what my ex, Harvey, could never achieve. The perfect balance of desperation and need, pleasure and pain. My wrists might sport bruises tomorrow, but I didn't care. I wanted this.

My climax ripped out of me, a cry of pleasure tumbling from my lips up into the glass dome ceiling above us. He kept his word. He made me scream. Seconds later, Brock trembled along with me, his body muscles tight as he pulsed inside me.

For a few moments afterward, I couldn't move. We stayed joined together, breathless and tired, our skin glistening under the starlight. I lifted my hand, brushing a damp strand of hair out of his face.

I missed him the moment he slipped out of me, which should have been a big red flashing sign, but I was already thinking about the next time. And how soon I could get him to slip his dick back inside me.

He rolled to the side, taking me with him so we faced each other, sprawled out from one end of the couch to the other. Swinging a possessive arm over me, he rested his hand at the small of my back. "You don't strike me as a cuddler," I told him.

His expression was relaxed and unguarded for once, and it made him appear younger. "Is that so? Maybe because you didn't give me a chance the first time."

My lips twitched. True. But in my defense, I never thought I would see him again.

His chest rubbed against my breasts, and I leaned forward, catching his lips with mine. I felt myself grow wet. When I ended the kiss, his eyes were dark. "Again? God, Firefly, you are not like most girls."

I flattened a hand on his chest and pushed slightly, but he didn't budge. "Thanks, I think. Just don't fall in love with me," I teased.

He chuckled, his hand tracing lazy circles over my back. "I don't believe in love."

"Good, because neither do I. I don't want this to get messy."

I liked things just the way they were. No strings attached. I didn't want him to expect anything from me. I wouldn't disappoint him then, and he wouldn't hurt me.

It seemed like a levelheaded approach.

But things rarely were ever that simple.

"Any chance next time we can make it to a bed?" I asked. That was twice I'd had sex with Brock on a couch. "Not that I'm complaining, but I'd really love to try this somewhere with an actual mattress." Not just any bed. I wanted to be surrounded by a room that was entirely his. I wanted to smell him on the sheets, and when I left, I wanted my scent to linger in his bed so every time he went to sleep, he thought of me.

I wanted to drive him as crazy as he drove me.

With a lazy grin, he shook his head. "You're insatiable. Besides, couches might be our thing. But... I think it could be arranged," he murmured.

If I stayed like this, entangled with him, I wouldn't be able to stop myself from touching him. It had been stupid to think I'd be rid of this need for him after one round. Sitting up, I searched the floor for my shirt. It was under his sweatpants. I stood up and slipped it on and turned to face him.

Bad idea.

His hair was rumpled from my fingers. The man had no shame, utterly comfortable in his skin. He owned his nakedness, and with the contours of his body and sculpted muscles, why shouldn't he? I tilted my head to the side as I unashamedly stared at him. "Is sleeping with you part of the Elite protection package?" I asked, joining him back on the couch. I couldn't stay away.

The corner of his mouth curved up, and he brushed my hair off my shoulder. "Hey, you came on to me."

My whole body jumped alive at his touch. "I did not. Besides, it's not like you complained."

"You're nothing like I expected."

Something in his voice made my heart skip.

His finger trailed down the column of my neck. "Do you have a problem with commitment?"

"Don't you?" I countered. "I mean, you have standby girls."

"I'm not talking about me," he replied levelheadedly.

"How about we just don't talk," I whispered.

The sensual curve of his mouth sent a round of tingles throughout me. "I couldn't agree more." He moved closer, leaning in to catch my mouth with his. I fell against his chest and stayed there. His heart hammered under my palm in time with mine.

Alone in his house, shut out from the rest of the world, it was so easy to pretend nothing else mattered. He was all mine... at least for the weekend. My fingers ran through his hair as his tongue slipped between my lips, and I let him in with a purr. His breath came as hard and fast as mine.

We never made it to the bed, not until he carried me up to his room to sleep.

* * *

I woke up late Sunday afternoon with a low beam of sunlight warming my face. It took a few groggy moments to remember where I was and what I'd done. A silent curse echoed in my head. What was just supposed to be a quick nap had turned into Brock and me dozing for a few hours. He was still asleep beside me, and after spending a creepy amount of time staring at him, I slipped out of bed to use the bathroom. These last few days with him seemed like a dream. Perhaps it was, considering half of it was spent in his bed.

He was still an asshole, just a more friendly, fun ass.

Stretching like a languorous cat, the temptation to crawl back into bed beside him wove within me. It had been months since I slept so soundly, if ever. I couldn't figure out if it was the sex, Brock, his bed, or all of the above that contributed to the soundless sleep.

Sprawled out over the bed, Brock's legs were tangled in the sheets so they only covered half his body. I'd never spent a night with a guy before, let alone a weekend. The opportunity had never been there, nor had I ever wanted to. My ex-boyfriend, Harvey, hadn't been serious, despite my losing my virginity to him. It had been more like a rite of passage. I didn't regret giving my virginity to Harvey, but things just got too complicated. I couldn't give him what he wanted. It was easier to end things with him than it should have been.

I didn't know what that said about me.

Nor did I know what would happen between Brock and me after this weekend.

What the hell had I been thinking, sleeping with him again? He made me lose my mind, but this couldn't happen again.

I grabbed one of his black T-shirts from the floor and slipped it on. Tiptoeing from his room, I headed downstairs into the kitchen to grab a bottle of water. It was strange having this huge-ass house to ourselves. I wasn't used to the silence. Sitting down at one of the kitchen stools, I thought about making him something to eat but decided against it.

That was too cozy of a gesture. Too girlfriend-like, and we were so not girlfriend-boyfriend material. The idea made me snort.

Unscrewing the water, I took a long drink. Today I went home. How sad that the thought filled me with such dread.

A stack of manila folders sat on the far end of the counter. I didn't think anything of them and yet... I was pretty sure they hadn't been there all weekend. Had they? I glanced back to the pile. They looked like just ordinary office files and were probably his parents'. They owned hotels all over the world or something. It wouldn't be unusual for them to bring their work home with them.

Just one quick peek to satisfy the curiosity that wouldn't be silent.

Was it wrong to snoop? Yes.

Was I going to do it anyway? Fuck, yes.

I grabbed the edge of a folder and tugged it toward me. My heart plummeted. Carter's name splashed across the tab in bold handwritten letters.

Okay, now I had an obligation to look inside.

I flipped open the file. My brows drew together as I stared at pictures of Carter and his father. Along with the pictures were photocopied bank records, emails, text messages, and other personal information.

"Oh, God," I whispered.

Snatching the other folders, I set them in front of me, looking at each one. Steven. Two other football players. And...

My name.

The pounding of my heart roared in my ears.

WTF.

Brock had a fucking investigation file on me?

The asshole.

I tore open the file and gasped as I stared at my own face. One by one, I went through the pictures, but it wasn't just me. There were images of my dad and mom too. Why the fuck did Brock have a file on me, my dad, and my mom? Carter and Steven, I understood, but me? How did that make sense? He had been investigating me prior to the wedding. I stared at myself in the most mundane situations. At school. Shopping with Ainsley or eating lunch. Stupid shit. How was any of this relevant to taking Carter down? That was the Elite's goal, wasn't it?

The kitchen door creaked open. "Why didn't you wake me?" His voice was sleepy and, God help me, sexy.

My gaze lifted, watching as Brock moved to the coffee maker. "What the fuck is this?" I asked, tossing my file open on the counter with the others.

He was slow to turn around, the tone in my voice giving away my anger. His eyes went to my face first before darting to the files. He scrubbed a hand through his hair and then let it run down the back of his head and around his neck. He blew out a long sigh. "It's not what you think?"

"Really, because it looks like you've been watching me and my family before I even moved into the Pattersons'. A file on

Carter makes sense, but a file on me? Explain it to me, Taylor."

He sunk back against the cabinet. "Your mom was having an affair with Carter's father."

This wasn't news to me and still didn't explain a full investigation into my life. "And? What does she have to do with Carter?"

He folded his arms over his chest, and that guarded expression was back into his eyes. "Look, you don't know the whole story, what he is capable of."

Emotions I didn't want to feel cut through me. Betrayal. Hurt. Had I actually begun to trust this asshole? "Oh, I think I know damn well just how far my stepbrother would go."

"Has he—?" Brock's voice broke off as if he couldn't bring himself to say the word. His eyes darkened, edging with anger that went deep.

I thought about Kenna. "Raped me?" I supplied. "No. But you saw to that." If it hadn't been for the Elite, Carter might have very well had his way with me.

Visible relief washed over his face, the tension in his body loosening as well. "Steven has been covering up his son's perversities for the last three years. This file was before I met you. I needed to know how far you or your mother would go to protect him."

I let out a short laugh. "You actually believe I would do something like that?"

He shook his head. "Not now. When I saw these pictures, I knew you would be Carter's next target."

"Why, because I look like her?" *Ooops. Damn!* The cat was

out of the bag. I would have to profusely apologize to Mads, but I was just so angry. The accusation hurtled off my lips, and there was no taking it back.

Surprise flicked over his features and was gone in the next instant. "You know about Kenna. Mads told you," he deduced correctly.

My fingers bunched together in my lap. "What if she did?"

"She shouldn't have," he said.

Whirling thoughts raced through my head as I recounted every encounter with Brock, every word spoken between us, but I kept going back to the night I first saw him. "Were you even supposed to be at the wedding?" I didn't know it at the time, but Carter and Brock weren't really friends. Teammates, yes. And the Elite had already started their deception to get Carter to let his guard down at that time. So why hadn't any of the other guys been at the wedding?

"No," he stated flatly.

My heart beat faster in my chest. "Why were you there?"

He didn't answer.

"Why were you there?" I asked again with more force, my nails digging into my palms.

"I wanted to see you for myself. See how you acted around Carter," he admitted, his voice lowering. Gone was the guy who had been so passionate. This was the Brock Taylor the rest of the world saw. I imagined very few people got to see the side I had this weekend. He had let his guard down briefly, but it was back in place and firmer than ever.

I glared at him, edging off the stool. "You slept with me as some sort of ploy against Carter. You used me!"

"It was nothing personal. Besides, the way I see it, we used each other that night."

I snorted in disgust, partially because I was upset with myself. He was right. I had used him that night, which didn't make me any better than him. My heart couldn't seem to grasp the concept. Somewhere along the way, I had grown to like Brock. He had come to mean something to me, but now... "I've got to go."

"Firefly, wait." He put a hand on my arm to stop me, but I shook it off, whirling to face him.

"Don't fucking touch me! And don't ever call me that again," I snapped, dashing from the room. I had to get the hell out of there.

My head was killing me as I grabbed my shit and left Brock's house. Of course, the bastard followed me out of the kitchen, ranting and swearing at me to listen. I did no such thing. I slammed out of the house, and relief poured into me when Brock didn't come after me.

How the hell had we gone from being so intimate to being cold and distant in nothing but a blink? It didn't seem real. The last thirty-six hours were nothing but a fantasy. This was real life. The pain. The disappointment. The hurt. The betrayal.

This was what people did to each other.

The walk home did little to soothe the throbbing at my temples, and the constant flashes of images flipping through my memory only fueled all those emotions. I was a mess by the time I opened the front door, dropping my bag in the entryway.

From the sounds coming down the hall, Angie and Steven

were back from their trip. I wandered into the house and swore, seeing the dining room table set for dinner. The scent of savory spices and fresh-baked bread wafted from the kitchen.

Fuck.

Sunday dinner.

I'd completely forgotten.

Mom stopped fussing with the tablecloth and glanced at me. A smile broke over her face. "Oh, good, honey. You're home. Did you have fun at your friend's?"

"It was fine," I said, sounding anything but happy. "I'm exhausted, Mom. Is all of this necessary?"

The smile on her face faltered. Dressed elegantly in black slacks and a sheer blouse with little black flowers embroidered on it, she looked like the picture-perfect upper Elmwood house-wife. "Yes. You promised, Josie. We need this. It is time this family started to act like a family."

"Do I have time to shower and change?"

Her smile brightened once again, pleased that I wasn't going to fight her on the matter. I was too emotionally exhausted to go a round with her. "Of course, that would be splendid. Dinner is served in an hour."

"Fine," I huffed, dragging myself upstairs.

Carter found me as I was about to enter my bedroom. "Where were you all weekend?" He looked better. The bruises were healing, the deep coloring lightening, but I could see on his features that his ribs were still bothering him and walking around took a toll on him.

"None of your business." My hand reached for the doorknob, but Carter, despite his injured ribs, moved faster than I anticipated.

His hand slammed onto the doorway, blocking me from entering my room.

I turned slightly to the side, glowering at him. "Carter, I'm not in the fucking mood. Back off, or I swear I will punch you in the ribs." The idea of causing him pain was appealing.

"You were with Brock, weren't you?" His blue eyes were flecked with disgust as they ran over me. "You fucked him, didn't you?" Carter sneered. "What, he is good enough to have between your legs, but I'm not?"

"You make me sick," I spat, elbowing him. He had been warned. I didn't hit him hard enough to do any further damage to his ribs, but enough to grab his attention.

He groaned, doubling over as he clutched his side, calling me a string of vile names I'd heard too many times from his lips.

With his hand no longer barricading the entrance to my bedroom, I rushed through, slamming the door in his face and quickly flipping the lock. My pulse raced, and I backed away, giving myself a moment to calm down. The back of my knees hit my bed, and I sat down, waiting for Carter to leave before I took that shower.

No way in hell was I going to get caught naked around him. And the prospect of a shower was both terrifying and necessary. My encounter with Carter left me feeling dirty, and despite my fear he would break into my room while I washed my hair, I had to scrub the stain of his words, of his eyes off me.

I'd been home for not even five minutes, and I already

wished I was back at Brock's. His betrayal was preferable to Carter's evil.

Twenty minutes later, I stood in the shower, the bathroom door locked securely, along with every door and window in my room. I washed my hair twice and my body numerous times, but it was the tears tracking down my cheeks that I couldn't seem to wash away. By the time I stepped out of the shower, my mental health was questionable, and I still had to make it through dinner.

I was the last one to show up to the table. It was a joke. The whole thing.

And the entire time I sat across from Carter, he watched me with that twisted smirk of his, making obscene gestures with his food or his fingers at me. I thought about hurling my drink in his face, or better yet, stabbing him with my knife. I'd love to chop off his dick.

Wow. Wouldn't that have been an interesting way to end dinner?

The idea made me giggle out loud, drawing everyone's eyes. *Holy crap. I'm losing it.*

Stirring my fork in my mashed potatoes, I pretended as if nothing had happened and scooped a pile into my mouth, covering up the smile that still tugged at my lips.

Angie and Steven monopolized the conversation with talk of their trip. Carter and Steven went on a football tangent, which was like speaking Greek to me. Steven asked Carter and me what we did all weekend, and my prick of a stepbrother smirked at me.

"Okay. I can't lie anymore. I'm sorry, Josie," Carter stated, the concerned expression on his face worthy of a Golden Globe performance. "But this is for your own good. It's dangerous for you to be hanging around them."

My fingers clenched onto the fork in my hand. He wouldn't dare. But his drawn brows said otherwise. *This asshole.*

"What are you talking about, Carter?" my mother asked, her eyes bouncing between Carter and me.

"Carter, you know the drill. There are no secrets in this house," Steven said, gaining his full attention.

I snorted, unable to control myself, regardless that I was about to be outed by my stepbrother. I didn't even care, and I glared at him boldly, lifting a brow. *Go for it, asshole.*

The scheming scum set down his fork and looked at Angie and his father. "She spent the weekend with Brock Taylor, and considering the way he feels about this family, I'm afraid he might be using her to hurt me."

The entire table fell silent as Carter just grinned at me.

Fuck, I hated him.

"Josie, is this true?" Steven asked sternly, a look of disbelief and disappointment shining in his blue eyes that looked so much like Carter's.

I wanted to tell them why I spent the weekend with Brock instead of at home, but it was a waste of breath. The truth would fall on deaf ears. "Yes," I said, meeting Steven's gaze head-on. I refused to flinch under his disapproving eyes.

Steven took a drink, but the wine didn't calm the anger burning in his eyes. He was unhappy with me and doing his best not to lose his cool. "I know this has been a difficult adjustment for you, but

I've done all I could to help you. Brock and his friends might be exceptional football players, but off the field, Josie, they are dangerous boys. It might not seem like it, but I am protecting you."

What a joke. I snorted, not meaning to do so out loud.

"Josephine," my mother scolded. "This is serious."

Carter continued to look smug in his seat across from me and it was nearly impossible to refrain from hitting him in the head with the pepper shaker.

"You leave us no choice. You are grounded. That means no parties, no car," Steven announced. "Edmond will drive you to and from school each day."

Like hell. "Are you shitting me?" I shrilled, my hands coming down on the table harder than I intended.

"Josephine," my mother hissed, smoothing the napkin in her lap to gain some semblance of control.

I bit down hard on my lip, fighting back the accusations that wanted to fly from my lips, but if I did, I would only dig myself a deeper grave.

"Fine," I bit out, shoving back from the table. "But when I turn eighteen, I'm leaving. I won't spend another night longer than I have to under the same roof as a monster." My eyes pinned Carter's. "And if your son lays one finger on me, I'll end him. I'll end you both. I won't run like Kenna."

Boom.

I dropped the bomb.

So much for staying silent. I couldn't let Carter intimidate me. I wasn't weak, and I was damn tired of being afraid of the jackass.

I tossed my napkin onto the table and stormed out of the room, leaving them gasping in my wake.

Good. I didn't have any more fucks to give when it came to this *family*.

* * *

It took an hour for me to calm down and stop pacing my bedroom floor. Finally, I took out my phone and opened my text app. I sent one to Mads, telling her to call me, and another to Brock.

I want in. That was the message I typed out to Brock. I stared at his name in my phone, my finger hovering over the send button. If I did this, helped the Elite take down Carter, there was no turning back.

I hit the button.

Whatever they were planning. I wanted in on it.

The phone buzzed a minute later. **No.**

Gah! He was so damn frustrating. He didn't even ask what I wanted in on, but it was safe to assume he guessed it had everything to do with Carter and those files I had found. **You don't get to decide for me. He needs to be punished. I can help bring him to justice.** I was giving him the okay to use me. It had been his plan to begin with. The only difference now was I knew about it and was giving him my fucking blessing.

Things have changed.

Maybe for him, but not Carter. My stepbrother still had every intention of hurting me. **What things? Because we

slept together? That's bullshit, Taylor, and you know it.

Perhaps. But it doesn't change my decision.

I grabbed a pillow and shoved it into my face, letting out a scream. God, he drove me crazy. Fine, if he wouldn't help me, then I'd go around him.

I still had Mads and the other guys. Some of them were bound to agree with me. And I'd start with my best friend and her cousin. Grayson should be the easiest of the four to convince. Kenna was his sister, after all. He would grab any means necessary to get justice for her.

My phone rang a few minutes later. It was Mads. "Hey," I answered, plopping onto my bed.

"So how was it?" she asked, fishing for juicy details about my weekend with Brock.

"Dinner tonight was a goddamn nightmare," I replied, knowing that wasn't the information she was looking for, but I couldn't stop myself from tormenting her.

"Josie!" she squealed. "Did you or did you not fuck Brock's brains out?"

Thank God I didn't have my phone on speaker. "What kind of girl do you take me for?"

"The kind who knows what she wants and goes after it." I could hear the smile in her voice.

"You know me so well," I grumbled, wishing some of Mads's happiness would rub off on me.

"So, how was it?" she asked, toning it down, sensing something was wrong.

My chest rose and fell as I let out a deep breath. "I've got to tell you something. You're not going to like it. And if you're mad at me, I'll totally understand, but I promise you, it was an accident. I didn't mean for it to slip out. He just made me so fucking mad."

"Brock has that effect on people. Look, you don't have to apologize. No one better than me understands how frustrating dealing with the Elite can be, especially Brock."

Her quick acceptance had my eyes narrowing. "You already know."

"That you mentioned Kenna? Yeah. Brock chewed my ass out for telling you."

"What a prick."

"You like him. That's the real problem," she said.

Maybe. But I wasn't ready to admit it. Not out loud, at least. "I totally don't deserve a favor, but I am going to ask anyway."

"I'm not going to like this, am I?" I could hear her frown.

"I need to talk to Grayson. Alone," I emphasized. "Without the others. Can you arrange it? I want you to be there too."

"This sounds mysterious." The pitch in her voice changed, going quieter.

"More like I'm going behind Brock's back."

"I'm in," she agreed, no hesitation. Just like that. And that was why this woman was one of my closest friends and only friend at the Academy. I hated keeping Ainsley out of the loop, but I didn't want her mixed up with Carter, and after what I learned he was capable of, she needed to stay as far away from me as possible.

Tucking a pillow underneath me, I leaned on it, keeping the phone pressed to my ear. "Okay. Text me the time and place, assuming Grayson agrees, but I think he will want to hear me out."

"This has to do with Kenna, doesn't it?" she asked.

"Yes," I replied.

"Are you in danger?"

"All the time," I admitted. But it wasn't just Carter I had to worry about. My mom. Brock. Steven. The Elite. It seemed as if I had very few people in my life I could trust. Ainsley was the only one who I knew without a doubt always had my back. I was pretty sure Mads was the same, but I couldn't discount who her family was.

CHAPTER TWENTY-TWO

I yawned. Of course, I slept like shit the first night back in my own bed. And despite being pissed at Brock, I missed the scent of him clinging to his sheets.

What it boiled down to... I missed the asshole.

I missed Brock.

Fuck me.

Mads, Grayson, and I were meeting after school at her house. While the other guys were at practice, the three of us would be plotting and scheming, the only thing it seemed I did this year. Grayson came up with some bullshit excuse to get out of practice that wouldn't raise any alarms, but Brock was suspicious by nature.

Brock and I hadn't talked much. I was still pissed at him. Not only had Brock lied to me, he then refused my help. I hadn't forgiven him... yet. However, that didn't stop him or the guys from walking me to class. They kept up the routine despite

Carter not returning to school until next week. The doctor ordered him to remain home for two weeks.

I was dreading the day.

Technically, I was grounded, which meant I was to go straight home from school. Screw that. Angie was too self-absorbed to notice I wasn't home until dinner, and even if she noticed, what would she do? Ground me longer?

So what?

After school, I met Mads at her car. She leaned against her little silver Mercedes, sporting our school uniform with ripped black tights, a cigarette dangling between her lips. "You ready, bitch?" she grinned, tossing the smoke to the ground before stomping on it with the heel of her combat boots.

"Fuck yes, get me the hell out of here." I exhaled, opening the passenger door and tossing my bag in the back seat.

"Good, because the suspense is literally killing me. I can't wait another minute," she said, sliding into the driver seat.

It took just a few minutes to get to her house, and Grayson's Jeep was already parked in the half-circle driveway. He hopped out of the car and waited for us, his lips pulled into a firm line. "This better be worth my time."

I couldn't help but roll my eyes.

"Chill out, Gray. You're so serious all the time," Mads said as we walked up to the house.

"Your point?" he retorted, expression unchanging.

I almost laughed.

Mads keyed in the door code, and the little light blinked green. "Forget it. Come on, let's go inside and get something to drink. My parents are still at work."

"Is Lucy here?" Grayson asked. Lucy was the Clarkes' housekeeper and cook. She basically ran the house.

"Yeah," she said over her shoulder, leading us down the hallway.

"Do you think she'd make us a batch of her chocolate chip cookies and a plate of nachos?" he asked.

Good lord. Typical boy. But I had to admit, it sounded amazing.

Mads paused at the kitchen threshold and threw Grayson a sidelong glance. "Are you high?"

He blinked. "No."

Her lips twitched. "Whatever. But only if you stop being a douchebag."

A hint of a smile cracked at the corner of his mouth. "That's like asking me to stop being me."

"And?" she prompted.

The three of us gathered around the patio table in her screened-in porch, not only for privacy from Lucy but also so Mads could puff away on her cancer sticks. A pitcher of lemonade sat in the middle of the table with three clear glasses.

"Got any vodka?" Grayson asked. "I have a feeling we're going to need it." His gaze slid to me.

"No shit," Mads muttered. "So, Sherlock Holmes, what's the big secret?"

Grayson poured drinks for each of us, passing them around. Odd. I hadn't thought he had a gentlemanly bone in his body. Perhaps that jerk inside him was just reserved for me. I still needed to have *that* conversation, but it would have to wait.

"I want to set up a trap for Carter," I announced, taking the glass Grayson held out to me.

"What do you have in mind?" Grayson didn't so much as blink at my suggestion, which meant this was probably something they'd already considered doing.

"Are you sure you should get involved? Won't that piss off Brock?" Mads pointed out.

"Definitely," Grayson and I said together.

We stared at each other, my smile slipping at the frown on his lips.

What was it about this particular Elite that made me want him to like me? It didn't make sense.

"The truth is, I can't live in that house with Carter. It's only a matter of time before he tries to hurt me." My brain shuddered at the thought. "And I've seen the files you have on the Pattersons," I revealed to Grayson. "I know Steven protects his son, which leaves me defenseless."

Neither of them had to ask about my mother. She was a worthless cause when it came to putting me before her rich husband. Some days I had to wonder how she could be my mother.

"You have us," Grayson stated with pinched brows, and I believed he meant it, despite the roughness in his features.

My heart squeezed at his offer, regardless of his reasons for offering me his protection. "Are you guys going to spend the night with me too?" School was one thing, but they couldn't be with me every second of the day. "Not to mention, Steven is onto you. He made it very clear I was not to associate with any of you."

"Okay, so what's your idea?" Mads prompted. "It's going to be reckless, isn't it?" she added, sighing.

"Probably," I admitted. "Can you handle it?" I challenged, looking them both in the eye. "You would be going behind Brock's back, lying to him." I needed them to understand the scope of my plan.

Grayson considered. "For Kenna, I would."

Not me. Kenna. I tried not to be hurt. Obviously, he didn't love me more than his sister.

I took a sip of my lemonade and swallowed, looking each of them in the eye. "Okay, you guys are in?"

Grayson nodded. "I am. But I don't like leaving Brock and the others out. I'm not sure that is the right approach."

"The fewer people that know, the better. This needs to be believable. Carter can't suspect anything or it won't work," I disputed. "He knows you guys are shadowing me. Mads?"

She took a long drag, holding the cigarette smoke inside her lungs before exhaling. "I need to hear the details first before I agree to anything. I don't like the idea of you being hurt."

We spent the next hour brainstorming, perfecting what we hoped was a foolproof plan, but honestly, there was no guarantee when dealing with someone as corrupt as Carter. He thought of himself as invincible, but hopefully that cockiness would work in our favor.

The plate of cookies and nachos Lucy brought out was nearly gone. Grayson scooped up one of the few remaining chips. "We'll set Carter up with the perfect opportunity. He won't be able to resist. Shit, he's already tried to drug you before."

I had a cookie halfway to my mouth. "What?!"

Mads's silver eyes narrowed.

But Grayson just shrugged. "It was at my back-to-school party this summer."

"Why didn't anyone tell me?"

"We knew who was supplying Carter with his drugs of choice. That information was easy to obtain, and we made sure he was at the party. One of us had an eye on him at all times. We were hoping to catch him slipping one into someone's drink. And he did." His face went dangerously dark. "Yours."

"Mine," I echoed, thinking back to the night. "How? I didn't feel anything. I would have known if I'd been drugged."

"You would have if Fynn hadn't switched out your drink," he explained.

"Fynn? Why did he switch my drink?" The Elite had wanted to catch Carter red-handed. That would have been the perfect chance. Not that I was complaining, but this all happened prior to the Elite knowing me. Was it because I reminded them of Kenna?

"You'll have to ask Brock, but I suspect it has something to do with the fact that the two of you slept together. He was the one who put Fynn on you. Brock told him to watch you because he had a feeling Carter would try something."

My cheeks grew warm. "Do I remind you of her?" I asked before I thought about what I was saying.

"Yeah, a little" Grayson admitted after a long minute of just staring at me as if he wasn't seeing me, but his sister. "But it's more complicated than that."

I tilted my head. "How so?"

He averted his eyes, staring at the table. "It's not important. What we need to do is make sure we have all our bases covered with this plan and nothing happens to you."

We all could agree on that. Especially me.

I was the bait, after all. Now we just needed Carter to take the hook, and he was too cocky to let the opportunity slip by.

* * *

I'd just cleared the school doors when Brock fell in step beside me. "Where did you disappear to yesterday?"

"Why do you care?" I shot back, picking up my pace. My ankle was finally feeling better, but I still wouldn't be able to ditch Brock.

"Firefly," he called, putting a hand on my arm and turning me around. "We need to talk. This silence, it's over." Annoyance flashed in those sea-green eyes.

I pulled my arm away and hugged my new laptop against my chest. Touching was a no-no. It weakened my resolve. I'd agreed I should keep my distance from Brock so he wouldn't uncover our plan, but it proved to be more difficult than I bargained for these last few days. Why did he have to be so damn attractive? It wasn't fair. "Why? Because you said so? Maybe I like the peace and quiet."

A lopsided grin graced lips I found myself staring at. "Don't fool yourself. We both know you miss me."

True. But I'd be damned if I'd admit it. "You wish, Taylor."

"You can't stay mad at me forever."

"Watch me," I said, moving past him, searching for Mads's car. I couldn't remember where she parked.

He stepped back into my path so all I could see was his face. "I'll drive you home."

The air shifted, blowing his scent toward me, and my insides turned to mush. God, I was so weak. "I'm not getting in your car. Besides, Steven's driver is picking me up. New rules."

"Don't test me, Firefly," he warned.

The parking lot was filling up, students rushing to get to their cars, their footsteps clattering past us. Engines purred to life. Someone shouted Brock's last name and honked as they drove by, but none of them mattered. It was just him and me. "Will you stop threatening me? I'm over it. I'm over you."

He moved so fast. I didn't have time to even register he'd moved at all or that I had as well until I was pressed up against a car, his body trapping me. "Are you really over me?" he whispered against my ear, his breath hot at my neck.

My body betrayed me, shivering. "I'm not Kenna," I said forcefully, shoving at his chest, but it was like shoving his Range Rover. I just couldn't do it.

He grimaced, steely eyes searching mine. "What are you talking about?"

"I know that I look like her and that you and she had a thing," I said, some of the tightness in my body fading.

"So you think I'm interested in you only because you remind me of Kenna?" His voice cooled. "Do I seem like the kind of guy who does that?"

I snorted.

"Okay, wait. Don't answer that." I tried to shove him off

me, but he was relentless. "Firefly, you need to hear this. I won't apologize for looking out for my family. Grayson, Fynn, and Micah... that's what they are to me. Family. What happened with Kenna royally fucked Grayson up. Hell, it fucked us all up. She wasn't like other girls. She was important."

My head tipped down, unable to look into his eyes as he spoke about her. "I get it. You had feelings for her."

His finger slid under my chin, forcing my gaze back to his. "Yes, but not so much in the way you believe. I wasn't in love with her, but I did let the entire school believe I was. It gave her protection. Or at least, I thought it did. Turns out I was wrong. Not only did she get shit from the girls in this school, but also some of the guys on the football team like Carter, who thought they could bend the rules, that there wouldn't be consequences for hurting one of us."

Brock didn't love her. It had been an act. Did Mads know that? No, otherwise she wouldn't have told me. "This doesn't change anything," I said, steeling my chin.

He cupped the side of my cheek in his palm, bringing his face close to mine. "Doesn't it?" he whispered against my lips in a deliberate dirty move.

My fingers curled into his shirt. "I haven't forgiven you yet." But I remembered what Grayson had told me, how he had saved me from Carter at his party.

"Perhaps I could change your mind." His lips pressed to mine in a soft kiss that was meant to destroy a person. I didn't think Brock was capable of such tenderness, and it threw me off balance.

"Not fair," I murmured, my eyes still closed when he ended the kiss.

"I never claimed to play fair."

Oh, yes. The Elite liked their games. Speaking of... "Don't you have practice?" I reminded him.

His fingers trailed down my arm to intertwine with my mine. "Yeah, stay and watch. We can grab dinner afterward," he offered with a wicked grin.

Someone cleared their throat beside us, presumably the driver of the car we were making out on. Brock gave the guy a nod and pulled me away from the car.

"Are you asking me out, Taylor?" I inquired as we walked.

He smirked. "You'll have to say yes to find out."

I shook my head, wishing I didn't have my laptop in my hands. "Only if you promise that the night ends with a milk-shake and sex in the back seat of your car."

He blinked and then promptly laughed. "Firefly, you're killing me. I'm going to have a boner all through practice thanks to you."

"Just doing my civic duty to every girl at Elmwood Academy."

He was leading me away from the parking lot toward the football field. "Is that so?"

"Doesn't matter. I was joking... about the milkshake," I said, not done tormenting him. I needed so much therapy.

He shook his head. "Stop. I'm serious, or I won't make it to practice and Coach will bench me for Friday's game."

"And that is bad how?"

"Scouts will be there," he answered, but something in his

tone was so... monotone, as if he didn't really care about scouts, but was supposed to because that was what everyone expected from him.

I chewed on my lip. "So you want to play professionally or something?" Carter did, but I guess I assumed Brock wasn't as serious.

"I don't know," he admitted, as if he hadn't thought too hard on the matter, and it made me wonder how much of his life was mapped out for him. "But I'd like to play in college."

We'd never talked about the future, what his plans were. In truth, Brock and I didn't do much talking when we were alone, and I realized there was so much I didn't know about him.

"You're buying me dinner. And we're not having sex... in the back of your car," I added, unable to help myself. Teasing him just became my new favorite obsession.

He groaned. "Enough sex talk. It's bad enough I think about you naked all day."

I brightened inside. This side of Brock was more dangerous than when he was scowling at me. This side of him was the part I could fall in love with.

No, Josie. That is not happening.

He left me on the edge of the field to head into the locker room and change. I debated for five minutes, deciding whether or not to stay. It was the offer of dinner that made me stay.

At least, that was what I told myself.

I was surprised by the number of people who hung around to watch the football team practice. This wasn't even a game, and yet the stands were stuffed with people. I took a seat in the bleachers as the players jogged onto the field, beginning their warmups. Micah waved to me, shooting me a wink before placing his helmet on. Grayson, on the other hand, scowled when his glacial stare landed on me. Fynn gave me a salute, and I returned the gesture with my middle finger. His laugh echoed over the field.

They made it clear who I was there for.

From a few rows below me, Ava and her bitches glared up at me. I smiled sweetly in return. *Suck on that, whores.*

Before Brock started on his drills, his eyes scoured the stands, landing on me. A roguish grin formed on those damn sensual lips.

After that, my eyes never left him.

CHAPTER TWENTY-THREE

When practice was over, I clattered down the bleacher steps to the field. Grayson waited for me, glaring at Ava from the corner of his eye while the rest of the team went to shower and change. "Brock will be out in a minute," he informed.

"Were you sent to guard me from the big bad wolf?" I asked, my gaze shifting to Ava and her band of bitches.

His football helmet dangled from his finger, beads of sweat gathered along the edges of his dark hairline. Just looking at him made me want to shower. "Something like that," he mumbled. He kept a close watch on Ava as she and her friends got up to leave.

Grayson's abhorrence for Ava was written in every line on his face. It was clear he didn't like her, but the Queen B herself seemed oblivious to the loathing emitting from Grayson. She grinned saucily in a way that made me want to cut off her lips—

not in jealousy, because my feelings for Grayson weren't stemmed from attraction, but more a protective sister, which was weird considering he barely tolerated me.

Ava ran the tip of her blazing red nail over Grayson's shoulder. "I'm having an intimate get-together at my place. You should come," she told him, her eyes devouring Grayson. "The others too." Then her eyes slashed to me. "But not you. I can't have my place stinking like trash." She and her friends giggled like Ava was the wittiest person on Earth.

It was like a light switch of pent-up anger flipped inside of me. I lunged straight for her, fists clenched and ready to throw down. I would have too if Grayson hadn't grabbed me around the waist and lifted me just off my feet, making it harder for me to struggle against him.

"She's not worth it," he murmured near my ear.

My breath came out in sharp pants like a raging bull's while Ava blinked and started to laugh. "You're insane."

Grayson's gaze whirled. "Get the fuck out of here, Ava, before I let Josie tear you apart." His voice came out clipped and cold.

She flipped her siren red hair and huffed, eyes narrowed to slits. "I don't see what your guys' obsession with her is. She's nothing. A no one."

Grayson kept his hands around my waist, but put my feet to the ground. "So were you until Brock decided you were good enough for a cheap fuck. Keep this shit up and you won't even be that anymore," he told her, his chest rumbling against my back.

Flanked by her two friends, she hissed like a little viper

before spinning around and storming off, her little minions close on her heels, mouths gaping.

When she and her friends disappeared behind the bleachers, Grayson finally released me. I turned on him. "You should have let me kick her ass."

He shook his head, a hint of a smirk pulling at his lips. "I believe you could. Ava has a sharp bite, but she doesn't have the claws you do."

Brock appeared beside me. I hadn't even seen him coming. "What did she want?" he asked Grayson.

Grayson's mouth thinned. "Nothing. Just stirring up trouble. Josie handled it."

Brock's heat seeped into me, and I felt a bulk of my anger leave my body. My lips twitched at Grayson.

"See you later," he said to Brock before those chocolate eyes flipped to me. "Try not to kill anyone tonight," he told me with a shred of a smirk.

"What just happened between you two?" Brock asked, noticing Grayson was a little less intense around me. Brock's perceptive nature missed little.

"Nothing." I shrugged, but he didn't believe me, so I resorted to poking fun at him, regardless that it bordered heavily on flirting. "How do you feel about sex in the guys' shower, because man, could you use one." I wrinkled my nose.

He had changed out of his uniform into gray sweats and a cotton tee. He stepped closer. "I thought the scent of a guy's pheromones drove girls crazy."

"There is a difference between good guy sweat and..." I plucked at his white T-shirt. "This."

He chuckled, tossing an arm around my neck and pulling me in close for a suffocating bear hug, but to my chagrin, his fucking sweat caused a bolt of instant lust.

"Where is this promise of food? I'm starving," I grumbled.

A knowing smile glinted in his gaze. "I just bet you are, Firefly."

I rolled my eyes, shoving at his chest. "Please. You don't stand a chance next to a pizza extravaganza."

"Is that so? I might just have to put that to the test." Brock did like a challenge.

I was bummed to see that there were a lot of kids from the Academy at Sammy's Pizza. It seemed like the place to be after football practice. If I didn't have such a weak spot for pizza, I would have skipped dinner or insisted we go somewhere quieter. But I had a feeling this was all intentional. Brock wanted everyone to see us together. I was just happy Ava hadn't come here before her *intimate gathering*. WTF. Just call it like it was. A ho party.

We were seated at a booth in the corner, offering a tad of privacy, but it meant we had to walk through the entire dining area, and everyone stared. Brock put his hand on the small of my back, guiding me with light pressure to keep moving. Being out in public with him was like being on display. Everyone stopped and gawked. The crazy part was that Brock seemed unaware of the attention he drew—that, or he was just so used to it that he was no longer fazed. What was it about this side of town that was so fascinated about the Elite?

Then I looked at Brock, and I remembered.

He was fucking gorgeous.

But that wasn't why. It helped, but there was more than just a pretty face behind his over-the-top popularity. Brock and his friends had made a name for themselves.

We were only seated for less than a minute when a server came over and dropped a strawberry shake in front of me and a Coke for Brock without ever taking our drink orders.

I glanced up at the guy in his early twenties, if that. "Uh, I didn't order this," I said politely, indicating to the milkshake.

He looked at Brock with a stupid grin on his face.

It dawned on me then, the reference to the milkshake I'd mentioned before practice. I turned slitted eyes on Brock, who leaned back in the booth, his long legs stretched out under the table so they touched mine. "You did this. Smooth, Taylor, smooth." I slid the tall glass toward me and took a long sip of the sweet berry-flavored shake. I couldn't stop the grin. "You're still not getting laid."

His lips twitched.

"What I want to know is how you pulled this off." We had been together the entire time from the moment we stepped into the pizza place.

His eyes heated and dropped to my lips. "I don't kiss and tell."

My body warmed, and I sucked down another gulp of shake. At this rate, we weren't going to make it through dinner. I had a mind to drag him into the back of his SUV and make good on all those threats I'd been issuing.

We shared a long look, filled with unspoken promises. I never wanted to hate and love someone all in the same breath as

I did this guy. I should have known at my mother's wedding he would be bad news.

The urge to close the distance between us and leap over the table became a pestering throb within me. That would give everyone something to talk about at school tomorrow. *Ohmygod, did you hear? Josie James jumped into Brock Taylor's lap last night and basically humped him while shoveling pizza in her mouth.*

Two pizzas arrived at our table, thankfully interrupting not only my inner monologue but also the mounting sexual tension hovering in the air between Brock and me. Trevor, our server, set one mushroom and sausage pizza on the table. The other was an extravaganza with literally everything you could imagine on a pizza.

I'd died.

Brock thanked Trevor after he dropped two plates onto the table for us and left.

Reaching across the table, I snagged a piece of pizza and plopped it on my plate to cool for a few seconds, because the shit was fresh and hot. "What the hell, Taylor? We didn't even order. Do you always get such premium service wherever you go?"

He considered, taking a piece from the other pizza for himself. "I guess. I don't really think about it."

And that was sad. He was so used to being treated like a god, it was natural.

"So you're not one of those girls that just eats one slice?" he asked when I helped myself to my third piece of pizza.

I laughed. "Uh, definitely not. I'm going to eat my weight in pizza." For someone who could be so intimidating, conversation with Brock was effortless. We clicked in more than in bed.

On the way home, I made him park a few houses down from mine, seeing as Angie and Steven would lose their shit if they saw him. Our house was officially anti-Elite after they put Carter in the hospital—except for me, of course. I was utterly team Brock.

He wasn't thrilled about not being able to drive me up to the house, and even in the dark car, I could see the deep frown lines on his forehead.

"I'll be fine," I said, reaching for the door handle. "If it makes you feel better, you can watch me from the car, and if anyone kidnaps me, I'll expect you to rescue me."

Brock wasn't laughing or smiling. "Promise me you'll stay out of this. He will hurt you if given the chance."

Shit. That was a promise I couldn't make, not without lying, but still, I nodded, because to do otherwise would make him suspicious.

Three weeks later, Grayson threw one of his legendary parties. *The* party.

It had been nearly impossible for the three of us to conspire *and* keep it from Brock. But tonight was the night. It was do or die. In this case, it could be literally.

The thought increased the trepidation I already felt.

I was a nervous mess. I'd have to be an idiot not to be. If anything went wrong, one little mistake or something we overlooked, I could be in deep dog shit. It was a risk I was willing to take because the alternative wasn't something I could live with. Each day under the same roof as Carter put me in danger, especially since he was feeling a helleva lot better.

He'd been talking about Grayson's party all week and couldn't wait to get rip roaring drunk. It had been too long since he'd had some fun. No one missed one of Grayson's parties, not even if these were the guys who had beat the crap out of him almost six weeks ago.

It was a testament to just how fucking stupid Carter really was. He wasn't coming alone and he was definitely there to fuck shit up, so he'd told multiple people. Carter wasn't good at keeping his vile lips shut.

Music played from one of the other rooms. I scanned the sea of people, looking for Brock, but he was nowhere to be found. That was good, right? I didn't want him to foil the plan, but somehow I felt more nervous without him here. I smeared my hands down my jeans, wiping away the sweat.

"You ready for this?" Grayson asked, handing me a drink. Cranberry juice, just like we discussed.

I nodded. "Promise you won't lose sight of me?"

Grayson clutched a drink in his hand, his eyes sharp as he took in the crowd. "And risk Brock killing me? Not happening."

I wouldn't say Grayson and I were friends, but we were on neutral territory tonight. We shared a common goal. This time when I was in his house, I noticed details that hadn't before, like the black-and-white canvas pictures of Grayson and Kenna. It was a strange feeling, staring at a girl who resembled me. I could see the similarities, but at the same time, I thought we looked nothing alike.

My fingers clung to the plastic cup, half afraid it would slip through my fingers. I pulled my eyes from the pictures and looked up at Grayson. "What if he doesn't try anything?"

"He will," he assured with more confidence than I felt.

A heavy sigh came off my chest.

The party tonight seemed livelier. There were definitely more people than there had been at the end of summer. Perhaps it had something to do with Halloween, which was just a week away. Everyone seemed amped up and ready to go wild.

As more kids from the Academy filtered in, I noticed a group had dressed up, wearing black masks and reaper cloaks. I assumed they were Public kids crashing. Maybe I should have worn a mask or dressed up. I stared down at my jeans and white shirt.

Someone snuck up behind me and lifted me in the air like I weighed ten pounds, and I went stiff in their arms until I heard their voice. "You ready to get fucked-up, JJ?" Micah more or less hollered in my ear. He had taken to calling me JJ over the last few weeks.

My ears rang as I demanded, "Put me down."

He chuckled, spinning us around. "Not until you swear to do a shot with me."

That was not on tonight's agenda, but Micah didn't know that. Only Grayson and Mads did. "If I refuse, do you plan on carrying me around all night?" I asked when he stopped spinning. Luckily, I somehow managed to keep the drink in my hand from spilling.

Micah set me down on my feet, the ground swaying for a moment, but he was right there, steadying me with a hand on my waist. "Absolutely." He grinned, flashing those hazardous dimples at me.

I rolled my eyes. "You're impossible. Grayson, give me a damn shot." It was important that we keep up the façade of things being normal. This was a party. We could let no one suspect that this was actually a trap.

Grayson scowled at Micah. "Don't you have some girl to screw?"

Micah turned those light blue eyes to me, slinging an arm around my shoulder. "You think Brock would mind?"

I snorted. "As if I'd sleep with you," I said, pushing away his arm.

Grayson knew just how to distract Micah. He was no longer thinking about that shot but who he was going to be bang tonight. No matter how cute Micah was, that girl wasn't going to be me.

Grayson punched him in the arm. "Dumb question, but it's your funeral, man. Besides, I'm on babysitting duties tonight, and that doesn't involve me watching you have sex with Josie. Where is Brock?"

Micah shrugged as a group of girls walked by giggling. "Dunno. Haven't seen him yet."

"Haven't seen who?" Mads asked, suddenly appearing between Micah and me. She was dressed in all black, her hair pulled into a high ponytail on the crown of her head. The faint traces of smoke clung to her clothes, masked by the fresh appli-cation of her perfume.

"Brock. Have you seen him?" I asked, chewing on the bottom of my lip.

Mads shook her head. "I just got here. What's up with the masks?" she asked, eyes narrowed on two guys who strolled past headed for the kitchen.

"The goth kids getting their freak on?" Micah suggested, not really paying them much attention. His focus had moved to Mads.

I was pretty sure it wasn't the goth kids, but who knew. Not being able to see their faces made me jumpy. Mads, Grayson, and I shared a look. This was a complication we hadn't foreseen.

Micah looked Mads over, a glint in his eyes. "Are we going to screw?" He gave her a cocky grin.

Mads wrinkled her freckled nose, making a face. "I made that mistake once. Never going to happen again," she stated adamantly.

Beside me, Grayson went stiff, and I knew before he even leaned over to whisper in my ear, "He's here."

I went still, my gaze going straight to Carter's like my body naturally sensed danger. He wasn't alone. Three of the football players were with him, including Shawn and Porter. Carter's conceited grin widened when he saw me. His eyes flicked to Grayson before returning to me, and he blew a kiss in my direction.

Every muscle in my body wanted to shudder, to step closer to Grayson, but I had to play my part and pretend like everything was normal. So just what would Josie do in this situation? She'd flip the fucker off, which I proudly did.

Oh, it is on, motherfucker.

"Stay calm," Grayson muttered.

Easy to say, except that I was shaking everywhere. The minutes seemed to drag on eternally. An hour went by and then another as I waited for Carter to toss back the beers. We made eye contact a few times from across the room, but he more or less avoided me. *Not* part of the plan.

Crash.

"Shit," Grayson muttered as the sound of glass smashing echoed from another room. "Stay here," he ordered before taking off toward the commotion. I didn't know how he or his parents put up with these parties. People had no regard for others' homes or possessions.

I sipped on my drink, eyes casually scanning the room for Carter. Shawn and Porter were in the corner with two of the Academy cheerleaders lounging on a couch. Where was Carter? Would one of them be his target instead of me? It seemed likely, and I wondered if he'd noticed how Grayson watched me. The plan was for Grayson to have eyes on me but leave me alone.

Gah.

This night was turning into a bust.

And just when I was about to call it a night, Izzy, one of the standby girls and Ava's friend, came rushing toward me looking frantic. Her makeup was messy, mascara smudged like she had been crying. Hazel eyes big and wide, she was out of breath when she stopped in front of me. "Ohmygod. I found you. It's Brock. Hurry." She tugged on my arm, pulling me away.

The second she said Brock's name, my heart plunged. I glanced over my shoulder, looking for Grayson or Mads. Dread dropped into my gut when I couldn't find them. "What happened? Is he okay?" I demanded.

She shook her head. "No. He is with Carter." Her voice was higher than normal, edged with hysteria.

"Shit," I muttered. That wasn't good. "Where?" I asked, going with her more willingly as she led me down the hallway.

"This way." She quickened her pace, weaving around our lingering peers and shoving one or two out of the way. She ignored any protests.

My mind was scrambling. What was Brock thinking? And tonight of all nights? He couldn't just leave my stepbrother alone for one night. Perhaps he was pissed that Carter showed up. It didn't matter. I had to stop Brock before he put Carter in the hospital again. This time Steven would press charges. There were too many witnesses at a place like this.

We turned the corner into a dimly lit room. "In here," Izzy instructed, pulling me harder through the door. Just as my foot stepped over the threshold, a sharp pain pierced my arm. I whirled. "What the hell. What was that?" I asked, my voice trembling as I rubbed at the fleshy part of my arm.

A masked figure stepped out from the shadow of the door, a needle in his hand. "Hey, sis."

Ah, fuck. Carter.

"Where's Brock?" I demanded, taking a step backward. I bumped into Izzy, who clasped her hands on my arms, digging her nails into my skin.

Carter slammed the door shut, removing the skeleton mask. "Not in here," he said, grinning like a superior asshole.

Chills raced down my back, the blood in my veins turning

cold, and I realized it was the drug working its way into my system. "What did you give me?" I rasped, my voice sounding off in my head.

"Just a little something to keep you calm," he informed me, his voice eerily even. "Can't have you screaming, at least not until I'm ready."

Shit.

I jerked out of Izzy's hold and staggered. Everything felt heavier, weaker. Carter caught me, anger glaring in his eyes. "Don't touch me," I hissed. His scent hit me, and fear dug its claws inside me.

Holy shit. This isn't happening. That bitch. I couldn't believe Izzy had set me up.

"I got you, sis," the voice from all my nightmares whispered. "Here, let's get this on." He took the skeleton mask and fitted it over my head.

My hand swung out at him, but nothing. I tried to twist, to avoid the mask, but I couldn't. Hands pinned my arms down, and the material descended down over my face. Carter adjusted it over my eyes, not that it did a whole lot of good. My vision wavered. I was going to pass out.

He secured something on my shoulders, followed by his arm for support. Then the bastard guided me out the door. I understood the masks now. In this guise, Carter and I were undetected, concealed by the Halloween costumes. "Brock is going to kill you," I mumbled, my lips hardly opening. I was dying to lie down, to close my eyes, but I was terrified of what would happen when I woke, where I'd be.

"I hope so," he said.

My stomach rolled over on itself. What did that mean? He wanted Brock to find us?

"I need you to stay awake," he whispered in my ear, jostling me as a gust of cold air washed over me, my feet dragging over the ground. "Just a little bit longer."

Good luck with that. I was so damn tired and all I wanted to do was sleep. I might have laughed or smiled. Delirium was setting in.

Finally, the drug won. Despite how much I fought to stay lucid, I could no longer fight the power of the liquid Carter had injected in my veins. Darkness swarmed me, heavy and thick like a blanket. Then there was nothing. No party. No Grayson. No Brock.

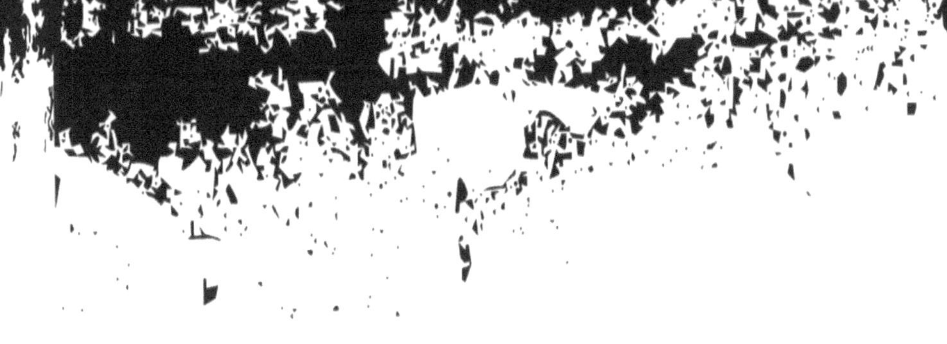

CHAPTER TWENTY-FOUR

The process of waking was slow and painful. By the time I was aware of where I was and what was happening, I just wanted to fall back into the blissful darkness of oblivion. My hands were bound in front of me, and when I tried to open my mouth to scream, I couldn't. Tape covered my lips, and all I could do was make muffled cries. Not that it mattered. Wherever I was, it was dark inside and cramped.

I realized the fucking mask was still over my head. Panic surged through me, and I gagged on it.

I had to get this off me, had to remove the tape before my anxiety became a living thing. Wedging my bound hands up toward my face, I grabbed hold of mask and frantically tugged at it until I was free, no longer suffocating.

Tick. Tick. Tick.

The repetitive noise of something echoed in my ears, and I turned my head, but the ground suddenly was moving underneath me. No. Not ground, for the surface was plush and cool, like leather. I was in a car. And the ticking I heard was the blinker.

My drug-induced cloud of confusion cleared, and I was thrust into reality. Turmoil rolled through me in waves.

Holy shit.

Not only did Carter inject me with drugs, the bastard kidnapped me.

Fuuckkk!

I was at the mercy of a psychopath—and probably a rapist too.

It took some time, my muscles still shaking off the drug in my body, but I managed to sit myself up in the seat. I recognized the inside of his SUV. Though my hands were bound in front of me, I lifted them to mouth, grabbing the corner of the duct tape and ripped it off. My eyes instantly watered from the pain, but I forced myself to breathe through it.

"Carter." My voice rasped, and I wondered if I had screamed while unconscious. Had he done anything to me? My clothes were still intact under the long black reaper cloak.

From the driver seat, Carter angled his head so he could look at me through the rearview mirror. "Oh, good. You're awake. I was hoping I didn't give you too much. That would have put a wrench in my plan."

Plan?

Carter had a plan.

No, I had a plan. Grayson, Mads, and I did. This wasn't supposed to be Carter's show. It was mine.

I met his eyes with a glare. "Untie me, Carter, or I swear to God I will press charges against you."

He laughed. "Funny. My dad won't let that happen. Besides, they'd never believe you. Kidnapping my own step-sister is a little farfetched, especially since I have every intention of returning you when I'm finished."

"Finished with what?" I dared ask, regardless that my heart was fucking about to jump out of my chest.

His lips curled in the mirror. "You'll see. I don't want to spoil the surprise."

"Screw you, Carter. Let me go. I swear I won't say anything," I bargained, not expecting him to take the offer, but it was worth a shot.

"Liar," he grinned.

It was true. I was lying through my teeth. Vague memories of the party drifted back to me, Carter laughing when I threatened that Brock would kill him. It froze my blood. He was up to something, and I was damn afraid it involved hurting the Elite in some fashion, Brock especially.

I couldn't let that happen.

But I also couldn't let Carter harm me.

What was I supposed to do? Were Grayson and Mads frantic? Were they looking for me?

Carter had managed to hijack our plan to formulate his own. *That fucker.*

I had to be smarter than him. It was the only way to swing this shit storm back in my favor. Or survive it.

Fumbling my knotted hands, I wiggled my hips to the side, attempting to reach my back pocket where my phone was stashed. The idiot hadn't thought to check my pockets. Bunching up the ends of the cloak, I navigated my phone into my hands. My call should be to 911, but I pressed the speed dial for Grayson, hastily reducing the volume as low as it went, that way Grayson could hear what was happening inside the car, but hopefully Carter wouldn't be able to pick up Grayson's voice.

I shoved the phone under my leg, keeping the speaker part sticking out and the cloak hiding my movements. "Carter," I said louder than before. "Where are you taking me?" I asked, scrambling to get any information that might help Grayson find me.

"Like I'd give you that information," he sneered, eyes back on the road.

I glanced out the dark tinted windows, looking to see if any of the landscape was familiar, but it was hard to see, no streetlights to illuminate the path. I caught the shapes of trees passing by. "Why are you doing this?" I seemed to be asking the same questions in rotation, praying for something.

"Because I can."

"That's a bullshit reason. I know what you did to Kenna," I said, looking for a reaction from him and boy did I get one.

His fingers tightened on the steering wheel so hard his knuckles turned white. "I can only imagine what you've heard. Let's set the record straight. She wanted it."

Says every rapist ever.

"If anything she was using me, trying to get back at Brock

for discarding her, just like he does with every girl. You'll be no different," he warned, so fucking sure he had it all figured out.

My inner voice told me not to listen, that everything out of his mouth was lies, but another voice, the insecure side, thought there might just be some truth to his words. Perhaps Kenna did have feelings for Brock and she hadn't been pretending like Brock had.

But then I remembered all the shitty things Carter had done to me, and I was back on Kenna's side. No way was Carter innocent in any of this.

He stopped the car, killing the engine. Scooting closer to the window, I pressed my nose to the glass. We were at some sort of empty parking lot. Keyword empty, and as I scanned the area, I noticed the nearest lit streetlight was faraway. All the ones in the Escalade's vicinity were out, like someone had broken them.

Shit.

"Why did you take me to a parking lot?" I asked loud and clear, not that it was much to go on. Was he planning to kill me? This definitely had killer vibes.

"The others should be here soon," he said.

"Others?" I prompted, sliding my hand around the door handle as inconspicuously as I could. It was locked; go figure.

"Enough talking. Or I'll tape your mouth shut again." He pulled out his phone and sent off a text.

I imagined he wanted to hear me scream, so he wasn't too concerned about silencing me. A few minutes later, a truck rolled up beside Carter's SUV, and two football players jumped out. Shawn Whitaker and Porter Beckman. Asshole one and asshole two. They were Carter's sidekicks.

And now I was outnumbered and in deep shit.

"You actually brought Porter and Shawn to help you. Pathetic." While his attention was focused on his friends' arrival, I hit the little unlock button and tried the door. A string of f-bombs went off in my head. He must have engaged the childproof locks.

Right now, I cussed out whoever came up with such a feature. Sure, it was great for keeping in kids, but it really sucked for victims trying to escape their captors.

"They're here in case something goes wrong. Now stay put," he ordered, taking the keys and exiting out the door. A second later, the car beeped as he relocked the doors.

I stared out the window, watching him walk over to Porter and Shawn. This was my chance. Fumbling to uncover my phone from underneath me, I enclosed my fingers over the device and hit speaker. "Grayson? Are you there?" *Please be there, please!*

From the other side of the speaker, I heard someone wrestling with the phone and then a deep voice said, "Josie? Are you okay?"

"Grayson." I sighed, double checking that Carter was still talking with asshole one and two. "I'm fine, for now. But Carter has me tied up in the back of his car."

"We're on our way. Hold on. We'll be there soon," he promised, and I was desperate to believe they would save me.

Carter was strutting back to the car. "I gotta go. Grayson, hurry." I quickly hit the end button and tossed the phone to the floor, covering it with my foot.

My car door opened, and I scrambled across the seat,

putting as much distance between us and his grabbing hands. "Don't be difficult, sis. You really don't want me to crawl in there with you."

Hell no, I didn't.

I couldn't avoid him, not for long, and that proved to be true when Shawn appeared on the other side. Carter's fingers attached themselves to my ankles, and he yanked me out of the car.

My nerves were a jangled mess, and yet, I fought him, doing anything I could to break free. It was futile. Porter was right there, followed moments later by Shawn. Even if I managed to get away, I wouldn't be able to outrun all three of them, but it was against my nature to just give in. I couldn't. Not when I knew Grayson and the others were on their way.

I just had to hold on to that thought.

Except... something occurred to me. How the fuck did Grayson know where I was? He said he was on his way.

I told myself not to think about the how. The Elite would find a way. They were the fucking Elite. The impossible was what they did.

Carter dragged me to the front of his SUV. Headlights beamed over the parking lot as he shoved me up against the grill, pinning me to the car with his body. "Shh," he cooed, putting a hand to my lips. "Calm down. You're going to hurt yourself."

"Now what?" I asked sarcastically. "You got me here. What's the plan?"

He ran a finger along my jawline before tucking a strand of hair behind my ear. The gesture was gentle, almost loving. "We wait. And in the meantime..." He grabbed the cloak and whipped it over my head, tossing it to Porter. His eyes dipped to the V in my shirt. "If you try anything, there will be a penalty."

I gagged. "You need help."

His finger traced down the column of my neck to my shoulder. "Don't we all. Welcome to the upper class, Josie."

I lifted my chin despite the tears that were threatening to spill. "If my hands weren't tied together, I'd deck you."

Shawn, Carter, and Porter all laughed. "She has such spirit," Porter said, his eyes skimming over my body. "Such a shame to have to break it. You really do look like her, Josie."

"You guys are idiots," I spat. I had to keep them talking, keep them busy.

Carter grabbed my jaw in his hand, and I cried out from the pain of his fingers. "Shawn, is everything in place?" he asked, Carter's eyes never leaving my face.

"Yeah. We're set to go," Shawn replied. "These bastards are going to get what's coming to them."

"Damn time too," Porter agreed. "I'm so sick of seeing their smug faces, thinking they own us."

Carter released my face, but the imprint of his fingers lingered. "Are you going to tell me why I'm here?" The bright lights from his headlights made it nearly impossible to see in the dark beyond the lighted beams. Time seemed to crawl while I waited for the Elite—assuming they found me.

"Get into position and stay out of sight. You know the signal," Carter instructed assholes one and two.

They both nodded and jumped back into the truck, taking off into the night. I watched the taillights of Shawn's car disappear behind a building, leaving me alone with my unhinged stepbrother. I almost wished they hadn't left.

My mind whirled. Was this some form a retaliation against the Elite? Carter hated being made a fool of, which the Elite had done the night they kicked his ass. "Do you want your ribs broken again?" I hissed through my teeth.

Carter's fingers dug into my arms. "If it means getting rid of them then it will be worth the price. Besides..." Carter fished into his back pocket and produced something slim and shiny. He flicked his wrist, and a wicked blade popped out. "I particularly like pain."

True fear hit me in the gut, immobilizing me for a few dreadful moments as I just stared at the blade too close to my face. Would he hurt me? Did he plan to hurt Brock? Or the rest of the guys? Panic spiraled inside of me. "Do you mean to kill them? You're insane. You'll go to jail, Carter," I managed to say, but my voice trembled over the words.

Carter let a soft laugh. "No. As much as I would like to see them dead, I'm going to do to them what they've been trying to do to me for over a year."

So he knew what the Elite had been up to, trying to get the proof they needed to make Carter pay for what he did to Kenna and put him behind bars. A laugh escaped—a hysterical one born of fear not just for myself, but for the Elite as well. "And you think kidnapping me is going to do that? You're insane."

"I am not," he spat. "I exploited their weakness to lure them here."

"They don't have a weakness, and you're stupider than I thought if you think it is me."

"Really?" my stepbrother said like a smug asshole who had a trick up his sleeve. And he did. I just wasn't sure it would work like he anticipated. "You look so much like her, but you already know that. Not exactly, of course, but close enough that if someone was drunk, they might mistake you for her."

"Is that another threat? That you will do to me what you did to her?" I shouldn't be baiting him.

He took the tip of his blade, catching it on the front of my shirt just above my breasts. "If you keep talking." I heard the material tear as he tugged the knife just slightly upward. "You never do know when to shut that pretty mouth of yours."

I swallowed, doing my best to stay still. I didn't trust Carter with a knife that close to my heart. Cutting my shirt was one thing, but God forbid if I breathed too deep and the blade pierced my chest. I wasn't overly fond of blood. Particularly my blood.

Carter's head jerked to the side as another set of headlights cut through the darkness. They headed this way, flying across the parking lot. My already pounding heart beat faster as the car came into view. Carter's grip tightened on me. The desire to bolt was so strong inside me, and I knew seeing Brock, Micah, Grayson, and Fynn's faces would ignite my will to be safe. Despite what everyone thought of them or the reputations they built, the four of them made me feel like no one would ever hurt me again. I might have chanced an escape if it weren't for the blade.

Grayson's Jeep came to a screeching halt in front of Carter's SUV, the headlights blinding me. I heard the car doors open, one by one. Then Brock, Grayson, Micah, and Fynn were all standing in front of us, each wearing similar expressions of murder. Even Micah wasn't sporting his usual smirk. Not tonight. His light blue eyes went from me to the knife in Carter's hands. "What the hell is going on, Carter?" Micah shoved his hands into his pockets.

"Took you guys long enough." Carter sounded annoyed. "I thought perhaps Josie and I might get to have some fun after all. But here we are." He ran the back of the blade down the column of my neck, and I shivered, icy dread forming in my gut.

"He drugged me," I rasped.

Dark anger defined Grayson's eyes as they flicked to my face. Our gazes clashed, and for a brief second, those cognac eyes flashed with regret. He had lost track of me at the party after promising not to, but it wasn't exactly his fault.

"I'm okay," I assured. "Just pissed off." And scared, but I wouldn't give Carter the satisfaction of voicing that emotion out loud.

Brock stepped forward, putting himself just in front of his friends. "Enough with the games, Carter. You got me out here, now what is it you want?" he demanded.

The ropes around my wrists cut into my skin as Carter jerked me forward. "I think it would be obvious. A trade."

How would that be obvious to anyone but him?

Brock crossed his arms over his chest, staring Carter down. Even now, he looked at my stepbrother as if he was worthless. Not a bone in Brock's body was intimidated by Carter or the weapon he held in his hand. "You don't have anything I want."

"Don't I?" Carter countered, a brow raised in my direction. "How many times have you dangled your relationship with

Josie in front of my face? Well, I finally figured it out. She's your kryptonite."

"I think you've seen too many superhero movies," Micah said, rocking back on his heels. The seriousness that had been on his face when he got out of the car was gone. Micah wore his I-don't-care-everything-is-a-joke mask like it was a shield—or maybe it was a battle tactic.

"Come on, Carter. You know a girl could never mean that much to me." Even as I saw the slightest flicker in Brock's eyes, his words still hurt, tearing through me like the storm churning in his eyes.

Carter reached up and grabbed me by the hair, yanking me forward. Pain prickled at each hair follicle, bringing tears to my eyes. "So this doesn't bother you?"

"Let me go, you bastard," I hissed, taking my knotted hands and thumping them against his chest.

Brock's face was made of stone, unyielding, unmoving despite the pleading in my eyes. "You think I care about her?" he said to Carter flatly, facing him squarely.

"Yeah, I do. You want her for the same reasons I do."

His eyes narrowed. "I've fucked more girls than you ever will in a lifetime. And not once did I have to force them."

"You're wrong about what happened between Kenna and me. She lied. I didn't do anything to her she didn't ask for." His voice snapped with hatred. "She used me to make you jealous, except you didn't care, not until she said that I assaulted her."

"Kenna wouldn't do that." Grayson seethed, a vein pulsing on his neck.

Carter shook his head. "I won't let you ruin my life."

Brock took another step closer. "So you plan to ruin mine instead, is that it? If your beef is with me, then let her go." His gaze just for just a fraction caught mine and then he was back focused on Carter.

My stepbrother waved the knife in the air, his other hand still tangled in my hair. "It's with all of you. I'm tired of the four of you thinking you're untouchable. You're not."

"Is that so?" Fynn baited.

"You know, Josie just offered to suck me off in the back seat of my car. Isn't that right, sis—"

Brock's fist flew so fast, I didn't know he hit Carter until I heard the crack of knuckles against bone. Carter's face whipped to the side, yet he still managed to keep his hold on me. He swore. I told myself to ignore the pain of fire shooting through my scalp, but I felt the hot tears roll down my cheeks.

A low, sickening laugh came from Carter as he swiped a pebble of blood on his lip with the back of his hand. "I bet that felt good, but not quite as good as fucking Josie."

God, he was just begging to get his ass kicked. At this point, I was primed to do it myself... once I got my strength back, that was. My damn muscles still felt like they were made of Jell-O.

The air thickened with tension. "What the fuck do you want, Carter?" Brock held my stepbrother's gaze. "You want me to promise to leave you alone, is that it?"

Carter's nostrils flared. "Give me the flash drive that you have on me and I'll let her go."

He failed to mention if he would let me go unharmed, but the wording wasn't lost on me. But then I registered what else he had said. Flash drive? What flash drive?

"I don't know what you're talking about," Brock replied, his voice cold.

"Don't bullshit me." Carter's hate for the Elite was right on the surface. Anyone could see it.

Brock's jaw hardened. "So you staged this whole thing to get a thumb drive that doesn't exist?"

"It does. And I want it. Everything on there is bullshit. None of it is true. I won't let you take everything away from me." Carter's desperation to keep his life was clear in the fury that trembled in his voice.

I looked between the four Elite.

Fynn stepped up beside Brock so they were shoulder to shoulder. "Pretty dumb of you to come alone." Micah and Grayson moved forward, forming a wall of Elite in front of Carter and me.

I heard rather than saw the smile curl on my stepbrother's lips as he said, "Who said I did?" He lifted his hand into the air and from somewhere in the dark parking lot, an engine roared.

Up until that moment, I'd forgotten about Porter and Shawn. The car's engine revved again, taunting us. "It's Shawn and Porter." I rushed out the words, knowing that Carter would silence me, and I braced myself for impact, squeezing my eyes shut.

"Shut up," Carter seethed, jerking me.

Brock's eyes were as dark as death. "Hurt her again and I'll kill you." And that was exactly what Carter had been looking for. That moment where Brock gave in, showing his emotions.

Carter shot him an I-win grin right before he screwed his lips to mine in a bruising kiss. I struggled, crying and twisting my head away from his mouth. When Carter pulled back, I spat in his face. The next thing I knew, blinding pain shot across my cheek, and my head whipped to the side. The bastard had hit me.

I wanted to crumble to the ground from the pain, but I made myself stay upright. The binds rubbed against my wrists as my fingers curled, digging into my palms as I fought against the sting that radiated over my cheek.

A primal roar erupted from Grayson. "That's my sister!" he yelled, and I lifted my eyes just in time to see him lunge for Carter.

"Oh shit," Micah muttered.

"Dammit, Grayson," Fynn grumbled.

In Grayson's eyes, this entire situation was a flashback to that night with Kenna. Me? Her? It was all jumbled together for him.

But Brock stood there, his eyes glaring past the fight taking place in front of him.

Grayson had Carter pinned up against my stepbrother's SUV and was repeatedly slamming Carter's hand against the car to dislodge the knife. My stepbrother was fucking relentless. He held on to the damn thing as if his life depended on it, and in a way, I guess it did, because Grayson looked like he wanted to murder Carter.

I screamed Grayson's name, but my voice was drowned out but an engine gunning across the parking lot.

Grayson sent an elbow flying into Carter's face, catching him on the nose. Blood gushed.

"Josie!" More than one voice cried over the roaring engine. I spun around, a horrible feeling weighing down my stomach, but all I saw was the blinding headlights. Someone hit me, arms wrapping around me as we went down to the ground, hard. A body landed on top of me, shielding me.

Then the car barreled past us, rumbling the hard surface under my body. My cheek pressed into the ground, more than one pebble digging into my skin, but considering the alternative of getting mowed over by a car, I'd take the scrapes and bruises.

Brock's arms stayed tight around me, his muscles rigid. Fury burned into me, rolling off him in sheets. He would kill Carter. Porter and Shawn too. Had they really tried to run me over in their truck? I couldn't believe it.

"Are you okay?" Brock asked, lifting off me just slightly.

I drew in a ragged breath, staring into Brock's face hovering above me. He had saved me. I tried to speak but I couldn't. My lips wouldn't form the words, so I just gave a small nod, my mouth quivering.

"Jesus Christ," he whispered, sitting up and crushing me against him.

Tires squealed, and for a second, I thought the truck was coming back for round two. Brock must have had the same thought. His muscles went rigid underneath me. He turned his focus to Fynn, Grayson, and Micah. "Where's the truck?" he demanded.

"They took off," Fynn answered. "Didn't even slow down."

"Do you want us to go after him?" Micah asked.

Brock shook his head. "No, just grab Grayson before he puts Patterson in the hospital again. We need to get out of here."

Brock lifted me into his arms and stood up, carrying me to Grayson's Jeep.

I buried my face into the crook of his neck, not wanting to see Carter. I never wanted to lay eyes on my stepbrother again. It might not have been a feasible request, but right now was all that mattered. My arms looped over Brock as he slid into the back seat, adjusting me on his lap. From outside the car, I could hear voices, but then Brock closed the door.

I couldn't stop trembling, even though in my head I knew I was safe. "How did you find me?" I whispered, my voice shaking as I continued to shiver.

"I put a tracker on your phone." His voice was gruff, and I could see from the tight lines on his face that he was fighting every impulse in his body not to jump out of the car and beat Carter to within an inch of his life.

Any other time I'd be pissed, but given the circumstances, I wanted to kiss him for invading my privacy. "Thank you," I whispered.

Brock shook his head. "Don't thank me. If it wasn't for me, you wouldn't be in this mess, but the plan the three of you concocted, that was stupid. Do you know what could have happened? Grayson never should have been so reckless."

I sighed. I didn't have any energy left in me to argue. "He did what you refused to."

"And what good did it do? We still don't have the evidence we need, and now I just want to kill him. He hurt you." His hand lightly touched my swelling cheek.

I winced, swallowing the pain. "I'm okay. You got there in time."

"Josie, don't ever go behind my back again…" His chest heaved. "I don't know what I'll do."

Nothing good.

"Grayson thought I was Kenna," I said somberly in his arms, seeing the shadows of Micah, Grayson, and Fynn walking toward the front of the Jeep.

"No, he knows exactly who you are. You *are* his sister—his other sister."

My brain had to be fried, because I swore Brock just said that Grayson Edwards was my brother, which meant Kenna was my… Ohmygod. "What did you say?"

Thank you for reading!
Brock and Josie will be back in
DISORDER

xoxo,
Jennifer

P.S. Join my VIP Readers email list and receive a bonus scene told from Zane's POV, as well as a free copy of Losing Emma and Breaking Emma, bonus books from my Divisa Series. You will also get notifications of what's new, giveaways, and new releases.
Visit here to sign up: www.jlweil.com

Don't forget to also join my Dark Divas FB Group and have

some fun with me and a fabulous, fun group of readers. There is games, prizes, and lots of book love.

Join Dark Divas

You can stop in and say hi to me on Facebook night and day. I pop in as often as I can: https://www.facebook.com/jenniferlweil/ I'd love to hear from you.

ELITE OF ELMWOOD ACADEMY

(New Adult Dark High School Romance)

Turmoil

DIVISA HUNTRESS

(New Adult Paranormal Romance)

Crown of Darkness

Inferno of Darkness

DRAGON DESCENDANTS SERIES

(Upper Teen Reverse Harem Fantasy)

Stealing Tranquility

Absorbing Poison

Taming Fire

Thawing Frost

THE DIVISA SERIES

(Full series completed – Teen Paranormal Romance)

Losing Emma: A Divisa novella

Saving Angel

Hunting Angel

Breaking Emma: A Divisa novella

Chasing Angel

Loving Angel

Redeeming Angel

LUMINESCENCE TRILOGY

(Full series completed – Teen Paranormal Romance)

Luminescence

Amethyst Tears

Moondust

Darkmist – A Luminescence novella

RAVEN SERIES

(Full series completed – Teen Paranormal Romance)

White Raven

Black Crow

Soul Symmetry

BEAUTY NEVER DIES CHRONICLES

(Teen Dystopian Romance)

Slumber

Entangled

Forsaken

NINE TAILS SERIES

(Teen Paranormal Romance)

First Shift

Storm Shift

Flame Shift

Time Shift

Void Shift

Spirit Shift

Tide Shift

Wind Shift

HAVENWOOD FALLS HIGH

(Teen Paranormal Romance)

Falling Deep

Ascending Darkness

SINGLE NOVELS

Starbound

(Teen Paranormal Romance)

Casting Dreams

(New Adult Paranormal Romance)

Ancient Tides

(New Adult Paranormal Romance)

For an updated list of my books, please visit my website:
www.jlweil.com

Join my VIP email list and I'll personally send you an email reminder as soon as my next book is out! Click here to sign up: www.jlweil.com

ABOUT THE AUTHOR

J.L. Weil is a USA TODAY Bestselling author of teen & new adult paranormal romance, fantasy, and urban fantasy books about spunky, smart mouth girls who always wind up in dire situations. For every sassy girl, there is an equally mouthwatering, overprotective guy.

You can visit her online at: www.jlweil.com or come hang out with her at JL Weil's Dark Divas on FB.

Stalk Me Online
www.jlweil.com
jenniferlweil@gmail.com